13 DAYS OF DECEMBER

Book Two

ENDURE

May

LEXI KINGSTON

Published by L. Kingston Books, LLC
Edited by Elaine York, Allusion Publishing
Proofread by Joy Editing
Cover Design by Elaine York, Allusion Publishing

 Created with Vellum

ENDURE
May

*For the fools like me, who refuse to give up on love
even after seeing the worst sides of it.*

PROLOGUE

Life is tricky. Complicated. Unfathomably and incomprehensibly messy. Every facet of who you are stems from the way in which you react to the rocks life throws at you. The potholes that appear in your path before you have time to blink, and before you know it, you've been thrown off the road, spinning out of control, and doing everything in your power to keep the world from flipping upside down on you. That is life. It sucks. It is the most unfair and inconsistent thing that will ever be. And yet, oftentimes, the uncontrollably fast-moving rollercoaster that we call life, the dark, the disturbed, the lonely, the *messy* pit of darkness that it can be... is the beauty of it.

1

TORI

I enjoy days like today more than any other. My brother isn't home, my sister is caught up doing God-knows-what with her devilishly handsome boyfriend, of whom I do not think about at all hours of the day, and my parents are out of town for some kind of surgeon retreat. I don't know what. All I heard was, "Your dad and I have to go out of town for a few weeks... we'll be back after... lasagna... freezer..." then checked out of the conversation. Is it my fault her monologues are so torturously long that she can't hold my attention for more than a few seconds at a time?

Today is one of those rare gems in May—it's warm, and the afternoon sun scorches my skin. I'm propped on a lounge chair, enjoying the first nice day we've had in a while, and just as my eyes drift closed, a person-shaped shadow forms above me, shading my entire body.

Seriously? How long has it been? Forty-five minutes and my peace and quiet is already being interrupted? It's rare for a day in early May to be this warm, and personally,

I'd like to enjoy it *in* the sun. I was hoping my siblings wouldn't be back for a few hours... or ever, if I were being honest.

I grit my teeth menacingly, wondering who I'll have to yell at this time in order to get some time to myself. Whether I'm in the living room or the kitchen or my car, I can never catch a break. Usually, it's my younger brother Dylan who irks me the most, always sticking his nose where it doesn't belong and cracking jokes with the sole intention of getting under my skin. He irritates me to the point of exhaustion. Just last week he snuck into my room and upended my entire closet because he had "nothing better to do."

Personally, I think he gets off on making my life as miserable as possible.

"You're blocking my sun," I advise, shimmying lower on the lounge chair. I have dibs on this specific one because it's positioned closest to the afternoon sun and requires the least amount of work to move.

There's no reply. Maybe if I keep my eyes closed long enough the sun-stealer will leave me be.

Time ticks by. Minutes. Hours. Centuries—okay, maybe it's only been a few seconds, but I can't take it any longer.

Ripping off my sunglasses, I shoot up in my seat. "Does anyone in this house—holy shit!" I screech. Above me looms a life-sized cutout of Jeremy Dean—the only cutout I don't already own, that is—the bass guitarist of my all-time favorite band, 13 Days of December, positioned at just the right angle to piss me off. Jeremy Dean also happens to be the bandmate of my sister's boyfriend, lead singer of said band, Carson James, of whom she didn't tell me she was dating until I found out from the *freaking late-night news station*. But I'm over that. Completely moved on. Doesn't even phase me.

I clutch my hand to my chest, letting my sunglasses clatter to the ground.

Laughter erupts from the kitchen, and my siblings stumble out, wheezing for breath as I bite the inside of my cheek to keep from screaming at them.

"Did you get it?" Dylan asks, straining to see Rylee's phone. She nods her head, tilting the screen toward him. He bends backward, cackling at the visual proof of why I hate my family.

"You should have seen your *face*," Dylan cries, dropping beside me on the lounge chair that is *not* big enough for two.

"I'm sorry I missed it," I say dryly, leaning to pick up my sunglasses. I silently pray they just stopped home for a quick little prank and will be out of my hair in no time. "I thought you two were gone for the day."

Rylee exchanges a glance with our little brother, sucking in her cheeks to hide a smile. "Carson insisted on throwing you a party. He rented a hall and everything."

My lips quirk upward. A party? For me? Thrown by none other than Carson Andrew James? I mean, I guess I could suffer through *one* night of partying instead of going out with my college friends like I'd planned...

"Invite Megan and Quinn?" I plead, batting my long lashes. I know exactly how Rylee feels about my friends, but I also know that no matter how much she dislikes them, they'll be at the party nonetheless. She only met them a few months ago because they wanted to meet *her*—it seems my sister has become somewhat of a celebrity since she started dating Carson.

Still, my stomach flops a little at my request, knowing a big part of me only wants them there because she doesn't. There has always been this side of me that revels in Rylee's misery, and I feel all the guiltier for not only being this way, but openly admitting it to myself without attempting to change. She and her celebrity boyfriend planned a party for me after all, and here I am trying to make her suffer for it.

Both my sister and Carson still feel exponentially guilty about keeping their relationship from me for so long, and who am I to stop them from wallowing in their guilt? The truth is, I'm over it—mostly—and have been for a while. But if she insists on planning little surprises for me here and there, and giving me chances to spend time with her superstar friends... well, I guess I can't do anything about that, now can I?

My sister's hopeful grin is replaced with a less enthusiastic one, and that's how I know I've gotten to her. Still, she agrees, trying her best to hide how she really feels.

Dylan doesn't even try to mask his eye roll. "Really? They're so annoying."

His guilt is harder to manipulate, probably because it wasn't him shacking up with the could-have-been love of my life. He still knew about it, though, and couldn't be bothered to tell me. Where Rylee keeps her mouth shut, Dylan speaks up, completely unafraid to call me out for being, well, who I am. And I know he would have made a more unpleasant comment on any other day to push my buttons—just not today. I smirk in satisfaction.

"What time?" I ask, feigning boredom.

Dylan watches me with a look I can read like the back of a book, while Rylee continues to act unaffected by my behavior. She's trying so hard to be better to me since we've worked out our kinks. "Six-thirty."

"Well, then, that means I have four hours and twenty-six minutes left to enjoy some quality sun time." I make a shooing motion with my hands, hoping they'll take the not-so-subtle hint, and get lost.

They both exchange a look at my dismissal. A look I pretend not to see, as per usual. Our family is like a rusty machine—we still function, but we also overlook the things that piss us off about each other the most to keep the peace. I ignore their shared glances and secret-keeping, and they don't bother to point out when I'm being rude—well, most of the time. My siblings are thick as thieves and think I'm the annoying, ungrateful one. They also think I don't give much thought to anything. If they only knew how calculating I really am. How not a single word leaves my mouth without being processed by my brain, ensuring it'll have the effect I want, that my face will give off the exact reaction I want people to perceive. I let people think they catch me off guard, when in reality, I hold the cards. Every. Last. One of them.

As Tweedledee and Tweedledum head back into the

house, I rescue a raft that was submerged under a pile of pool noodles and boogie boards, trying my hardest to shake it off in case any spiders decided to make it their new home between last night when I sat on it and this morning.

As I'm settling into the raft, careful so only my feet touch the chilly water and my raft doesn't tip, I see a shadow pass over me on the deck. I should have known better than to think I'd actually be left alone. In this house, it's always something.

Heavy rock music erupts from the speakers mounted on our patio, scaring me so bad my raft rocks on the water. I grab each side to steady myself and hold on until I've regained my balance.

"Don't you dare," I warn, eyeing my brother, who is the king of bad intentions and mischievous smiles, just like the one he's eyeing me with right now. "Dylan... Dylan, I'm warning you..." He pretends not to hear me, though, and continues walking along the pool's edge threateningly. "Dylan!"

Just as his name rolls off my tongue—though rolls isn't really the right word, is it? More like his name is *shot* from my tongue. *Blasted*—he springs off his tree-stump legs, landing far enough away that he doesn't hit me, but close enough so his cannonball drenches me from head to toe in freezing cold pool water.

"You little rat!" I scream, catapulting myself at him, but he's already swimming in the opposite direction. And let's face it, there's no way in this world I'd ever catch him even on my best day. He's way too fast.

I sigh, dumping my body back on the plastic raft, and watch him walk away as if he's not completely and utterly satisfied that his piss-Tori-off-to-no-end mission was a success.

"Oh, and Tor?" Dylan turns halfway, shooting me a wicked grin. "Happy birthday."

2

TORI

I guess tonight is as good a time as any to throw a party, considering I'm now at the legal drinking age... but a party with my siblings on my twenty-first birthday isn't exactly what I had in mind. If it wasn't for the fact that Carson planned it, which means he'll be there, which means the rest of the band will be there, I wouldn't go at all.

Despite what I say, I really do love Rylee and Dylan, but I tend to get left out when I'm with them—feelings I cover with sass and disinterest. They have this bond that I'm not a part of, and as much as I'd love to blame it on the fact that Rylee snuck behind my back with the man I fantasized about meeting my entire life, it started long before Carson James became part of the picture. I don't know exactly when or how it started—if I pushed Rylee away and she gravitated toward Dylan, or if it was just bound to happen either way—but I just don't *fit*.

Ry and I used to be close. And I mean, tell each other everything, blood promise, die for each other close. Okay, maybe not blood promise, because *ew*. Still, something changed, and suddenly she didn't tell me everything anymore. She was secretive about her relationship with her skeevy ex-boyfriend, who for a while I ragged on her for dumping even though it was for the best. She stopped wanting to hang around me and my friends at sleepovers... oh, and then there's the whole part where she *lied* to me about falling in love with the world-famous singer/songwriter I'd planned my whole wedding around, but who's counting, am I right?

Maybe she grew up and reached an age where I wasn't the cool older sister anymore, but instead just her older sister. Nothing special about it. Maybe it's partly my fault for handling it poorly and making high school hell for her. Either way, there's been a divide between us, and no matter what we do or how much ice is broken, it won't go away.

I thought after she let me in, back in Cali, that we'd start to rebuild our sisterhood. I was mistaken. I mean, she's trying, and for a while, things were actually pretty good between us, but I'm not sure it's enough. Not only that, I'm not sure if *I'm* trying hard enough.

"Can I borrow your silver hoops?" I ask, peeking through the open sliver in her doorway.

She nods her head, motioning me into the room, holding a phone between her cheek and shoulder. "Yeah, I know, but do you think it's enough? I mean, your fans are pretty hard to please. After everything you've put them through these last few months, a break from interviews and social media may not be the way to go... well, sure, they'll be excited about new music, but we're talking a small hiatus here, and—okay, this is why I like talking these things out with Elizabeth. Stop distracting me!"

Even if Rylee's voice was on mute, which would be my preference, I'd have known who she was talking to by her cheeky grin and ogling stare that glazes over her eyes. The way she tucks her chin and scoops her light brown hair behind her ear, before biting her bottom lip, trying and failing to hold back a smile. It's unmistakable. You can see it in her eyes.

That look is precisely why I pushed her to chase after Carson when she broke things off. For me. It's also why when I ran into Jamie LeMont at a café in California, instead of taking time to fangirl and soak in the once-in-a-lifetime experience, I gave him the letter of apology Rylee had been so desperately trying to get to Carson. How could I deny her this happiness when he made her smile brighter than I've ever seen from her? I'm a lot of things, but heinous isn't one of them.

She giggles, and a pang I try to push down burns in my chest.

Be happy for her. I tell myself. *You should be happy for her.*

Even after all of that, I'm not. And I'm selfish because I want what she has more than she'll ever know.

"I don't know..." She looks around the room as if it holds the answer to world hunger. "I just..."

"Eh-hem," I clear my throat. Startled, she looks my way, clearly having forgotten I'm here.

"I have to go; I'll see you later." Rylee bites her lip, tucking her hair behind her ear like clockwork. Typical.

It'd be cute if it didn't make me want to throw up in my mouth a little. "Love you too, bye."

"Earrings?" I quirk my lips expectantly the second her thumb taps her screen, suddenly anxious to leave the room. I silently wonder how many times Carson was in here and I had no idea, sitting bored out of my mind in my bedroom across the hall.

"In the jewelry box." She points to the small marble box on her dresser, by far the most glamorous thing she owns. Naturally, it was a gift from Carson.

Sure enough, the pair of earrings I'm after is right inside, next to the best friends charm I bought for her eleventh birthday. I purse my lips and close the lid, not wanting to look at it any longer, and halfway wishing I hadn't seen it at all—halfway glad I did because that means she hasn't thrown it away along with the rest of our relationship.

"Thanks," I mutter and head toward the door. I expect her to stop me by offering up something else I can use, it's sort of become a pattern. I need something, she gives it to me, plus the offer of something more.

Except she doesn't try to stop me, and I don't turn around.

There's a tiny voice in my head that whispers words I don't want to hear:

She's giving up on you.

If only that was enough to make me give in. But giving in isn't in my nature. Rylee is the practical one, where I'm unreasonable, and unlike her, I can't give in even when I know I'm wrong.

"Hello there, gorgeous." Kris whistles, waggling his brows. His eyes roam every inch of my sister, only finding me when Carson gives him the look that says *eye her one more time and I'll bury you.*

Rylee just laughs, used to Kris's humor and sexual innuendos, not a blush on her cheeks.

Carson attaches his gaze to something on the other end of the hall, probably so he doesn't have to continue watching his best friend hit on his girlfriend. Voicing my thoughts, he says, "Don't you have anything better to do other than check out my girlfriend?"

"'Course," Kris smirks, turning his attention on me, "I can check out her sister. Happy birthday, by the way."

I roll my eyes, pushing my purse into his chest as he tries to lean in for a hug, not having the time or energy to find a better place to put it. "Take this. I need a drink."

"I second that," Dylan agrees, following behind me across Ambler's *only* local event hall.

"Nice try, Dumbledore. The Coke's over there." I point to a table with under-twenty-one drinks and shove him in that direction. "Don't get too crazy." I smirk as he mumbles unintelligible words under his breath. I'm about to ask when I decide I'm better off not knowing.

As I watch him walk off, I'm hit with a surge of regret. I wish I hadn't pushed him away, because as I look around the room, I find myself alone in a sea of strangers. My eyes circle the ballroom, scanning every happy and fun-loving face. Some I know, some I wish I didn't, and others I've never seen before in my life.

Carson and Rylee were snagged by someone back at the doorway, and Kris has disappeared, too, probably losing interest in me now that Rylee isn't here to impress.

My chest aches. I don't need them. I was perfectly fine mingling with strangers before my sister went and did a three-sixty on our lives, I can be fine again. I can't count the number of times I lost track of my friends at parties and was forced to make friends with the people around me—so I'm not sure why it's bothering me now, here, on my birthday. My *twenty-first* birthday.

Pull it together. You're a hard-ass-bitch, Tori. You thrive in these kinds of settings.

Lately, the things I used to feel most at home doing are like walking in a stranger's skin.

"You look lost." A voice disrupts my solid attempt at standing alone at a party. More and more people stream through the back door, filling the room with double the number of people I either hardly know or don't like—all of whom are here for me. A year ago, I would have taken every opportunity to shove my life in the faces of those who smiled to my face and bitched behind my back, but now I just don't see a point. Sure, I could brag about my life, talk up my celebrity friends, make them all jealous, but then what? What's the point in making them envious of me? They'll still talk behind my back, and I still won't care. What good does it do to try and change the minds of people who will never care enough to accept you? The real you?

"Nope." I bite my lip, refraining from turning around. "Just taking in the crowd."

My right hand toys with the bracelet on my wrist, a gift from Rylee before the party. It's beautiful, and in fact, the exact thing I'd wanted—or so I told her a month ago when it popped up in the March edition of *Teen Queen*. She'd been so excited to give it to me, and I'm sure she can afford it now with her new, fancy job working as Junior Publicist for a goddamn boy band, but I don't want expensive things. Okay, I want expensive things more than I want a real-life Carson James willingly in my bed, but it's different, and I can't explain why. It's complicated. It's...

Jealousy?

Pretty much. Okay, so it's not so complicated. She's living the life I've pictured for myself since I was a child, and her buying me expensive gifts feels like an even bigger reminder that she has what I want. And I hate it. I hate it so much. I don't want to be jealous of my little sister, but the fact is, in the last five months she's gotten absolutely everything I've ever wanted. *Everything.* And, yes, now I'm part of it, no longer excluded by her need for self-preservation, but I'm just not *there*. I'm not at a place to let it go, yet, and even though she tries, I'm not part of the group. She and Dylan have had so much time with the band that they're practically members, and I'm left out here standing in the cold. Invited, but never really included.

"You're standing alone at a party thrown in your honor," Jamie remarks in a tone I don't appreciate.

"Well, from the looks of it, so are you." I swivel on the

balls of my feet to absorb all six feet of his brooding stare and long, messy hair, styled to sexy perfection. It's like every inch of him screams *Sexy Drummer God.* No... not God. He looks much too sinful to be a god. He's more like a *Sexy Drummer Devil.*

My cheeks heat a little when I become aware of the prevalent thoughts on my mind, and I lean back on my heels a bit, wishing someone would swoop through the crowd and whisk me away from this nightmare.

"That would be inaccurate, because I'm standing here talking to you," he replies, raising an eyebrow. This bastard just loves to be right, doesn't he?

I gnaw the skin on my inner lip. "Then it looks like *I'm* standing here talking to *you.*"

Jamie blinks once, then twice. "Are you just repeating what I say?"

"I don't know, am I?" I say in a mocking tone I'd usually only use with Dylan, and on occasion, Rylee. He stares at me dumbly, and I find myself looking anywhere but his face.

"Do you mind?" I chastise, brushing past him. "I have guests to mingle with."

"How many of their names do you know?" he hollers after me, but I'm already swallowed by the restless crowd, deep enough that I can play it off like I didn't hear his remark.

I suck on my cheeks, not so much hating that he's right, but that he got to me. He was trying to be an ass and I let him get under my skin. Worse, I let him *see* that he did.

Right then, the lights dim, and the room is lit with technicolor streams and fog from the stage where the DJ is playing typical party songs. And just like at any party, when the lights go down everyone screams, excited to have their scandalous dance moves and risky make-outs masked by the darkness and lost in the neon.

"She's Got It," a single from the band's upcoming album, blares so loud I can feel their vocals vibrating through my body, so strong it almost feels like the music is coming out of me, and it low-key makes me feel like a bad bitch.

"Tori!" someone calls, and I turn abruptly, squinting through the murky air and hot bodies moving in rhythm. My chest releases at the sight of a familiar face, and I lurch at her.

"Megan!" I squeal, locking hands with my best friend. "You made it! I wasn't sure Rylee would actually invite you!"

"Yeah! Quinn will be here soon, she's just getting off work," she responds, adjusting the strap of her outfit so it tightens around her boobs, making them pop more than they do without the extra assistance.

I nod, taking in her leather jumpsuit, unzipped down past her bra so anyone who looks can't help but get a face full of cleavage. I can't judge, though. Megan is a fashionista, and as much as I hate to admit it, I couldn't pull off half of the looks she does. It's why I admire her. She doesn't care who judges her, and she most definitely always makes a statement. Whether it's her clothes or her eyeliner or her attitude, Megan never disappoints.

"This is fucking insane," she says, gesturing to the moving bodies all around, and the grind line that seems to have started up at the front. It's mostly girls, and all the guys have taken position, watching as their bodies gyrate off one another's. I can't remember the last time I had that much fun at a party. So drunk and carelessly fun that consequences meant nothing, and if there were any, I wouldn't remember in the morning anyway.

I peel my eyes from the fun and glance at Megan's gleaming ones. She's a partier in the truest sense of the word. I'm all for a good time, but there's no such thing as a slow night when she gets a couple drinks in her hand. She is, by dictionary definition, the life of the party. "It's definitely something."

"Something? *Something?*" Meg slaps my arm, giving me a little shove. "Babe, this is what we've always dreamed our lives would be like—and look at you! You're killing it. Let's have some fun. Kiss a cute stranger. Where's the beer?"

I grit my teeth, unsure of why I'm in such a bad mood on what should be one of the best nights of my life. I open my mouth to give her a snarky response, but she knows me too well.

"Tori. Shut up. Have fun. So what if you have to ride on your sister's coattails to get you to the top... all that matters is that you're standing above her in the end." She raises her brows, knowing she's right as ever.

And then, just like Megan, she's off to the next thought, eyes scanning the room for the beverage table, of course. And naturally, I catch sight of Dylan slinking behind it. I hope that poor kid never robs a bank because he would never get away with it. There isn't a stealthy bone in his running-back body.

My dumb-as-shit brother looks around twice before snagging two cans of Bud Light from the tin bowl of ice, and attempts to inconspicuously drop them into his front pockets. Except he can't get his jean pockets open without a free hand.

I roll my eyes, trailing behind Megan as she swerves through the thickening crowd.

"Dylan," I hiss, stomping over and snatching the beer from his fumbling hands. "What the hell do you think you're doing?"

He looks at me, then casts his eyes over the rest of probably underage drinkers in the crowd. "What everyone else is doing...?"

"And almost everyone else is of age." I cock my head to the side. He knows I've got him there. He only turned sixteen last month.

"Whatever you say," he mocks, handing me the other beer. I crack one for Megan, and then one for myself.

I sigh, leaning my back against the wall, narrowly avoiding a couple getting a little too into the slow song that's just started.

"This party is beat," I mumble, taking a swig of the drink in my hand. My brother quirks a brow, eyeing what was supposed to be his drink, but knows better than to steal it back.

He scoots between me and the table, lightly tapping his elbow to my arm. "Looks to me like you're the only one not having fun, sis."

My jaw drops, and I close it quickly so he doesn't see when he turns back to look at me, quirking his lips. I hate him for being right. Why am I the only one not enjoying myself? Megan's still sober as I've ever seen her and *she's* having a good time, and everyone knows she can't party without alcohol. Her motto is *No booze = party blues.*

"I know what'll cheer you up." She winks, glancing up, then adjusting the top of—or lack thereof—her V-neck.

As if on cue, a body appears beside me, and I find myself gawking at the ungodly perfect man blessing my eyes. How is it possible for someone to be that beautiful? It just isn't. It's physically impossible and yet, here he is, with his soft curls and blue eyes that seem to glow in the blacklight.

"Enjoying the party?" Carson asks, grinning down at me with the light of a thousand suns brightening his face.

My stomach twists and I feel the sudden urge to puke, blinded by his perfect white teeth. When Rylee's around, it's easy for me to feign indifference. But when he tries to talk to me when she's not...

Pull it together. Don't act like a fool.

Giggling lightly, I twist my hair around my fingers, flitting my lashes twice, three times. "Of course, I am, you planned it."

A throat clears to my left, forcing me to peel my eyes away from Carson. Megan's there, tugging on my arm with Quinn at her side—when she got here is lost on me—both giving me wide, pleading eyes. They want to meet Carson. If only there was enough of him to go around...

Maybe Rylee's willing to go split-zies? A sister discount?

"Uh, Carson, these are my friends, M—"

"Oh my God," Megan blurts, shoving past me so hard I'm surprised her boobs don't flop out of her jumpsuit. "Hi, I'm Megan, and I love you so, so, so much, you have no idea... will you go to prom with me?"

Carson gives her an easy smile, probably all too used to fans acting like this around him. Before he gets the chance to respond though, he's being interrupted.

"Meg, you're not even in high school anymore," Quinn accuses, yanking her friend away. "Sorry about her, she gets a little excited." Quinn smooths the hips of the tight little dress that barely meets her thighs, and bites on the inside of her lip. "I'm definitely *way* more mature than she is."

"Says the girl who still sleeps with a nightlight." Megan lets out a *humph* sound, puffing out her lips in satisfaction, happy to have taken back the upper hand.

Quinn grits her teeth in a forced smile, once again shoving Megan back, who has somehow maneuvered her way in front. "Well, at least I never made out with his face pillow!"

"Okay." I clap my hands, ushering Carson away from my friends before things get ugly. And yes, I mean *get* ugly, as in that was nowhere near what it could become.

The *one* time Rylee isn't hovering over him, I swear.

It doesn't take much effort to pull Carson away, though. He seems more than happy to comply, probably eager to get away from my crazy friends. I don't know what possesses them to act the way they do sometimes.

"I'm so sorry," I mumble once we're a safe distance

away, my cheeks reddening at both the scene my friends created, and the one I made back when I asked Carson what his lips felt like. My stomach churns again. I still can't believe I said that. I guess I can't be too mad at Megan and Quinn, considering I was definitely just as bad. Either way, it's a different feeling being on the other side of things. Rylee's side of things.

Ever since I found out the truth about her and Carson, I've been trying to imagine what it was like for her all those weeks, because I want to understand why she did what she did, and why she lied to me. Watching my friends just now, I kind of understand. She was embarrassed. Of me. And she didn't trust me not to interfere.

"It's all good. If I remember correctly, you were once a crazy fangirl yourself." Carson smirks, his eyes roaming through the swarms of people. There's no doubt in my mind who he's looking for.

"Hi, Tori!" A few girls stumble as I pass by, hanging limply on their dates. I smile and wave in their general direction but can't see who they are with all the other people bumping into me at every angle.

"Hey, where've you been?" Rylee greets us once we break away from the crowd into a little corner where she stands with Dylan and the rest of our friends—*her friends*. Carson gives her a peck on the cheek as if he hasn't seen her in hours. It's been, what, ten minutes? I highly doubt that deserved a greeting, but whatever.

Don't be petty, that's why you're in this mess.

"Around," I sigh, eyeing up the mountain of presents

I'm just now noticing. "Are those all for me?" I screech, shoving past everyone to admire the mound of humungous boxes, each wrapped with a different kind of paper.

They nod their heads, and I feel the urge to jump up and down with joy. It's like Christmas!

"Do we want to cut the cake now, or wait?" Kirsten asks, untangling herself from Jer's arms. And I thought Rylee and Carson were inseparable, Jer and Kirsten never leave each other's side. I guess I wouldn't want to either if my boyfriend spent most of his time traveling the world without me, meeting new girls in every city, and doing God-knows-what with them.

I feel for Rylee. Truly. Carson's whole life revolves around traveling, and the strain of long distance is already hard enough on her, and his tour is over. Next time it might be longer, more places, more commitment, and he won't be able to see her nearly as much. Though, I am kind of envious of the jet he can jaunt off in whenever he wants, because who doesn't want a celebrity boyfriend who's willing to fly from Tokyo to see you at a moment's notice?

I realize after a moment that everyone's looking at me, waiting for me to decide when to cut the cake. "Um," I toy with my bracelet. "I don't think anyone's going to want to stop dancing for cake..."

Rylee whispers something up to Carson, and he nods thoughtfully. "We can do it downstairs," she offers. "There's a smaller, private party room down there."

Shrugging my shoulders, I nod, because I could really

go for some cake right now. I also really want to break away from this crowd and breathe some fresh air, even if said air is in the basement. Anything is better than sweat and booze.

The guys gather a few more of our close friends and lead us to the private room, weaving through yet another clump of people who seem to be migrating their way around the entire room. I catch sight of a couple making out on the back couch and thank the Lord our family party was a separate event last weekend before Mom and Dad had to take off.

"You look beautiful," one of the boys' sisters whispers in my ear, tugging on the maroon gown I'm wearing. She moves past me quickly, and I think I recognize her as Carmina. I give her a smile before she moves on, up beside Jer's younger sister Justice, who has outdone everyone tonight in her silver dress and sky-high heels. I admire her fashion much like I do Megan's. She's not afraid to make a statement.

I glance behind me to find that Quinn and Meg are lagging a bit, probably trying to get a good look at the guys' asses. I roll my eyes at that. Not probably, they most definitely are.

We finally reach a small room, furnished with nothing but a long, rectangular table surrounded by chairs with rose-colored cushions. It doesn't look like this part of the hall is used too often, and I can understand why. Not only is the room drab, but the above ballroom runs circles around the tiny space. No one in their right mind would want to hunker down here instead of on the dance floor.

I take a seat around the large wooden table at the center of the room. Everyone fills in around me, chatting and grabbing plates. Laughing, having genuine fun. Everyone's having fun, and I've spent most of the night thinking about my sister and her boyfriend. God, am I lame. How is it that after five months my mind still revolves around that one stupid thing? The thing that I'm completely understanding of, and is mostly my fault? Every time I think I've made my peace with what happened, my jealousy revives itself and nags me until I'm so submerged in my envy that my mood is ruined.

And here I am. Still thinking. Still obsessing. Still the only one in the room not having a good time.

"You have to blow them," Jer whispers in my ear, snapping me from my obsessive thoughts.

"What?" I choke on the swig of water in my mouth.

He chuckles, nodding his head toward the cake, with twenty-one little flames dancing atop. "The candles. You're supposed to blow them out."

"Right." I breathe, adjusting the skirt of my dress, which feels twice as tight now that I'm sitting. No one else seems to be suffocated by their choice of attire, either that, or they're having way too much fun to notice.

Never in my life have I felt so out of place, let alone at a party thrown for me.

3

TORI

I can say with absolute certainty that I've never heard "Happy Birthday" sung with so much harmony in my life. I almost melted into a puddle on the floor. It's safe to say that it was undoubtedly the highlight of my night. *Hell,* that was probably the highlight of my *life.* After we had cake, the guys had the DJ pause the music and sang to me again, along with everyone else at the party. It's also safe to say that after their performance I was in a significantly better mood.

"Thank you, guys!" I say, throwing my arms around each of the boys. It's two in the morning, and the party is just now starting to break up. Mostly everyone has gone, and the boys are tasked with locking up the doors and returning the keys to the owner. I guess when you have multiple multiplatinum records, businesses don't require supervision when they rent out their hall. Either that, or Carson's well-known, humble, hometown-boy personality is enough for anyone to put trust in him. I mean, I definitely see the appeal.

"Thank Rylee." Jamie nods in my sister's direction. "This was all her."

I bite my lip, eyeing the concrete before I turn my attention to her. She'd made it sound like Carson did all the work.

That was probably just so you'd come.

She smiles slightly, averting her eyes. "It was nothing."

"Well, thanks." I bump her shoulder with mine, because I don't know what else to say or how else to act around her.

We're so strained. After our talk in California, I expected us to go back to how we were in middle school, but I guess we're not the same people as we were back then. I miss when life was that easy, despite how hard and trying we made it seem at the time. I'd give anything to go back there. I'd give anything to change how I acted toward her because I let my jealousy get in the way. Even with this remission, I still let my jealousy get the better of me when it comes to her, instead of trying to smooth things over. We slapped an old Band-Aid over a wound that needs stitches, and it's starting to fall off again. Our one night of talking wasn't enough to fix the long, tearing gash that is our sisterhood. It needs care and work that I'm just not ready to put in. I want to be. I just... I don't know how.

I give my last hug to Jamie, who sways a little when I latch onto him. Of all the band members, he's the one I don't particularly like—which I never could have imagined in my wildest dreams. I've only been around him a handful of times. In the last few months, whenever the band had a weekend off, they'd fly here for a day or two—Jamie stayed locked in his room the whole time, hardly socializing, or doing anything other than lying in bed all day, but he was better then than he is now. Or maybe I'm just seeing more of him than I did then.

I pull away and meet his eyes, which rest unfocused above my head looking up at the skyline. He tries to take a step backward and loses his balance, clutching onto my hips for balance.

"Are you okay?" I ask, dipping my head to catch his eyes, now focused on the worn gravel beneath our shoes.

"Peachy." He smirks, his breath a cloud of alcohol so thick I hold back the urge to gag. He lifts a finger and bops me on the nose. "As long as the *birthday girl* had a good night," he slurs, backing away with more caution and balance this time, trying so hard to be aware of every move he makes so he doesn't stumble again.

"Why'd you say it like that?" I ask, unsure of what he means, and a little perturbed at his tone. Drunk or not, I've only ever known Jamie to be a grade-A ass, and whenever it comes to me, he's just a downright douche.

He shrugs carelessly, slowly dragging himself to his car (which Carson is driving) with amusement dancing in his eyes. "Your sister gave you everything you wanted tonight, and you look like all you want to do is whine about it."

"Excuse me?" I spat, but it's too late. He's already tripping into the car and slamming the door. I don't know why the words of a drunk idiot felt like such a slap in the face, but my chest burns where the insult hit. I stare after the band's vehicle as it drives away, and count to ten. Five times. It doesn't work, though. My anger is still boiling.

"You coming, Tor?" Dylan calls from Rylee's car. Her head is bent past his and she's looking out the window with concern.

"You okay?" she calls. A drop of rain lands on my forehead, sliding down my cheek. I look up at the dark sky, taking a slow, deep breath.

"Yep, coming!" I call, jogging through the light rain that's now splashing on the ground. "Carson's not coming with us?" I ask once I'm safe inside the car. It's become a habit that Carson stays at our house. Mom and Dad don't particularly like it, but they'd rather him stay here than her sleep in his hotel room with three other guys. Plus, when he's hardly ever around, they can't exactly deny their daughter the right to see her boyfriend whenever he has a free moment, which normally is late at night when rehearsals and recording sessions are finished. Even then, sometimes he's stuck working until the wee hours of the morning, and I know it bugs her.

"I think he and Jamie are coming back after they drop off Kris and Jer." She shifts the car into reverse, glancing at the camera on the dashboard, then at both sideview mirrors.

"Great," I sigh, running a hand through my damp hair.

"Huh?" she questions, pausing before pulling out onto the road, even though no one else is out this late.

Another habit: Jamie always tags along with Carson. Wherever he goes. No matter what. I do kind of understand, though. The two of them basically got the band together, and they've grown closest over the years. Carson doesn't want Jamie to be alone right now. Not after the tragic accident with his sister. That's the only pass I give him for being a complete and total jerk. Almost five months ago, Jamie's older sister Mara was shot and killed by her drug dealer when she failed to pay him her dues, and I didn't know Jamie before that happened—thanks, sis!—but from what I gather, he hasn't been the same since.

"I said great," I repeat, sounding more annoyed than I mean to.

"Punch buggy!" Dylan yells, leaning over the center console to punch me.

Clutching my arm where he hit me, I groan in pain. "Ow. What is your problem? There weren't even any cars!"

"Yes, but it is approximately two-thirty, which means your birthday is over, *which means* I no longer have to be nice to you." He grins so mischievously I could slap him. I could slap him so hard.

"I hate you." I shake my head, looking out the window at the passing trees.

"You couldn't if you wanted to," he remarks, satisfaction skating through his sarcasm.

Where Rylee has been nicer to me, Dylan has made up for in snide comments. "Would it kill you to be nice to me, you know, just because?"

He looks back at me with sad eyes. "I'm sorry, Tori, but I don't want to die young."

At that Rylee snickers, then clears her throat, changing the subject. "Hey, so I was thinking."

What now?

"Jamie is starting a charity foundation where he'll collection donations for—" she pauses, clearing her throat, "—for Mara, and he's using the profits to help build and design homes to help recovering addicts get back on their feet. I thought it would be a good thing for you to do, you know with your real estate interests and interior design niche. I thought maybe you could get in on it. I'm handling all the social media and marketing angles, but he could really use some creative inspiration."

Rylee looks at me through the review mirror, uncertainty in her eyes.

"And why would I do that?"

"It pays thirty-five dollars an hour."

"Why not." I give her a stretched, fake smile.

Truthfully, I have nothing better to do now that school is out for the summer, and I don't exactly have a job anymore after I cussed out a customer for leaving a penny as a tip... And though I'd never, ever, ever admit it, this could really be a leg up for me to get my name out there, not only with a good cause, but with Jamie's influence and reputation, too. Though, with the amount of alcohol he consumes on a daily basis, I'm not sure how clean that reputation is anymore.

"For real?" Her voice rises an octave. As if I'd turn down that kind of money.

"Do you want me to change my mind?" I threaten, and her face falls a little. Not a ton, but enough for me to notice and feel a pang of guilt in my chest. *She's only trying to help,* I remind myself. "Thanks, Ry."

She just nods, turning her attention back to the road ahead, lit by nothing but her bright headlights.

My eyes dart to Dylan, who is uncharacteristically quiet. He's fiddling with the bracelet Dad gave him, and it makes me look down at my own wrist, at the bracelet from Rylee I've been absentmindedly playing with all night.

I open the window, hoping some fresh air will rid the car of unwanted tension.

It doesn't.

4

TORI

"Is he okay?"

Rylee's sitting cross-legged on the couch, her eyes boring into Jamie, who's slumped over the kitchen counter, milking a glass of water.

Carson shakes his head, eyes following hers to where his friend is basically passed out—the cup he's holding is the only indication that he's not. An unreadable expression crosses Carson's face. Concern? Fear? Denial? His ocean eyes clear a bit, and he finally speaks. "Everyone keeps saying it's going to get better."

"And what do you think?" she prods. Though, it's not so much prodding given how in sync they are. She's not searching for answers, she's trying to help him lay out his thoughts as I've often seen him do with her. They actually value each other's opinion, and in my experience, that's rare. She almost helps him understand what he's feeling, even if he's unsure himself.

His cheeks puff out with air, and he releases it at once,

looking younger than his sharp features make him out to be. "I think he needs help." His voice cracks when he talks, and an ache stings my chest seeing him this way. Rylee doesn't hesitate, though, resting her cheek on his shoulder like it belongs there.

"We'll figure it out. Even if we have to go against what he wants," she mumbles, pressing her lips against the exposed divot in his collarbone where his shirt is twisted to reveal a small sliver of golden skin.

"Jealous?" Hot breath tickles my ear, making my hairs stand on edge. I clutch my chest, turning to find Jamie uncomfortably close.

"How did you get over here so fast?" I gasp, glancing at the now-empty chair, slightly askew at the kitchen island. It's a miracle Jamie managed to sneak up on me in his state.

"I'm not that drunk." He winces, sliding down the wall so he's on the floor.

Rylee glances over Carson and says something softly so only he can hear. I tear my eyes from them, feeling a little embarrassed that I was caught watching their interaction so closely. Besides the jealousy and longing I feel when I see them together, I also feel something else I can't quite pinpoint. When Carson is around, I get to see a side of my sister I hadn't known existed. She's suddenly not my little sister, but a woman paving her own way through life as someone I don't recognize.

And that's the part that both stuns me and saddens me the most.

There's a clicking sound, and the smell of smoke wafts

up to my nose. I wrinkle it, looking around for the source of the smell when my gaze rests on *him*.

"What do you think you're doing?" I hiss, snatching the cigarette from Jamie's mouth and tossing it into a nearby trashcan after smothering the end. "My mother is a bloodhound. She'll smell your smoke all the way from Utah." I shake my head, disgusted. "And you're already drunk, why do you need to smoke?"

He shrugs, brushing his long hair from his face. "Dunno. Feels good."

"Well, it's gross."

"Then it's a good thing it's not your problem."

"*Well, I'm next to you,* so it kind of is my problem when I have to *sit here* and smell your—"

"Tori," Rylee calls. I look up to find her standing in the hallway, motioning for me. I roll my eyes, and pluck a second cigarette from Jamie's hand, throwing it in the trash before he gets the chance to light it.

"If there's a third one when I come back, I'm lighting your jacket on fire," I threaten sweetly, leaning in close enough to smell the stale alcohol on his breath. He glances down at the black leather and scoots away from me a bit. I smirk in satisfaction. With all the times he's bitched at me, this was long overdue.

When I finally reach the hallway, I can tell Rylee has something to say by the way she licks her lips and averts eye contact. I only watched her do it for a month when she was lying to me about Carson. She's a horrible liar, but a genius with cover stories... not to mention she had my brother's help—the king of deception.

"What is it now?" I await her convictions, spreading my arms wide. "What did I do this time, Little Miss Perfect?" Dylan appears then from the bathroom, wiping his hands on a towel. Guilt floods me instantly, shame washing away the anger I feel toward my sister. He hates when I'm mean to Rylee. Most of our arguments stem from his annoyance with my comments at our sister, arguments I usually blame on her for inadvertently starting.

"I was going to say take it easy on Jamie because he's going through a lot right now, but you know what? Just do whatever you want, Tori. You always do. I don't even care anymore." Rylee shakes her head a little, lifting her arms in surrender. Turning sharply, she continues up the stairs to her room.

"Rylee!" My voice cracks when I call her name. I messed up, once again. "What?" I shake my head at Dylan's disapproving look. It's like he thinks he's my dad or something, when he's actually five years younger than me. He's only in high school, and somehow gets the idea that he's above me.

Dylan scratches the back of his head, clearly debating whether to say what he really wants to. I don't know why he considers it when we both know he will. "You know, she's really trying. Maybe you could give her a break."

I scoff, closing my eyes to keep from crying. The anger I feel mixes with my remorse, and my eyelids are the only things keeping the tears from escaping. "Why does everyone keep telling me that?"

"Maybe because it's time you start listening." He shrugs, following the same path Rylee took up the stairs.

"She's only going to try for so long, Tori. So if you keep pushing her away, you're really going to lose her."

"Well, everyone just has words of wisdom tonight, don't they?" I scoff again, sounding immature. I can't help it.

Carson walks past me without saying a word, and I'm not even sure where he came from. Why would he say anything? What would he even say? It's not like he's going to try to make me feel better for insulting his girlfriend.

The second they're gone, I let my shoulders fall, face crumbling in my hands. I'm a terrible person. Dylan's right, Rylee is trying, and I just find every excuse possible to hate her for the things she does. Like the party. I didn't enjoy it because I spent the entire night hating that it was a party full of strangers... I mean, I love that. That's exactly what I want, where I thrive. The things she hates about Carson's life are the things I *want* out of it. I want the attention and the publicity. I want every girl in the world to despise me because I have the man of their dreams. I'd give anything for the world to know my name and recognize me as Carson's girl. I want to be controversial and have people question me just so I can put them in their place.

It's toxic.

I'm toxic. And yet, I still can't bring myself to change.

And the truly worst part? In all my anger and frustration, I never really thanked Rylee for tonight, either. I mean, I sort of did, but I didn't mean it. I could argue with her that I did and that I meant it, but we'd both know that's one of the many lies I tell her just to feel better about everything else I've done.

Sulking back into the living room, I plop on the couch where Jamie's made himself at home, sprawled out across most of the cushions. The last thing I want to do is sit here with him, but I don't feel like going to bed and being alone right now, even if the only other option is sitting in silence with an intoxicated jackass. I truly don't get why Rylee is so protective of him. I just don't see the broken boy she does, I guess. Which is surprising considering a year ago I'd have done anything, and I mean *anything,* for the chance to know Jamie LeMont.

"I'm sorry," he mumbles, looking at me. I look over my shoulder just in case there's someone else there he could be talking to. There's not.

I blink slowly, crossing my feet beneath me for warmth, and so I have something to focus on besides his heavy stare. "For what?"

"The things I said earlier. Your relationship with Rylee is none of my business."

"You're right." I bite my lip, and since we're handing out confessions, "About both things. It *is* none of your business... but I was also a bitch to her tonight."

He laughs, low and deep. "That you were."

Jamie tosses something across the space between us, and it lands in my lap, right on top of the stretched material between my thighs where my shins cross. It's a small, cardboard box. I recognize what it is the second I pick it up.

"What the...?"

"Help me quit, and I'll help you be nicer to your sister." He proposes, sitting up a little, then sliding right back down. He might be lucid, but he's in no way sober. "We'll keep each other in check."

I shrug, knowing he's way too drunk to remember this in the morning. "But don't you just have another pack of cigarettes at the hotel?"

It's his turn to shrug.

Great.

"I guess it'll work since I'm your new interior designer," I say thoughtfully, picking at my thumbnail.

"She asked you?" He raises a brow, surprised. "Even after how you treated her?"

I shoot him a warning glare. Just because we're making nice doesn't mean I want his judgmental opinions. He can keep those to himself.

"Hey, it's my job to make you aware of the situation." He smirks sinisterly, jerking his chin so the strands of hair that fall in his face move from his line of vision. "And I don't think you realize how much she cares about you."

I laugh bitterly. I can't help the next words that spew from my mouth. "Enough to tell me about her and Carson."

He groans, trying to sit up again, and finally succeeds. Jamie rests his elbows on his knees, hands over his face in exasperation. "See, that's your problem. Right there."

"What do you mean?" How is that my problem? If anything, he should be able to agree with me on that. I deserved to know, and instead I was tricked and lied to and made into a fool.

"What I mean is… it was none of your business. It's Rylee's life and she made the choice to keep her personal life, well, personal. You're not *entitled* to know everything about her. Plus, you do realize Dylan figured it out, she never planned on telling him, either." He raises his brows challengingly, and I scrunch my nose at the way he says *entitled,* as if I'm a princess, exactly like he called me earlier. A remark I won't soon forget.

"For a blubbering drunk, you have some pretty decent advice," I observe, squinting. I hate admitting there's a possibility he's right. It's not like I haven't thought the same thing many times, but I keep pushing it down and allowing jealousy to fuel my actions instead of my moral compass.

"Eh, alcohol doesn't affect me for long anymore."

"Because you drink too much?" I assert, hoping I haven't crossed a line. Actually—who cares? He crosses them all the time with me and feels no remorse. And since when do I care about crossing lines, anyway?

"We all have our demons." He shrugs, standing and snatching the cigarette pack from my lap. "I'm going for a walk."

"Uh-uh. Give it back," I order, grabbing his arm.

The dark grin he gives me sends tingles down my spine. "I was just testing you," he winks before turning back, tossing the pack over his shoulder and onto the table.

I couldn't have made that if I was looking, let alone with my back turned *and* intoxicated.

5

JAMIE

The cool, wet air is like a punch in the gut, knocking every ounce of air from my lungs. It hurts. Burns. Claws at me until my insides feel as though they're going to collapse on themselves.

You can't keep doing this. A voice whispers in my head. *I can't, I can't, I can't.*

She wouldn't want this. She wouldn't, she wouldn't, she wouldn't.

Except she's not here, so it doesn't fucking matter what she wants, now does it?

No. Didn't think so.

At the end of the circular housing plan, far enough so the nearest house can't see me, I stop just on the edge of the woods, scream, and thrust my fist into an oak. I groan, knowing the tree I chose to be the recipient of my anger doesn't hurt nearly as much as my hand does now. I clutch it to my stomach, holding it against me to ease the pain. My head clouds over from either the alcohol or the pain, so I lean against the tree while heaving in shallow breaths to calm my mind.

Might as well add this to the list of interrogative questions Elizabeth will have for me tomorrow morning when she gets into town. She wants to talk about our next album, which we haven't started—minus the *two* songs we've managed to scrounge up based on old, unreleased songs, and one Carson wrote for Rylee. Yeah, that's right, we used old, discarded ideas to stitch together a new song because we had literally nothing else. Of course, the rest of the guys want to stay here and get "inspiration" from the humble small town, i.e., stay here to be close to Rylee. Not that I mind. I like her just as much as the next guy... well, maybe a little more. It's complicated, but sleeping so close to where Mara—to where she—

Shit.

It's been half a year, Jamie, pull it together.

I can't, I can't, I can't.

This isn't what she would want for you.

She was my sister. My best friend. I should have seen it coming. I should have known. I should have stopped her, done something that those pointless rehab centers couldn't—just taking our money and sending her back to us before she was truly clean. As if they didn't know Jordan, her drug dealer and killer, could funnel drugs inside. How stupid were they? How stupid am I? Then, by some miracle, the final center she admitted herself to worked. At least, it seemed to. I guess now we'll never know.

You did this to her.

No. No, no, no. Please no.

If I hadn't been so scared of the consequences of paying off a drug dealer, and what it might do to my and the band's reputations, she might still be alive. I could have saved her. I could have done something. Goddammit, I *should* have done something.

If only I had seen the signs and immediately realized there was something more going on with her than she let on. If I had, if I had seen through her lies the day she spontaneously showed up at our suite, maybe things would have turned out differently...

The suite doors open smoothly, revealing an empty, calm room. I'm relieved to have a moment to myself before the chaos starts when the others come back. I'm walking in when I freeze, shocked to see my sister lounging on our couch. "Mara?"

"Hey there, little brother." She smiles that brilliant smile that gets all the guys talking. Her hair is currently raven black, though that'll change soon enough, it always does. I have to say I prefer this, her natural color, best. She's been talking about going platinum, though, so I better get used to the idea of that drastic change.

Mara jumps into my arms, squeezing me as tight as her frail arms can muster. I wrap my own around her and tighten my grip, rocking her gently back and forth.

"What are you doing here?" I laugh, lifting her from the ground.

She pretends to be offended. She's never been a good actress. "Can't a sister just miss her brother?"

"I missed you, too," I mumble, burying my face in her hair. It always smells like strawberries.

When we were growing up, our dad's job required us to travel a lot, and on top of that, our parents both often had multiple-day business trips, too. So aside from nannies we'd often been pawned off to, it was just Mara and me. All we had was each other until I met Carson. If anyone changed my life, it's him—taking us in whenever our parents were away and making sure we always had a place to stay when we needed it. Even if we just needed a little break from reality for a while, Carson and his parents offered us an escape. He always had our backs. Still does.

"So, how's it going... anything new?" she prods. "How many hearts have you broken this week?"

"None." I roll my eyes. "We've been in Texas for a day, Mar."

Her hands rise in surrender, and she laughs, the sound making my chest swell. This is the longest we've ever been apart since I was born. Seven months.

"How's that tool of yours?" I can't say his name. It puts a sour taste in my mouth.

As if a switch flips, Mara is no longer smiling. She looks at me seriously, shaking her head. Normally she'd correct me, "His name's Danny," or "I'm happy, isn't that enough for you?" but not this time. This time, her face turns a modest shade of pink, and she tucks a big clump of midnight hair behind her studded ears, more piercings than I can count lining up her pale flesh.

"We're done," she says instead, brushing me off. "How's the concert lineup looking so far?"

"No. Don't do that. Don't change the subject. What happened? Last time I saw you, you were practically ringing wedding bells."

"Things change, Jamie. Let it go."

"No. What did he do?" I know for a fact a lowlife like that wouldn't dump my sister. He couldn't afford to. There's no way in hell he'd find another girl like her to show even a minuscule amount of interest in him. And oh, did she ever. Mara was head over heels for that prick, so for them to be over... something happened.

Her head shakes, and she turns away from me, eyes filling with tears.

"He used to just push me around a little," she chokes, holding her breath. Mara doesn't like to cry, and when other people cry, she gets uncomfortable. She always used to tell me there was something about the vulnerability of tears that bonded you with another person, and she never wanted to give that much of herself away to someone. "But not, not last time."

"He hurt you." It's not a question.

"No. It's fine."

"Mara."

"Jamie, it's fine. It's handled. We're done, okay? That's the end of it." Her fingers trace the tears that have leaked out, making the bags beneath her eyes more prominent.

"Where is he?"

"What?" She blinks. "He's back in Nashville, Jamie. Let it go, I shouldn't have told you."

"I'm going to kill him."

"No, you aren't," she sighs, standing up to watch me pace the room. Finally, I grab my jacket and move toward the door, having made up my mind. I'm definitely going to kill him.

"And how do you think you're getting to Tennessee from here? You can't just take the band jet."

"A plane," I grunt, steam rolling from my ears as my rage grows.

"You need a ticket."

"I'll just get one from Ticket Master or whatever!" I scream.

Mara blinks rapidly. "Jamie, they only sell event tickets."

"Well, is murder an event?" My arms flail wildly, and she grabs onto them, holding my forearms against my chest. I probably look like a madman, but I don't care. The bastard hurt my sister, and he won't get away with it.

I'm expecting a lecture, or an eye roll, or even a slap upside the head. She hugs me, instead, and my anger melts away a little.

"I'm okay, and he's taken care of. That's all that matters," she whispers, smoothing back my hair, which is in desperate need of a trim. "Can I crash with you and the guys for a while, though? I haven't told Mom and Dad, and I really don't feel like going back home alone."

"Whatever you need." I frame her face with my hands, searching her tired eyes and frowning lips. "Whatever you need."

6

TORI

"Tori!" A pillow smacks me in the face.

"Ahh, what? Don't kill me, please!" Shielding my face, I take a quick peek at my assaulter. "Oh. It's you."

"Where's Jamie?" Rylee crosses her arms. Her face is blank, but last night's anger still brims in her eyes.

"I don't know, he went for a walk after you guys left." I roll over, smacking my face on something hard. "Ow! What the f—" I squint at the solid arm of the... couch? Am I in the living room? I must have fallen asleep.

"Tori, that was last night. Jamie's not in a place right now to be going on walks alone in the dark! What were you thinking?!"

Rolling off the couch, I grab my jacket and slide on my slippers, following a panicking Rylee out the front door and hustling to keep up with her as she jogs down the sidewalk. "I was *thinking* he's a twenty-one-year-old man who can handle going on a late-night walk to get some air."

"Before, yes, but now... not after Mara. Now we need to find him before Carson wakes up and realizes he's gone."

My stomach sinks. Mara. Of course. How could I be so dumb? His sister is dead, and I spent most of the day insulting him. Everyone but him has seemed to move on, so I don't think much about her anymore. I didn't even go to the funeral because I'd never met her, but from what I heard, it was worse than I could imagine.

"Jamie?" Rylee whispers loudly, scanning the street and peering down the grass walkways between houses.

I nod my head approvingly. "Oh yeah, that'll do it. Good job, Rylee. Maybe I should run back in and grab some treats for him? Bottle of bourbon, maybe? That should perk his ears right up."

She stops midstride and laughs bitterly to herself. "Can you not? Please, for once?"

"Sorry." I bite my lip, sucking in the hollows of my cheeks.

"How many times do you have to say sorry before you mean it, Tori? Honestly, it's like you can't even talk to me anymore. I thought we worked all of this out in Cali. What's your deal?"

"I don't know," I whisper honestly, pursing my lips. Despite my anger and the bubbling jealousy I can't explain, I feel the sudden urge to cry.

I don't know.

She doesn't say anything more, just keeps walking and searching for Jamie like he's her lost dog. I snicker to myself when I picture her stapling LOST DRUMMER posters on every telephone pole for miles, but keep that amusing thought to myself.

We continue throughout the rest of the plan, turning around and backtracking to the opposite end until we stumble across Jamie, slumped uncomfortably against a wide tree. His shirt is unbuttoned and has bright red smudges messily slopped on the front of it. I grit my teeth, squinting my eyes to get a better look at the hand he cradles in his lap.

"Is that blood?" I gag, turning away before I throw up what's left of last night's birthday cake. Luckily, it looks as if most of it came from his fist, which is still oozing thickly.

"Oh God," my sister says. "Jamie, what did you do?"

His eyes open as she grabs onto his face with both hands. "Got in a fight with Mrs. Oakwood. She's a dirty woman. Splinters and all."

Rylee lifts him from the ground easily, and for as small as she is, I'm shocked she's able to lift him at all considering I don't think he's much help with carrying any of own his weight.

"Here." I grab under his other arm and help her pull him away from the tree a little more. We balance him between us, struggling to keep him from tipping forward and backward between incomprehensible ramblings. "Can you try to walk?"

He shakes his head, a tear leaking from his eyes. He throws his head back toward the sky, the jerking movement causing one of his carelessly tied shoes to slip from beneath him. It takes every ounce of my strength to keep the both of us standing straight. Jamie's hand clamps down on my hip for balance, clutching onto a fistful of the dress I never changed out of.

Rylee glances at me helplessly, and I shrug, not knowing what to do any more than she does.

"Tori, stay with him, I'm getting the car. We'll never be able to carry him all the way back to the house like this."

I nod, easing Jamie back to the ground as Rylee takes off in a jog back down the road.

Biting my lip, I rack my brain for a way to distract him, and, well, myself. "You suck at your end of the bargain, I hope you know that."

"What do you mean?" he groans, taking some of his weight back. His back was still leaning against my arm before he shifted, and I'm surprised he manages to sit on his own, though I catch him wincing with each movement.

"Rylee's pissed because I let you leave last night, and you never came back." His job is to help me be nicer to Rylee, not to give her more reasons to disown me.

He chuckles, but it sounds hollow and lifeless. There's no humor behind his forced laugh. "You're not too hot at this either."

Confusion stirs my thoughts as he fumbles in his pants pockets, until he finds a small white box, half the cigarettes missing. So, he *does* remember our deal.

Honestly, when I brought it up, I didn't think he'd have a clue what I was talking about.

"Seriously?" It shouldn't be funny, but for some reason I can't help but laugh. "We suck."

Laughing, he bops my nose like he did last night, just

with less mockery this time, then tosses something else into my lap. "That we do, birthday girl."

"Don't touch my nose," I order, a slight grin cracking through my serious exterior. I refrain from telling him it's no longer my birthday.

My eyes find a small bottle in my lap, and I groan inwardly when I realize he must have stolen it from our cabinet before he left. Mom and Dad travel a lot, so they keep a stash of travel-sized alcohol in the small cabinet above the fridge. I only know this because I have, on several occasions, stolen a few from the back as well.

Jamie positions his finger above my nose so it's hovering like a challenge. His brow quirks.

My expression turns serious as I raise two of my own eyebrows in warning. I don't have the energy to be mad at him at the moment. "Don't do it."

"And what if I do?" he threatens, words slurring as if he's talking in cursive.

"Just don't." I'm unable to hold in the smirk that wants to splay across my face. "Don't do it, Jamie."

"You sound like my mom," he jokes, and as I'm distracted, he bops my nose with his finger, then tries to get away.

In retrospect, I'm not sure what in the world made him think he could get away from me in his state, but he sure as heck tried... and didn't even make it off the ground.

I snatch his box of cigarettes and toss them farther than my eyes can see, much less his.

"You've got an arm," he concludes, scanning me up and down in surprise. The pack of cigarettes is completely forgotten. Just as well, I'm sure he has plenty more where that came from.

If only he knew I couldn't even throw a crumpled piece of paper from my bed to the trashcan below it.

Suddenly, he grumbles, sliding away from me to grab the shoe that flew off in his attempt to flee my wrath. "Here comes the cavalry."

At first, I'm confused, because I think he's talking about my sister and Carson, but then I see it. A bright, cherry red Audi R8 Spyder cruising down the road. No wonder it took Rylee so long to get the car.

Jamie and I both look at each other, dread etched into his slack face, and say, "Elizabeth."

"God help us," he moans, pulling a spare cigarette from his pocket, and lighting it.

7

TORI

If there was a medal for the most disgusted, disapproving look, Elizabeth would hold the world record for most awards. There's a fine line between pissed off and annoyed, and she has definitely crossed over both thresholds and is now headed directly into crazy territory.

"Lizzy-bear, I think you're blowing this a tad out of proportion. My mans was just getting acquainted with nature, finding his chi, if you will?"

"Stop talking." Elizabeth holds up her hand, silencing Kris as he babbles on. His idea of help isn't as helpful as he thinks it is. "Jamie." She turns her attention to the hot mess sitting on our couch, looking as if he'd rather be anywhere but here. I mean, I get it. He messed up. Again. I don't see, however, why the entire band needed to come here to talk about it. Not only is that humiliating, but there's a good chance he has a major hangover and stiff neck from sleeping against a tree—and don't even get me started on his bloody hand. Now isn't the best time for accusations. "What were you thinking? What if there were paparazzi? Don't you remember December? The last time you were intoxicated in front of cameras?"

Jamie sucks in his cheeks, spreading his legs and propping them on the coffee table. His hands open upward as if to insinuate he remembers just fine. "Yes. It's no big deal. I'm good."

I stare at his dirty shoes and cringe, knowing if Rylee and I don't clean that thing spotless, Mom will have a coronary. Though, I figure now isn't the best time to shove myself into the conversation just to ask him to be polite.

"No. Not good, because last time you were almost sued for assault and battery, Jamie. This needs to stop." She pauses momentarily to look at each of the boys. Her lips sag more than usual, and now she looks like *she'd* rather be anywhere but here. "This was posted on a media blog last night. I tried to have it taken down, but they refused because it wasn't out of context."

Jamie squints at the screen Elizabeth has turned his way, and by the looks of his dour expression, he doesn't like what he sees.

"Lindsay Birmingham, is it? The two of you couldn't find a less public place to make out?"

"It's not my fault, I was—" Jamie pauses, dropping his face in his hands, kneading the heels of his palms into his eye sockets. "I was drunk."

Elizabeth closes her eyes and takes a seat beside him on the couch. She folds her hands around his much larger ones, waiting until he looks at her to continue. "I know things have been tough. And I think that's mostly why the tabloids aren't all over this yet, but you've got to pull yourself together. The label wants me to do something about your behavior because it's damaging the band's image. I don't want to get involved, I'd rather let you figure things out on your own, but they aren't giving me much of a choice, and honestly, neither are you."

"Are they gonna drop us?" Kris asks in the most serious tone I've ever heard from him. His jaw clenches tight and he stands rigid, trying to hide the worry lines creeping across his features.

I furrow my brow, wondering why they'd have to be concerned about the label dropping them at all when their success has proven to dominate that of anyone else's. I mean, they'd just get picked up by another label. But after staring around at all of their somber faces, I realize that in their minds, they're still a band of young boys trying to keep their heads above water.

Elizabeth shakes her head shortly. "No, but we don't want things to get bad enough that they have to consider it."

I'm not sure why, but I hold my breath while Elizabeth talks. Friendships aside, I've followed 13 Days of December since the moment I heard their first single on the radio. I was in love. Irrevocably drawn to their sound and their looks. Not only that, I was drawn to their image. They weren't typical Hollywood celebrities in it for the money or the fame, putting on a façade the world would eat up. They were genuine and real—so much more like everyday people than I ever imagined anyone of their status could be. I just wish they had more faith in themselves.

"That kind of goes along with what me and Ry have been talking about." Carson sticks his neck out. Every head in the room turns to look at him and my sister, leaning against the kitchen island with Dylan at their side. The Three Musketeers. "I think that we should all settle down somewhere and take some time to sort things out, focus on our next album—because let's be honest, it's not coming along very well, and we're all exhausted from the tour."

"For the record," Rylee claims, raising her hands, "from a professional standpoint, I don't condone this."

"But?" Elizabeth sighs, and I'm surprised at how willing she is to hear my sister's opinion. If I so much as open my mouth, her eyes roll back in her head.

What surprises me more is how good Rylee is at this job.

"But... as a friend and girlfriend, I think a break might be healthy. The fans won't like it, not after they just thought they were losing him because of, well, me." She shrugs her shoulders carelessly. "When any band takes time off, rumors start up about breakups and tension between members, so we'd have to be careful about how we promote it, especially since a lot of people will argue that they just had a break over the holiday. We could say being here for Christmas made Carson want to go back to his roots and rediscover the small-town boy inside. The fans will eat up the wholesome act, and we can keep the media in the loop, tease new music so they don't feel closed off from them... because we don't want that again."

"Act?" Carson dips his head to get a better look at Rylee.

She looks up, scrunched brows creating little frown lines around her eyes. "Huh?

He blinks, offended. "Wholesome *act?*"

"You know what I mean." She smirks, bumping him with her hip.

Jer quirks his lips smugly. "Come on, Car, we all know you're not wholesome in the bedr—"

Dylan's eyebrows raise a mile, and Jer clamps his mouth shut really quick, looking around the room at all of our faces. I find that even my eyes are popping from my skull. I've never seen my sister so uncomfortable, or Carson, for that matter.

Jer looks to Kris for help, probably because he's usually the one who takes his jokes too far. "Don't look at me. You dug the grave, you can lay in it by yourself."

Everyone laughs to themselves, and I catch Dylan mouthing threatening words at Carson. Rylee must yell at him because he clenches his jaw and growls lowly.

"*Anyway,*" Elizabeth breathes, smoothing her jet-black pantsuit. "If that's what you *all* want," she eyes my sister like she's the sole reason behind this plan, "then I'm okay with it."

Everyone is silent in shock. It was that easy?

In all honesty, Elizabeth probably needs a break more than any of the boys do. All she does is damage control when they screw up, which seems to be a lot more often than I ever thought. I guess that means she's good at her job, because I know everything that's ever happened to them—in a totally non-creepy way, of course—and I never hear about this sort of stuff.

"What about charity work?" My voice strikes loudly in the quiet room. They all look at me, confused. I clear my throat, wiping sweaty hands on the joggers I changed into earlier. "I mean, that'll look good, right? You're already starting the—that foundation." I stumble on my words, afraid of saying her name. My eyes bounce to Jamie nervously. "So, isn't that good publicity?"

Carson is the first to speak, glancing back and forth between me and Jamie. "Yes, but it's not enough. Anyone can throw money into something and wash their hands of it. Celebrities do it all the time. We'd need footage of you actively being involved and living your day-to-day life. We need to make it look like you're getting your life together."

Jamie scoffs. "Gee, thanks."

"Hey, it's your mess, I'm just cleaning it up," Carson snaps, and once again, you could hear a pin drop in the room. Rylee's hand finds Carson's, and she gives it a squeeze, which seems to physically remove the tension in his shoulders. He lets out a long breath and shakes his head. "I'm sorry."

It's evident Jamie's behavior has the whole band on edge, yet they're trying to be understanding and supportive. He's been through a lot, but in any case, there's only so much people are willing to take before enough is enough. And putting their reputation on the line, not to mention their record deal... I think it's safe to say that they have all reached *enough* by now.

"You're right." Jamie shakes his head in defeat. "If that counts for anything."

He sucks in his cheeks, looking anything but happy about his life being called a "mess."

"I have an idea." Dylan stands, stretching his arms. There's an arrogant gleam in his eye that sends shivers up my spine.

"Dylan..." Rylee drags, looking scared of what crazy thing he might say.

"Everyone's obsessed with *Ryson* or whatever," his fingers quote around *Ryson*—the cutesy name the fans came up with combining both Rylee's and Carson's name —as he makes a gagging gesture, "so why not give Jamie that same image?"

"I am not dating them both," Rylee expresses, raising her hands in the air.

"No, not you." Dylan rolls his eyes in exasperation. "Someone else. Someone who could give off that same kind of image. Someone... like..."

My brother's eyes rest on me and I fight the urge to dive under the table and hide where no one can see me.

"Me?" I deadpan. "You're kidding me. Just because we share the same last name doesn't mean people will view us with the same respect."

"Then you make them. All the fans have done a three-sixty and think Rylee is good for Carson. If they see Miss Humble Beauty's sister with Mr. Hot Mess—no offense, Jamie —then maybe they'll start to think the same thing about you."

Is it bad that the idea... intrigues me? Dating—or fake

dating—Jamie LeMont would be absolutely perfect. I'd finally be even with Rylee. We'd be tied.

"And we could add a bonus to your paycheck for the foundation, too. That way you wouldn't be doing it for nothing," Rylee suggests.

"I'm not fake dating her," Jamie states. "No way. We sort of did that with Stacy and Carson, and we all saw how that turned out. She's psychotic."

My eyes blink rapidly. "Excuse me?" I squeak, and at the same time he says, "No offense, love."

"I like it," says their manager. "I like it a lot. Having a stable relationship will be great for publicity. It'll make you look like you have an anchor." And with that said, she exits the room, grabbing her keys off the decorative table in our hallway. "I better not see or hear from any of you for a while."

"She means, 'don't fuck up,'" Kris mumbles in my ear. I stifle a laugh, dropping my head.

Jamie's the next to stand, looking pale as a ghost. He looks around the room as if weighing his options, even though he doesn't really have any.

"I don't open doors," he grunts and bumps into my shoulder as he walks by, dropping an empty cigarette pack in the garbage can.

"And I don't put up with bullshit," I sass, turning on my heels and tugging on the back of his leather jacket. "So, you might wanna watch yourself."

"Ooh shit." Kris whistles, eyeing Jer and Carson. "She's got a little spunk of her own."

Dylan drapes his arm across Kris' shoulders. "It runs in the family."

8

TORI

Oh, the life of dating a pop star.

Fake dating.

F-ating?

Yeah fating, that sounds good. I like it.

Actually, I hate it. This is the dumbest possible thing in the world.

Have I dreamt my entire life about going on a date with Jamie LeMont? Yes. In my most mystical and fantastical dreams did I imagine he'd only be here because he was forced to be? Absolutely not.

But I can improvise. Fate led me halfway, now I've gotta do the leg work.

"I want a hat," I pout, punching him in the arm. "Jamie. Jamie? Oh, for God's sake, put the cigarette down!"

His fingers enclose mine as I try to yank it from his hand. He stares at me heatedly, closes his eyes, then reluctantly releases it into my care, clenching his empty fist around the air.

"And the rest?"

He gives me a long look, removing a half-empty pack of cigarettes from his pocket and giving it to me, as well.

"Don't let anything happen to them," he pleads. "That's all I ask."

"I'll burn them all," I say dryly. "How much longer do we have to sit here?"

"Until the paparazzi find us." The burger he's munching on drops to the table, and he brushes crumbs from his hands. "Who the hell's idea was it to get spotted in McDonald's anyway?"

"Whose do you think?" Honestly, who else would come up with that other than my lovesick sister and her halfwit boyfriend? "All things aside, they had really shitty luck in this place." I wrinkle my nose at the stuffy floors and dirty tables. Sure, the end result was great, I guess, but a lot of bad came out of the media's quick response. "What kind of stable relationship starts here?"

Jamie's lips spread into a thin, bitter line. "I could name one."

"I don't get it," I say finally, stepping through the open door—or more like forcing my way through a small crack. I've been dying to dig into that deep, dark mind of his. "You love Rylee."

The straw of his iced tea escapes his lips, spraying directly up his nose. Jamie chokes, motioning for the napkins on my tray.

"Drink much?" He gives me a sour look as I drop the napkins in his hand, the other catching the remaining tea dripping from his chin. "And Carson's your best friend. So why do you get so defensive whenever their relationship is brought up?"

"I don't get defensive," he scowls.

"Yes, you do."

"No, I don't."

"You're getting defensive right now!"

"I am not." He stands abruptly, grabbing his trash and crushing it into his to-go bag with the rest of his half-eaten fries. "I'm telling Elizabeth this isn't working. I don't know why I ever thought it would. I'm not Carson, people don't gravitate toward me the way they do him."

"Well, then, we'll have to try something else," I suggest, grabbing his hand. He freezes, rotating to look at me. The side door opens, and a rush of air blows his hair from his face. I swallow, standing up to meet him. "And that's not true, anyway."

Jamie scratches at the slight stubble peeking through his skin, making me well-aware that I'm still holding onto his hand. I should probably let go.

"I just wish everyone didn't care so much about my image. My sister's dead. Can't they let me be?"

His fingers squeeze mine before he submerges them deep in his pockets. I blink away the fog that's clouded around my thoughts and try to get back to where we were, but it's pointless. I can't remember. His eyes search my face, probably waiting for a snarky comment or witty comeback. I don't have either.

He swallows hard, glancing at the counter where a few girls stand inconspicuously with their cameras tilted toward us, whispering beneath excited breaths. Jamie's voice is rough when he speaks. "I think someone spotted us."

"If only we knew we just had to cause a scene. We'd have been out of here a while ago." The door opens again, sending in a fresh wave of cold air that replaces the settling warmth around us.

"Yeah," he agrees, seeming uncomfortable. He won't look at me.

Nice going, Tori, you just had to grab his hand and make things weird.

His words from earlier creep up my spine. *We sort of did that with Stacy and Carson, and we all saw how that turned out. She's psychotic.* Does he think I'm psychotic? That I might turn into her? That I am like her?

I hope not. Not that it even matters, we're only fating after all. Besides, what the hell do I care if Jamie thinks I'm a little bonkers?

"Should we...?" I nod to the side door suggestively.

He nods his head "We can go. If they didn't already get pictures, they will."

"'Kay," I whisper. While I'm sliding my arms through the burgundy sleeves of my winter jacket, Jamie removes the deep green beanie holding his messy hair in place and fits it to my head.

"What are you doing?" I whisper, just about choking on the words.

He shrugs, throwing my trash away—besides the few fries I have left over—then picks up my purse and slides it on my shoulder. His fingers trail down my arm until they touch tips with mine. He hovers for a second before taking them in his, height towering over me. "Ready?"

"For what?" I breathe, knowing what he has in mind can't be remotely close to what I'm hoping for.

"The cameras? Your face to be plastered on every social media platform, every news station?" He smirks, tilting the beanie on my head. His teeth snag on his bottom lip seductively. "What did you think I meant?"

Oh, he's good.

A little too good.

"That's what I thought," I say dumbly, blinking swiftly and tilting my head. His cheeks turn rosy, and he dips his chin to the side. I take the opportunity to get close enough so I can whisper low in his ear. "What did *you* think I meant?"

Yeah... I'm good, too.

He pushes open the doors and a cool breeze hugs my skin, making me shiver. "I draw the line at giving you my jacket," he whispers, but not rudely, more whimsical. There's a humor in his voice I've never heard before.

"You sure know how to put on a show," I remark offhandedly.

He tilts his head up at the stars, savoring the calm before the storm. "You're not so bad yourself."

"Jamie!" a voice calls from a car up ahead.

"Here we go." He smiles through clenched teeth. "Don't trip."

Smirking, I take the first step toward madness, sticking my foot *just* in front of his. He stumbles slightly over my wedges, catching himself at the last second.

"Jeez, walk much?" I blow a kiss at the cameraman closest to me and he melts like putty in my hands.

Before I realize it, a dozen cameras swarm around us, blocking our path across the sidewalk. Each of them yells out questions, accusations, some even just ask him to look directly at their camera so they can get the best shot.

I plaster on my best smile, though with the excitement bubbling in my chest, it's not hard to force.

"Jamie, who's the girl?"

"What happened to the model?"

"Are you guys exclusive?"

"Do you think Mara would approve?"

"Does this mean you're tied down, too?"

I skirt my eyes across the unfamiliar faces. There's no way we're going to make it to the car. Jamie must have the same thought, because he tugs on my fingers, pulling me back the way we came.

We round the back of the building at the end of the parking lot, but the paparazzi aren't far behind.

"You're gonna have to move faster than that," he warns, picking up his pace to one I can hardly match. Panic sets in and I lean down to unstrap my shoes, all the while being yanked by a long-legged Jamie. "Oh, for God's sake," he mumbles, stopping. I stand up, confused, with half of my shoe unbuckled. "Come here." He pulls my arms around his neck and lifts me onto his back in one swift motion.

"Jamie, put me down!" I screech, clasping his neck so tight I'm probably choking him. He runs across the pavement faster than I ever could have, opens the car door, and turns so I can slide off his back and onto the seat.

After closing the door, he runs around to the driver's side, narrowly avoiding the cameras closing in.

"This doesn't happen to you, huh?" I mock, trying to catch my breath.

Jamie opens his mouth to speak, then closes it again, deciding better of what he wanted to say.

My heart's racing out of my chest. Part of me is terrified because, holy crap, that was intense. Way more so than I ever could have predicted.

But there's another part that's enthralled. How could Rylee hate the spotlight that much when it's all I want? The *only* thing I want. There's something about it that makes me feel empowered.

"That was so cool," I say in awe, peering out the back window at the stumbling fools trying to keep up with his Ford.

Jamie's eyes widen, his head snapping in my direction. "That's your idea of fun? What else do you like? Stubbing your toe? Giving yourself little paper cuts between your fingers?"

I roll my eyes, relieving my feet by taking off the beige, checkered wedges that have been suffocating my toes all evening. "Don't be ridiculous. I only give other people paper cuts."

"Ha." His laugh rings throughout the car. Smells of fast food waft to my nose, and I remember I have a handful of fries I haven't finished. I unravel the bag and succumb to salty goodness, wishing Jamie hadn't thrown the rest of his away.

"How does Rylee hate that?" I wonder aloud, chomping down on a fistful of crunchy perfection.

Jamie peeks at me as he flicks on his turn signal. "Maybe because she was bullied and threatened. You've got it easy now that she paved the way for you."

"Of course, make it sound like I wouldn't be here without her."

"Would you?"

"I'd have found a way," I defend, not helping my case. My defenses resolve, and I give in, knowing I only sound like an ungrateful brat. "No. Probably not."

"You hate that," he notices, pulling down a side road I'm not familiar with. "You hate that she got you here."

I bite my lip, mixed feelings swarming in my stomach. No one's actually asked me why I hold such resentment toward my sister, and honestly, I'm not sure I have a reason. At least, not a good enough one to justify the way I treat her, unless jealousy counts. "I don't know, I guess I just hate that she's so... Rylee?"

"You mean perfect?"

"She's not, I mean she's—yeah." I crack the passenger window for some fresh air and breathe deeply as the scent of pine envelops my senses. I love that smell. It reminds me of Christmas and home. My lips pucker as I stare off into the distance, letting the wind whip through my hair, getting rid of all the insecurities clinging to my skin. "She's everything I'm not."

"That's not true, you know." Jamie's only trying to

make me feel better, but I think we both know I'm not Rylee. I could never be her no matter how hard I tried. I often think that's why I act the way I do—I'm always in her shadow. Ever since we were kids, she's gotten everything I've ever wanted. Good grades, talent, our parents' trust. She never had to earn it; it was just *there.* No matter what I did, I could never measure up. And I know she didn't have everything handed to her, and her life wasn't always easy, no thanks to me, but it just never felt fair. I felt overlooked, so I turned myself into someone who couldn't be ignored, even if that meant being the bitch. Then, at some point, it wasn't an act so much as who I was. Who I became. Who I am now.

"Yeah, it is." I blow out a puff of air, hoping my voice gets lost in the wind. "She knows exactly who she is, and I've always been a little lost."

9

JAMIE

The steering wheel digs into my palms, cutting off the circulation in my fingers.

I've always been a little lost.

I've never heard another person sound so much like Mara. When Tori spoke, she sounded so small, so sad.

Gnawing my lip, I try to keep my attention on the road.

Just look at the road. Not at her.

But I want to look at her. Just like I wanted to kiss her earlier in McDonald's. If she hadn't called me out on being an ass, I just might have.

I'm drawn to something about Tori that goes deeper than the surface. The façade she puts on to mask her vulnerability... I can't help but be reminded of Mara.

"Are you doing okay?" I inquire.

Mara's sprawled out on my bed, pieces of paper coating the comforter. She's trying to make a portfolio to submit with her application to be qualified for a writing scholarship. She's been traveling with me and the band since she showed up at my hotel room that day a few months ago and decided to start dedicating more time to her future—visiting schools with excellent art and writing programs wherever we go.

My sister is phenomenal with words, a gift that skipped right over me when I was born. If I could write like her I could contribute so much more to the band than banging sticks around. Carson has the real gift out of us all. You can't just have a drummer on stage, or a guitarist. You can't just be able to write songs. You need the voice. That fresh, new sound no one's heard before and everyone wants more of. Carson is all those things in one. I'm not unaware of the fact that he doesn't need any of us at all. He could be a one-man show, have a band that plays the rest of the instruments in the background of the stage that he only acknowledges during a musical rift in one of his songs. But no, he makes sure we're right up there with him, experiencing it all. I will forever be grateful for that.

My sister reaches for me, and I take her hands in mine, sitting beside her on the soft mattress. This hotel room is different from the others. Where there are normally browning walls and crappy TVs, there's a granite backsplash and a flatscreen mounted on the wall—the first sign that we're getting better at what we do.

"I'm all right," she sighs. "Just trudging through the day."

"You'll get it. You're too talented not to." Encouraging Mara has become part of my daily agenda. I'm not sure what's *changed in her life, but that light I used to see when she walked into a room is gone. Vanished with her lively smile and wired eyes. She never used to sleep, forever a wild child at heart, and now it's all she does. I thought she was just sad about her breakup, but it's starting to seem like much more than that... but she won't talk to me.*

"What if I'm not good enough?" she asks finally, staring up at the ceiling, as if she stares long enough the answers will flake from the drywall.

"Then they're stupid for passing you up." I lean over to read a small slip of paper with her admission statement scrawled in small italics. "'When I write, I take a feeling, a momentary, fleeting feeling, and flourish it, deepen it, and turn it into a world of emotional possibilities.' Mara, if that alone doesn't get you in, then I think this school needs a reality check."

"Thanks." She opens her striking eyes, sitting up to pull me into a hug. "I don't deserve you," she mumbles into my shoulder.

Mara pulls away after a long moment, but her knitted sleeve catches on the button of my flannel.

"Shit," she curses, fumbling with the pulled thread.

"Here, I got it." I push her sleeve up a little to see what I'm dealing with, but my eyes catch on three pink circles dotting her forearm. My thumb scrapes over them, and she stiffens, pulling back the second she realizes the thread has been detangled.

"What are those?" I ask, reaching for her arm again.

Her head shakes rapidly, and she stands, collecting all her papers and putting them in a thick folder. "Nothing. Just bug bites from being outside."

She steps across the room into the small ray of sunlight

peeking through the curtains. "I've gotta get to the school and drop these off before we leave tomorrow, see you later."

"Jamie—"

"Jamie!"

Tori grabs the wheel, swerving us back onto our side of the road as bright headlights barrel straight toward us. My foot slams on the brakes, knocking everything in the car to the floor with a *swoosh*. I close my eyes and bang the steering wheel, only to curse in pain because that's my bad hand. The same hand I used to abuse that poor tree a few nights ago.

"Are you okay?" I ask, looking at Tori. Her face is ashen, and she's gripping the seatbelt so tightly her knuckles are white. I reach over, pulling them away one by one with my good hand, the one that's not throbbing in pain. She swallows, blinking a few times before gazing out the window.

Finally, she nods her head. "No thanks to you." There's no conviction in her voice, though, no humor, no anger. She's scared shitless, and I can't blame her. I reach over and take a big gulp out of my McDonald's cup.

"What's in that cup?" she questions, yanking it from my hands.

"Iced tea," I grab for it, but she's too quick. "You watched me get a refill."

"No, I didn't. I went to the bathroom while you were

getting a refill," she reminds me, and I silently curse. "Tori, don't—"

Her lips close around the straw, resulting in a sour expression. "You're drinking? Are you kidding me right now? When the hell did you mix this with—bourbon?"

"How'd you know it was bourbon? Your birthday was this past weekend, and we didn't have whiskey at the party." I reroute the conversation, hoping I can piss her off and distract her at the same time. Anything to get her off my scent. She's like a freaking bloodhound.

"Don't you dare turn this around on me, you jackass. Get out of the car." She whips her door open, leaving it that way so I don't drive off without her. She bangs her fist on my window so hard it has to hurt. "Get out of the car, Jamie."

Sucking on the insides of my cheeks, I hop out of my sister's old car, towering in front of her. I lean in close, teasing her with my sexiest smirk—or so I've been told. "Happy?"

The words are barely out of my mouth before she smacks me straight upside the head, shoving past me and closing the driver's side door. The little minx is smart, too, because she locks it so I can't lift her out. "Tori, I had three sips since we left McDonald's, you're being ridiculous. I'm not even buzzed."

"I'm starting to think I've never seen you sober. Get in the car," she demands through the glass, but I pretend I can't hear her. Not a smart idea.

Tori opens the door with intended force, clipping me in the side, and then shutting it once more. "I said, get in the car!" she screams, crossing her arms in front of her chest. I'm not sure if she's that angry or trying really hard not to cry.

"Get out of the car, get into the car, what the hell do you want from me?" I mumble as I'm walking past the hood, and classic Tori, beeps the goddamn horn so loud I slip.

"I'm not even drunk," I defend once again when I'm tucked safely in the car, away from any horns or fists or flying doors. I crack my neck and work out the dull ache in my side from where the door hit. I'd be crazy if I thought that's what she was aiming for—she was definitely hoping it would hit my head.

Tori clenches her jaw, her face scrunching up like a bunny's. Then, she slaps me. Again. "Oh yeah, is that why you were driving into oncoming traffic? The only reason I'm doing this is to help *you,* but I wouldn't have agreed had I known I'd be in constant danger."

"I think we both know you only did this for yourself," I spit angrily, saying whatever I think might hurt her. She laughs, shifting the car into drive, and then back into park. I flinch, afraid she's going to hit me again. Or worse, clock me with a shovel and bury me beneath the trees.

"At least I'm sober enough to do my job and not screw up everyone else's lives," she says, voice low. Her green eyes bore into my soul. I should have known better than to fight dirty with Victoria Green. Not when she already lives in the mud.

Shutting my eyes, I bang my head against the headrest,

rolling it to the side so I can see her—her striking eyes and her tight mouth, the trembling hands she tries to hide.

"I'm sorry," I whisper, gut twisting in unexplainable guilt. What is wrong with me? How can I blame her for being mad when I'm acting so stupid? If Mara were here... "I'm sorry."

"Just shut up," she orders.

I have no other choice.

I obey.

10

JAMIE

Tori storms through the front door with me on her heels.
I'm not sure why I'm even following her, to be honest, but I
am. For some reason, I can't shake the inexplicable need I
have to make her understand, to stop her from being mad
at me.

"Tori, wait!" I call, and struggle to catch the door
before it slams me in the face. She marches up the steps,
me close behind her, and closes her bedroom door before
I can stop her. "Tori, please." I turn and press my back to it,
banging my head to mirror the anger I feel. "I fucked up,
I'm sorry."

A throat clears from across the hall, and I look up to
see Rylee standing in her doorway, brows raised.

"Looks like you woke the beast." She smirks, crossing
her arms and leaning against the doorframe. Her hair falls
perfectly, angling her angelic face. Her fuzzy blue pajamas
make her skin look porcelain in the orange light pouring
from her bedroom.

"You mean we haven't been getting the beast this whole time?" I gape, making her giggle.

"No, you've been getting Tolerable Tori. I haven't seen her so furious she didn't stick around to argue since eighth grade."

"Oh, we argued plenty, don't worry. What happened in eighth grade?" I prod, curious as to what else has made Tori this mad, and also, maybe what fixed it.

"Dylan spilled chocolate milk down her favorite white silk blouse from our grandmother."

So, me drinking and driving is the equivalent of a stained shirt? I almost say this out loud before I catch myself. Tori's overdramatic, but I know Rylee won't forgive me for putting her sister in danger.

Tori's door opens abruptly behind me, and I have to grab the frame on either side to keep myself from falling. She had to have done that on purpose.

"Give me the bottle," she orders, holding out her hands.

11

TORI

"Give me the bottle."

I'd really hoped he would fall when I opened the door. Oh well. Win some, lose some.

He sneaks a glance at Rylee before pretending like he doesn't know what I'm asking.

"Where is it?" I yank on his jacket and start searching his pockets. Rylee cups her palm over her mouth to stifle a laugh. If only she knew. My hands frisk him, roaming his body, every crevice, every pocket, until I get to his jeans.

"Hey, hey, okay. Okay. Here, Handsy. You happy?" He pulls a mini bottle of brown liquid from his back pocket, dangling it in front of my face. Oh, thank goodness I didn't have to feel up his ass just to find a bottle of alcohol.

"You should've let her keep going," Dylan coos from his bedroom. I swear, there's no privacy in this house at all. I give Rylee props for that, she somehow managed to keep everyone in the dark about Carson... except Dylan, the nosiest of us all.

There are so many insults I could use against my brother, but I opt against all of them, not exactly in the mood for fake-witty banter that we use to shield ourselves from how we really feel about each other.

"Come here." I grab Jamie by the collar and yank. After shoving him onto my bed, I grab the door handle and push it closed.

"Doors open at least six inches at all times!" Dylan calls, then cackles at his own joke. He's such a goon.

"Tori, please, I—" Jamie goes silent the second I clamp my hand over his mouth. He probably thinks I'm going to kill him. He's lucky my siblings are home.

"Do I look like I want to hear your excuses?" I ask, tilting his chin up with my other hand. He shakes his head shortly, eyes wide. When I'm sure he's going to listen, I release my grip. "I didn't think so. Now, we need to get a few things straight. I'm being paid to make you look like a better person than you are, not to sit in the passenger seat of a car while you swerve into the other lane because you've been drinking—which got you into this mess in the first place, I might add. I'm giving you one more chance that you don't deserve, and if you screw it up again, I'm done. No more chances."

He nods again, swallowing hard. "It won't happen again. I swear."

"Good," I sit beside him, lacing my fingers between my knees. I hadn't expected him to give in so willingly. I thought he would defend his actions above all else, no matter what. It's what I would have done. In fact, it's what I *have* done for most of my life. No matter how wrong I was, no matter who I hurt for whatever selfish reason, I always, always put myself above apologizing to someone in order to defend my own actions. I shiver in thought of the many horrid memories I have from high school, some torturing my conscience more than others.

"I really am sorry." He meets my eyes with his apologetic, Bambi-like ones, and I scoff. My mind is already drifting back in time.

Addison sits by my window, on the small lip sticking out just far enough to be considered a seat. Her blonde streaks glisten in the sun against the brown and black ones mixed in. Since the moment I met her, I thought her hair combination was ridiculous and messy, but it's her choice if she wants to look like a raccoon. Don't get me started on her eyeliner. "Are you sure he said that? It was about me?"

I rise, walking up behind her and resting a comforting hand on her shoulder. "How could I mistake something like that Addy? He's clearly into you, just go for it."

"I don't know," she sighs, guilting me with those Bambi-brown eyes, so wide and naïve.

"Trust me," I say sweetly. "Follow your heart."

"You know what? I will." She smiles up at me, rising to her feet with renowned confidence. "I can't thank you enough, Tori." Addison throws her arms around me in a hug, then rushes downstairs in excitement, looking forward to tomorrow.

I pull out my phone and call Quinn, "Hey, do me a favor? Keep an eye on Cory tomorrow."

"Anything for you," she singsongs back to me.
Anything for me.

My stomach sours at the memory. The worst memory I have. What I did to that girl... well, it was worse than trying to ruin my sister so everyone would like me instead. Destroying Rylee's social life was a slower, more thought-out process, but either way, it haunts me just the same.

I defended my actions that day for years. No one questioned me—they never did—but I questioned myself. Every day. I'd like to say I was also young and naïve, but I wasn't. I was a sophomore, and stupid, and no matter what I feel, Addison will never forgive me for what I did to her.

"Are you okay?" Jamie notices the tears running down my cheeks, and he suddenly looks guiltier than he did before. "Tori, I mean it. I'm so, so sorry. I'm an idiot. What I did was reckless and getting mad at you for it didn't help."

"It's not that," I whisper, standing. He joins me. "It's just—I have no room to judge you, or Rylee. I'm not a good person, Jamie, no matter how you try to spin it. I've done some messed up things to people."

I'm not sure why I admit this to him, or why, all of a sudden, after all these years, thoughts of Addison have resurfaced, but it feels good to finally get it off of my chest. I've never told anyone about what happened between us, but I can assume everyone figured out I was behind it.

"Like what?" he prods, pressing his fingers into my wrist as the memories assault me just like it was yesterday.

The bell for class rings just as the door closes behind me. I find Addison crying in the last stall of our tiny upstairs bathroom— the one nobody ever uses. She opens the door, cheeks colored with tears. There's a pink stain on her shirt that wasn't there this morning, as well as in her hair. I recognize it as one of our cafeteria's strawberry smoothies.

"Are you okay?" I question, reaching out my arms for a hug. Her eyes harden to stone.

"You bitch!" she yells, shoving me away. "You lied to me. He doesn't like me, he likes you!"

I'm quiet. Pursing my lips, I adjust the purse strap on my shoulder, staring at her unblinkingly, playing coy.

"But you already knew that," she clarifies, wiping away smudges of eyeliner, understanding clearing her vision. "You wanted me to ask him out so I'd make a fool of myself. Your little friend Quinn did this to me, by the way—" she gestures to the smoothie sticking in her hair, "—so you know who to give the credit to. What does she get, Tori? A gold star? A seat at the cool kids' table?"

I shrug my shoulders, tilting my head to the left, admiring my friend's handiwork. I almost feel bad for ruining Addison's shirt. Although, there's a possibility I did her a favor.

"I don't understand," her voice cracks, water filling her tear ducts. "I've been nothing but your friend. I did everything you asked, I—"

"That's the problem. You're not," I inform her bitterly. "You're not one of us, and you never will be. So back off and stay away from Cory."

I leave her there, crying on the bathroom floor, without a shred of remorse for what I did.

———

Things only got worse for Addison after my little stunt. I had liked Cory, the boy I told her to go after. Leading up to the smoothie incident, I'd rag on her appearance and her personality to my friends, so that when the time came, I knew I could count on them to do what I needed. They were always susceptible. If I didn't like someone and said it enough times, they'd begin to feel the same. It's like I could embed ideas into their brains and they'd go along with anything I said.

The truth? I was jealous of Addison. Cory didn't chase after me like all the other boys, and he's the one I wanted. So, when beautiful, perfect Addison came along with her winning smile, sweet personality, and adorable crush on Cory, I jumped at the chance to destroy her, afraid that if I didn't, he might pick her over me. I told Quinn to humiliate her, make fun of her in front of him when she went to ask him to our Winter Snowball dance. I had no idea she'd take things so far, and still, I did nothing about it but tell my friend she did well. And let her take a seat beside me at our lunch table.

After that, everyone harassed Addison to no end. She transferred schools the next year, and last I heard, she'd overdosed on sleeping pills the doctors prescribed because she wasn't sleeping from all the bullying she endured. From the nightmares I gave her. I've never been able to find out if that was true, or just another rumor my friends spread for their petty amusement. Though, who am I to judge? I founded our little group that terrorized the school. The same group that made some kids wish they were homeschooled.

In some ways, I got mine for what I did to her. Cory and I dated for two months, until he made a point to kiss Erica Goodman right in front of me—*of all girls!*—at the Winter Snowball. That was his way of telling me he wanted to break up. I guess neither Addison nor I had exceptional taste in men. The karma part was that I never lived it down. For the next two years, I was the victim of Cory jokes and brutal harassment from my friends. They thought it was funny but playing with someone's heart is never a game. I'd been really hurt by what he did, and everyone took amusement out of it, burning me with their harsh one-liners that just got old after so many uses. Ironic, isn't it?

I realized a little too late that Addison was the only real friend I'd had. The only friend who wouldn't have laughed at my broken heart. The only one who would have listened and stood by me no matter what anyone else thought. And I broke her. Every morning I'd show up at my locker, expecting to see her overly peppy face and thickly lined eyes waiting for me with a new quote of the day. That was her thing. I pretended to hate them, but I secretly envied her optimistic outlook on life.

I've done a lot of bad things, and I know that... though nothing compares to the regret I feel when I think about the look on her face. She would have been fine if a stupid sixteen-year-old boy didn't feel the same. It was my betrayal that broke her heart.

"What I've done doesn't matter anymore," I tell Jamie, instead of the truth. "You can't change the past."

"Maybe not, but it's eating at you." He accesses me carefully. "What did you do?"

I heave a sigh, closing my eyes to will the tears to stop.

"I've done a lot," I say honestly, not about to rehash every mean thing I've ever said or done to someone, my sister included. "But this one time I hurt someone in a way I couldn't take back. She never forgave me. I can't blame her. I wouldn't forgive me."

"You're trying to be better, that's what really counts." Jamie wipes a tear from my cheek, and I shiver, holding in the sobs that so desperately want to come out.

I shake my head. "But I'm not. I've been trying so hard with Rylee, but it feels like I'm not getting anywhere. I keep letting my jealousy get in the way, and it's ruining everything."

"Then stop," he whispers, his breath warming the cold tears on my cheeks. "You have to want to be better."

"So do you." He has nothing to say at that, so I turn to face the window in the corner of my room. "You should probably go. But take an Uber or something."

"I'll have Rylee drive me," he whispers, and I begin to wonder how me wanting to poke his eyes out turned into him attempting to comfort me.

The sound of the clicking door is like a weight being lifted from my shoulders. I know I should have driven him home because Rylee's already in bed, but I can't handle any more suffocating conversations. Jamie tries to talk to me in a way no one has before, and it scares me because he might just be the one person who can understand how I feel. I don't want him to, because that means he'll see the real me, and chances are he won't like that Tori Green.

He barely likes this one.

12

TORI

The next morning, I wake up grumpier than usual. I've never been good at feelings, let alone expressing them. Pissing people off? Sure. Being sarcastic? Absolutely. Annoying someone to the point of speechlessness? No doubt my secret superpower. But feelings... well, let's just say I'd rather embrace my ever-seething anger. And don't even get me started on the conundrum of admitting them to myself because that is a severe work in progress... or more like a sinking ship. It's like I got the rotten end of the Green sibling gene pool. I'm the prototype, the first model that hasn't yet been perfected. I'm the roughest draft of a novel, not entirely in order, and still fairly incomplete.

Squinting my eyes against the sun rays peeking through my pastel curtains, I shuffle to my vanity and plop down, turning on the makeup mirror that illuminates every blemish on my face. Puffing out a mouthful of air, I decide against putting on makeup like I normally would. I'm going to make today a me-day. A day to relax and watch movies and eat ice cream. In my opinion, every girl should have a self-pity day at some point or another in order to let go of all the responsibilities and demands put on her shoulders.

After I throw on a pair of around-the-house-shorts and a lazy-day-tank-top with inside-only-slippers I bounce downstairs, avoiding the mirror along the far wall as I tug my hair into a messy bun. I like the idea of a no-makeup-me-day—I never said I'd like to see said results.

"Tori, wait until you see this." Dylan snatches me the second I enter the kitchen. "I paused it for you."

His words make my stomach sink, though I don't know why. Everything went as planned last night. Well, almost everything. "Why do I get the feeling I'm gonna hate this?"

"Just watch." He clicks play on the remote, settling into the spot on the couch with his assigned butt groove.

A thin newscaster with dark hair and makeup for days stands prim, speaking in the typical, modulated voice people on the news have. "Okay, and next we have an interesting story: Jamie LeMont was seen with who sources say is Victoria Green, sister of America's sweetest girlfriend, Rylee Green. Except, it doesn't seem like Victoria takes after her sister. Take a look at this clip found of the pair looking quite tense during a quick meal at McDonald's."

The screen shifts to a video of me rolling my eyes and leaning back in my chair with crossed arms. I look disgusted at whatever Jamie said, though I have no idea at what point this was taken.

"Looks like Jamie has his hands full with that one.

Next up—" Dylan mutes the TV, pursing his lips. Rylee joined us at some point during the story, standing in front of the couch, and looking at me as if she's not sure how I'm going to react.

I open my mouth, then close it, and open it again. I'm at a loss for words. "That's the story they're telling? What about when we stood up and he took my hand and gave me my purse, or when he carried me on his back all the way to the car because my heels were too high to walk fast? Th-that's not even the whole story, that's only part of it."

Rylee scoffs, shaking her head. "Welcome to my world. Not so glamorous now, is it?"

"That woman just *lied*!"

"Technically, she didn't. That's how they get you. They only show part of the story with enough implications to let the world come to their own conclusions. It's genius, actually. Then, if the truth is revealed they're not liable for providing their audience with misinformation." Rylee plops down on a chair, unwrapping the paper towel stuck to a freshly heated sausage, egg, and cheese biscuit.

Her microwaved breakfast smells delicious, but the longing growl in my stomach misses Mom's cooking. The worst part about our parents being away? No home-cooked food. We're forced to live off of frozen food and Kraft Macaroni & Cheese. Dylan has no quarrels about this, but he's also a bottomless pit and would eat grass with enough coaxing.

I stand, making my way to the kitchen to find

something to fill my stomach—preferably that doesn't require any effort on my part.

"It's conniving, that's what it is," I grumble, slamming the cabinet shut and scuffling my feet back to the couch, box of Honey Nut Cheerios in hand. Dylan starts to speak, but I cut him off. "No, I don't want a bowl, and yes, I'm going to eat it dry, straight from the box."

"I-I was just going to say good morning," he stutters and gives me a cheeky grin.

"Sure you were." I squint my eyes, unraveling the rolled-up bag.

The moment I'm settled, Dylan grabs his phone from the carpet, giving us a tiny wave. "I'll see you guys later."

"Where are you going?" Rylee asks playfully, squinting her hazel eyes in suspicion. She takes a giant bite of her sandwich, resulting in a sliver of egg hanging from her chin. I roll my eyes at the sight of her.

"I'm meeting a friend before school. Believe it or not, I have a life outside of your endless drama," he snarks, walking out the door without another word.

"He's totally going to see a girl." Rylee laughs, shaking her head at our brother's knack for privacy. As nosy as he is, he has a hard time opening up to anyone, except maybe Rylee. But I'm here, so of course he won't say where he's really going.

"I bet it's that girl from the end of tour party, the one who's going to spend the summer with us in their house?" I suggest, drawing a blank on her name. Kris' sister, I think. She's gorgeous. Undoubtedly.

"Wait, Carmina? Oh my gosh, I bet you're right. I'm

pretty sure she's still in town." She sits forward in her chair, crumpling up a napkin.

The boys had planned to stay at their beach house in Miami following the tour party a little over a week ago, and my siblings and I were going to join them in June, but the guys like it here, and Carson wanted to spend more time with Rylee since they'd been apart for most of his tour. So, they decided to spend a few more weeks here with us until we all go on vacation.

"I wonder how Kris feels about that?" Rylee says as an afterthought, concentration wrinkling her forehead.

"I wonder if he knows," I add mischievously, and we both giggle. Leave it to our brother to have an interest in his best friend's sister.

"How's the fating going?" Rylee asks. She throws the napkin and misses the garbage can by a mile. "Damn," she curses, as though either of us thought she'd make it. As if she's *ever* made it. My sister is perfect in every way possible, but sports are not her forte. They're not mine either, but I'm not exceptionally great at so many other things that my lack of coordination is as noticeable as hers.

"You call it that, too?" I express, laughter bubbling in my chest. I thought I was the only one socially deprived enough to think up something that ridiculous.

"Well, yeah, you're *fake dating*. At least if you say it like that you don't risk anyone else finding out it's a lie." She shrugs, slouching into the armchair. I'd never thought of it that way, but she's right. If anyone gets wind of us "fake dating" it's over. That would be worse publicity for the band as a whole than it is for Jamie.

"Do you want to watch a movie or something?" I ask, my chest burning with nerves. How could I be so nervous about asking my not-so-little sister to spend time with me?

She looks taken aback, her lips separating slightly in surprise. "Oh, um, I—"

"Have plans with Carson," I finish for her. "That's fine. Go have fun," I say sincerely, despite my natural instinct to resort to jealousy.

She stands up, holding her phone in front of her chest like there's an ultimatum involved. She turns to walk away, then stops, and looks back at me.

"I do, after school." She smiles, though it's somewhat forced. "Actually, a movie sounds... relaxing."

A few hours later, when Rylee gets home from school, she runs upstairs and comes back a few minutes later in sweats and a t-shirt, holding a bag of popcorn. "I keep an extra box in my room so Dylan can't eat it all."

She's so lucky. I wish I had gotten work-release when I was in high school, but I didn't have a job. It doesn't matter if she works only one day a week, she still gets to leave school at the same time, and getting out as early as ten-thirty?—yes, please.

Once the popcorn is fully popped, she drops down beside me, placing a bowl between us and clearing her throat. We haven't watched a movie together in... four years? Five? Honestly, it's been so long that I can't remember.

"What should we watch?" I ask, flipping through Netflix, and then on to Hulu.

"Is that even a question?" Rylee asks in disgust. I smile. I'd been hoping she would remember.

"Dirty Dancing," we say in unison.

Rylee cracks a smile, rolling her eyes a little before snuggling her legs to her chest. "You remember."

It was our favorite movie growing up. Our parents had to bribe us with ice cream so we would watch something else as a family. And even then, it was touch and go—one of us would always try to steal the remote from Dad's lap, where he kept it, so it was harder for us to get our grubby fingers on it.

"Of course, I do," I snort, as if her accusation is ridiculous. "I'd never forget that."

13

TORI

Three movies—*Dirty Dancing, How to Lose a Guy in 10 Days,* and *When We First Met*—and two TV shows later—three episodes of *The Vampire Diaries* and six of *Friends*—we settle on *Nancy Drew,* the new CW drama I've been hearing a lot about. I hadn't been expecting so many jump scares in a teenage detective show, though.

During one of the longest commercials of my life, my phone rings. Glancing at the screen, I see Jamie's name dancing across the top, making my stomach churn. Five months ago, I'd have done absolutely anything to get his number, but I guess there's some truth to what my sister said after all: their lives aren't all glamour and fancy clothes and adoring fans. It's much more complicated than that, which I realized for the first time this morning when the news told a half-truth. I didn't understand the big deal before. So what? They tell little white lies. Who cares, right? But now... now I understand. Having someone you've never met tell fabricated and overdramatized stories about your personal life to anyone willing to listen is... overwhelming.

What I don't understand is that they're the most beloved band in the world, stealing hearts all over the place. Their sound is so evolved and new, yet tells beautifully architected stories. Everyone listens to it, even if they're not hard-core Decembers like I was. Truth be told, since meeting the band, I don't exactly feel like a super-fan anymore. Anyway, I guess my point is... how aren't their lives as glamorous as I imagined? Is that yet another fabrication to make them seem more appealing to, well, dreamers like me?

"Are you going to answer that, or stare at it all day?" Rylee asks, her voice drawing me out of my daze. She blinks a few times, her brows furrowed in confusion. It's not often I hesitate to answer my phone. Normally, I'm happy for the distraction because it pulls me away from whatever undesired situation I'm in but answering Jamie's call has the potential to release a load of emotions I don't feel like dealing with or dissecting today.

I pucker my lips thoughtfully, weighing my options. Truth is, I'm not sure I want to let Jamie any closer than he already is. I mean, I want to, but I don't...

He sees right through me the way Rylee and Dylan do. And much like them, he's unafraid to call me on it. Part of me thinks that's a good thing because I'm trying to be better, and what better way to do that than to have someone keep you in check? Yet, there's another part of me that doesn't particularly enjoy needing to have my guard up higher than normal, just so he can't climb over it.

"Tori?" Rylee nudges my thigh with her blue-painted toes. "You okay?"

Having made up my mind, I swallow, and finally click ignore. "Yeah."

My voice comes out breathy and unsure, and I can tell Rylee is not at all convinced. And again, I'm torn in two. Torn between wanting to trust in my sister, because I know whatever I say will stay between us—another perfect Rylee quality—and between keeping my feelings to myself. Because the last thing I want is her judgment, or worse, her pity.

"Is this about—"

"Jamie," I blurt before she can finish, then silently scold myself.

She sucks in her cheeks, smiling slightly. "I was just going to say last night."

"Oh."

"What's going on, Tor?" Rylee picks up the remote, pausing the show just as Nancy is about to unveil a new truth she's learned. "You've seemed off all day."

"Wh—how?" I argue defensively, widening my eyes.

Rylee looks at me dumbly, and when she realizes I won't be baited, speaks the obvious truth. "Well, for one, you asked me to hang out with you. And you also haven't made any snippy, snide, or sarcastic comments to me yet, and now that I think about it, you've barely said a word at all. You'd normally be dying to brag about your date with a superstar—fake or not."

The worst, most disgusting thing about my flawless little sister is that you can't even hate her. Not even a little. Because if you do, it makes you selfish and ignorant because she has the kindest heart and is always, annoyingly, *frustratingly* right. And even when she's wrong, she has this clear logic behind her words or actions that takes away any justified anger you feel. Take Carson, for example. She lied to me, over and over, yet the more time that passes, I realize that I gave her every reason not to tell me, and that she wasn't wrong to want to keep their relationship to herself for a while. He was her sanctuary. Her shining star in a dark abyss of letdowns and disappointment. Our whole family knowing the truth would have put a huge pressure on her that she didn't need. She'd already had the media hounding her, let alone my judgment and our parents' most likely disapproval.

"Fine, don't tell me. I don't blame you." She sighs, making my guilt feel heavier and more potent.

"I'm happy for you," I say so fast that my words practically smush together in one incoherent sentence.

"What?" She turns her attention back to me, and I swear there's a sliver of hope in her glowing eyes.

"I am. And I don't blame you for not telling me anymore. So stop feeling guilty. Please."

Clenching my jaw, I fold my hands into fists, forcing myself to breathe slowly. The truth comes just as awkwardly to me as emotions. I've spent most of my life holding closed the doors I use to shut everyone out. Unlocking the rusty hinges is like releasing a tidal wave I've let sit still for too long when it really just wishes to be free.

Here goes nothing.

"Okay." I breathe shakily, cracking my knuckles before wiping them on my pants. "So, like, Jamie is so messed up. Past the point of caring about anything but the blame he puts on himself. Last night, he spiked his iced tea and then got behind the wheel. He drifted into the other lane and almost hit someone."

Rylee's face is one of pure shock and disbelief, though she doesn't interrupt, just lets me talk.

"I was pissed until I—I remembered all the things I've done and realized they're so much worse. He's a lot more like me than I ever would have thought."

"He is," she agrees. "You both hold people at arm's length."

It's easier to keep people away, because then if they hurt you, they're not close enough to leave scars. "He doesn't have the perception in life that everything is going to be okay and that things work out for the best. And he doesn't look at me like I'm a bitch who hates everyone and hurts my sister to feel better about herself, but as someone who's trying to change, like he is. I don't like how that makes me feel."

My fists push down into my thighs, creating little sweat wrinkles in the fabric of my pants. I don't like feeling so naked.

Rylee crosses her legs in front of her, moving closer so she can take my hands in hers. "Look, I can't tell you how to feel about Jamie, but you don't always have to be perfect. It's okay to let people in."

That's how they hurt you.

"I can't. It's too hard." I shake my head rapidly, ferociously fighting off my feelings of embarrassment.

She squeezes my hands, her eyes as earnest as I've ever seen them. I find it amazing how willing she is to help me after everything I've done. I don't deserve it. "It won't happen all at once, Tor. Baby steps."

A small, breathy laugh escapes me. "Does this count?"

"Yes." She nudges my shoulder, smiling warmly at me. I'm supposed to be the big sister giving her advice, not the other way around. "Getting hurt is part of life, but it helps you learn and grow and become who you are."

"But how do you move on from it?"

"Somehow you just do. But you always keep that feeling tucked away as a reminder to never let anyone hurt you in that way again, and you let it fuel you." My phone buzzes beside me with a text from Jamie. "Don't let your fear get in the way of something that has the potential to be great."

Suddenly, the doorbell rings, and in comes Carson... with Jamie trailing casually behind him. Rylee never takes her eyes off me, though, searching my face to ensure I'm okay. I give her a small smile, nodding slightly.

"Hey, gorgeous." Carson bends, pressing his lips to Rylee's. It's like every time he sees her it's the first time, and I just now discovered how much I envy that. The way he looks at her, talks to her. It's so... pure. You'd never have to second guess him or his intentions, he just simply, undoubtedly loves her.

"Hey, sorry I canceled on our plans." She kisses him

again, threading her fingers in his hair. It's as if the whole world falls away, and it's just the two of them.

"It's okay, the guys and I actually got some writing done. Finished a few songs." He smiles proudly, and her grin grows to match his.

"Now all we have to do is record them," Jamie adds, his own eyes watching their exchange. "Elizabeth will be happy."

"Well, at least we can prove something's coming out of this hiatus." Rylee rolls her eyes and pulls Carson down on the other side of her. Jamie leans against the back of the couch, his shadow covering over me like a blanket. He hasn't looked at me once, or even acknowledged my presence, and suddenly I feel guilty for ignoring him all day. Once again, I was only worried about my feelings, not how what I do could affect someone else's.

The temporary break announcement went out this afternoon, and so far, the fans seem eager for new music, but it won't be long until they get restless waiting for the album release and tour information. Hopefully the prospect of new music is enough for now. At least when they go to Miami for the summer, they'll still be participating in talk shows and releasing the music they're recording now, which will keep the fans satisfied until their new album's tour next fall. Oddly enough, their actual summer vacation is less of a break than their time in Ambler will be.

"You guys want to watch a movie?" Rylee asks, looking at each of the boys.

Jamie shrugs, and Carson puts his arm around my

sister's shoulder, pulling her to his chest. "I'm just here to spend time with you. I could care less what we do." He kisses the top of her head affectionately, and my heart soars for her. She gives so much to everyone else—she deserves to keep a little for herself sometimes. She deserves this. To be happy. To be loved.

I hope to someday feel like I deserve the same.

"Why'd you come?" I question Jamie as he rounds the couch. I scoot closer to Rylee, unsure if he's going to join us, or sit in the adjoining chair.

He ruffles the side of his hair, adding more body to its long length. Shrugging uncommitted, he takes the seat next to me. "I don't know, I was bored."

"Hmm," I say because I have nothing else to offer. He's so close I can feel the heat radiating from his shoulder to mine. If I moved an inch, they'd be touching.

"Popcorn?" I blurt, and rise, grabbing the white bowl Ry and I used to make some earlier. I walk casually as possible down the hallway, and then sprint up the steps to Rylee's room. Except I don't even bother looking for the popcorn, I just drop down on her bed, releasing a huge breath of air.

After a few moments, I glance up to find Rylee standing in the doorway. She watches me for a moment, and then goes to her closet, digging to the very back where her popcorn must be stashed.

"He's Jamie LeMont," I say, as if saying it out loud makes any difference.

"He's just a person, like you and me." Her back is to me, so her voice sounds muffled and far away.

"I know." I bite my lip, willing my hands to stop shaking. "It's just, I've never been so unsure about anything before." I pause again, now fiddling with the hair tie on my wrist. My hair had been up in a messy bun, but I let it down the moment they walked through the door. When did my irritation of him turn into mixed feelings? "You know, I'm tired, and it's like ten-thirty, maybe I should just go to bed."

My sister stands and reaches for me, shaking her head at my poor attempt at chickening out of what's turning into a "date night." Once Rylee has my hands in hers, she just... hugs me. I'm not sure how to react at first, but I eventually give in, wrapping my arms around her lean figure. "Just be yourself, Tori."

14

TORI

While the two lovers are snuggled on their end of the couch, I'm stiff as a board, making sure to keep my appendages attached to me at all at times to avoid any unwanted collisions with Jamie. My mind is a battlefield, and I can safely say I'm not on the winning side.

What is wrong with you? You're supposed to be fake dating him, and you're afraid to accidentally touch him?

"Are you all right?" Jamie leans over, whispering in my ear. His hair falls onto my face as he speaks, and his arm is fully pressed against mine. Our hands are also too close.

My eyes revert to the bowl of popcorn, too full to need a refill. There goes my escape plan.

"Hmm? Yeah. Just, uh, hot. It's warm in here, is anyone else warm?" My eyes dart to Rylee and Carson, cozy under a thick, wool blanket. They both look at me with raised eyebrows. Humor shines in Rylee's eyes. Of course, no one's hot, it's sixty degrees outside, so Dylan turned the air conditioner on because he's ridiculous. Therefore, I'm the only one sweating through my t-shirt. And also, the only one acting like an idiot.

A bright light shines through the black living room, which was only lit by the dim glow of the movie we're watching. The brightness disappears with the sound of a closing door, and footsteps echo down the hall as Dylan appears with Kris behind him, just as the end credits are rolling.

"So you weren't with a girl," Rylee scrutinizes, looking skeptical.

"Nope." Dylan grins wickedly, turning toward the TV. "So how are the love birds doing this evening?"

I roll my eyes and Rylee laughs, throwing her empty water bottle at his head. "Get out."

"I wasn't talking to you." He winks. With that said, he's officially done his part in making the night awkward. "Remember: six inches. Thin walls."

My cheeks burn hot, and I thank the Lord the lights aren't on because I probably look like a cherry tomato.

Kris's grin mirrors my brother's, but he's a little better at keeping himself in check. He clears his throat, nodding toward his bandmates. "I'm heading back to the hotel... anyone need a ride?"

Carson shakes his head. "I'm staying here tonight."

As if we didn't all know that already. Kris's attention moves to Jamie, who says nothing, but gives a tiny shrug. "All right, then. Good night, everybody."

He turns his back and walks until we can't see him anymore. "Damn, if I want to get myself a Green, I'm gonna have to settle for Dylan." He gags loudly, slamming the door behind him.

"On that note." Rylee stands, thrusting the blanket at my head. "I'm going to bed. 'Night, guys."

"'Night," Carson says at the same time we do, looking groggy with sleep and trailing behind my sister. She stops dead in the middle of the hallway, so he runs into her, then cackles loudly. Carson grabs Rylee around the waist and lifts her up while she screeches in protest. For once, I'm not jealous. Instead, I find that I'm sad Carson is pulling Rylee away from me. That's progress if I've ever seen any.

"Good day?" Jamie asks, startling me out of my daze. I'd completely missed the fact that it's just the two of us now. Goddammit, Rylee definitely did that on purpose.

"What do you mean?"

"You're smiling." He nods at my upturned lips. I press them together immediately.

I guess I was smiling. "Better than yesterday," I say, scooting so there's more couch between us than skin.

"About that, I truly—"

"Jamie, if I have to hear you apologize one more time, I might just hit you."

He winces, presumably at the memory of the last time I hit him. Twice. "Right."

"Thank you." Suddenly it's easier to breathe. Sarcasm is a defense mechanism that's always been easier for me than anything else, but I also use it when I'm being my most honest. Falling back into that comfort zone feels like a weight being lifted from my chest, and suddenly, I'm not so nervous. "Have you tarnished your lungs yet today? Or your liver, for that matter?"

His shoulders fall, and his lips turn up in a knowing smirk. He visibly relaxes, and I realize he was just as tense as me.

"I haven't smoked," he insists, meeting my eyes. I think I believe him.

"But you drank," I prod.

"Just with dinner," he swears. I'm not buying it. "And maybe one with lunch." I pierce him with my stare. "And breakfast, okay, yes, I drank. It's not a big deal. Baby steps."

"I suppose you're right," I agree, and when he doesn't respond, I sip my bottle of water slowly, to avoid filling the settling silence. I'm good at pulling insults out of my ass, not casual conversation.

"Do you think you could come by the Foundation property tomorrow and tell me what you think? The contractor said the framework is mostly finished, so you should be able to get a feel for the kind of space you'll be working with." His index finger finds the shredded hole in his jeans, his eyes following as it weaves in and out.

"Sure, what time?"

"I'll pick you up. Ten?" He looks up at me and I nod.

With nothing left to say, I pick up the remote, desperate for anything to occupy our time. It doesn't seem like he plans on leaving anytime soon, and I'd rather fill the silence with a movie than with strained conversation. "Preference?"

"*Mission Impossible*," he says a little too quickly. I smirk, scrunching my nose. "What? I watch them with my mom."

He shifts uncomfortably under my stare, resting his elbow on the arm of the couch. Who knew Jamie LeMont, drummer of D of D, could be bashful?

"Stop judging me."

"I'm not judging you," I defend, my voice raising a few octaves.

"Yes, you are, you're judging me."

"No, I'm not."

Jamie refuses to believe me, rightfully so because I was totally judging, so I give up, pressing play on the movie. I rest my feet on the coffee table, wrapping the blanket around my shoulders for protection—from what, I don't know, but it makes me feel better. I used to make fun of Rylee for being awkward around guys, and here she is totally winning at life, and I'm having a mini panic attack because the guy I'm in a fake relationship with is sitting on my couch. It feels like middle school all over again, including the fake relationship, because let's be honest, were any at that age real?

The movie is of no interest to me, and I find myself studying my fuzzy socks, noticing Jamie's knee moving closer as he spreads his legs. I'd moved away, but not as far as I should have. His knee brushes against me, and instead of pulling away, he leaves it there, just barely touching my thigh. I swallow hard, forcing my eyes to stay glued to the TV screen.

Oh man. It's about to be a long night.

15

JAMIE

She's completely freaking out. I freaked her out. I don't know why I came tonight, but it most definitely wasn't to start something with Rylee's sister. And still, my leg finds hers as if gravity pulled me to it. *To her.* She's clearly uncomfortable but pulling away now would seem more intentional than my leg touching hers from our proximity.

I wish I was better at this, whatever it may be. All I know is when Tori is near me, I don't think about Mara as much, and yet I feel like I'm closer to her all the same. Maybe it's just because she's so annoying.

Regardless, Tori makes me feel like I'm in control... or at least like I can regain it. Someday. Somehow.

Before her, only Mara ever made me feel that way.

Mara came home today. Just in time, too, because we're announcing the Wild Heart Tour next month, and are leaving for our holiday vacation in Pennsylvania the month after. Soon, I'll be traveling more than I already do, and I couldn't live with myself if I left her in that rehab center all alone while I gallivant around the world, living out my dream. Luckily, the doctors agreed she was ready to be released.

The day I saw the needle marks on her arms felt like the end of the world. Convincing her she needed help was hell. She's been in and out of rehab for the past two years, relapsed more times than I can count, but this time is different. This time she was serious about getting clean.

Mara's doing good, she seems stronger. This is the most genuine smile I've seen on her in a very long time, and somehow, I think this time it's going to stick. She's finally done it. I think my sister is finally clean, and happier for it.

"I'm so proud of you." I squeeze her shoulders from behind, smashing her in a backward hug. The last time she was with me I was holding her unconscious body in my arms, screaming for someone to call 911. She took too many pills and passed out in the bathtub. That was when I knew she needed more than just a rehab center. She needed the best one there was.

"I couldn't have done it without your support." She takes my hand and grips it tightly. "Honestly, you've been my rock through all of this. I wouldn't be here if it weren't for you. Maybe even literally."

"Don't say that." I stroke her hair, the fear I've been pushing down all of these months claws at my gut. "You've made so much progress. That's all in the past, now we can look toward the future."

Mara had to put her writing and art dreams on hold while she got her life together, not that any of it mattered to her while her life was falling apart, either. Now she can devote all her time and effort to getting into college, specifically a school in New York that is only forty-five minutes from the rehab facility, in case she ever needs help again. Plus, it's only a few hours' drive from the small town we're staying in during the holidays, which means she can come visit once her applications are all submitted for the fall semester.

Mara's face falls, her eyes are full of shame and regret that I wish I could take away. "I owe him money, Jamie. A lot of it."

"If I take too much out of my account at once, it's going to raise red flags. I can't risk having my name attached with a drug dealer. And once he knows we're willing to pay, he might blackmail me for more." What I don't say is that I'm afraid if Mara has that much cash in her hands, and is standing face to face with her ex-drug dealer, that she might break down. Give in. I can't lose my sister again, not when she's finally getting her life together.

"I know. I've been saving what I have, I'll sell the house I've been holding onto back in Nashville. We'll work this out. Jordan doesn't need it all at once. I've been a loyal customer anyway; he'll be more lenient on me."

Jordan was her dealer. I don't know how they met, but only that it was after her ex beat her, and she was in a rough place. He took advantage of her pain and used it for his own profit. From what Mara understands, Jordan doesn't even do drugs himself, just exploits other people and ruins their lives to make a quick buck.

"Hey, if it comes to it, I'll take the money out. I'd just rather that be a last resort. Give him what you have saved for now while I try to figure out how to get the rest quietly."

"You can't control everything and everyone no matter how hard you try. Just let me handle this, Jamie." She smiles sadly, her eyes transporting her somewhere else, somewhere darker. "You know why I kept my Southern accent, even after I moved in with you?"

I'm totally lost as to how we got on this topic, but I find myself thinking of a time when she, Carson, and I all thought we could be country singers, so we pretended to have accents, but only when we talked to each other because we needed "practice." Then, when Mara moved to Nashville a few years back, she started to pick up a Southern lilt.

"I kept it because when things got bad, it was the one thing in my life I could control. It gave me a sense of security. We can't control everything, but we can control who we are. You taught me that with your strength these past few months. I'll never be able to repay you for that."

Mara lays down on her bed, and closes her eyes, looking content for the first time in a long while. "You never have to, Mara."

16

TORI

There's an unholy brightness in the room for such an early hour. I pull the blanket up to my forehead, clutching the material between my fists to keep warm and block away the light swarming the living room. A low clicking noise sounds from behind me, indicating someone's in the kitchen, and I know it's not Mom because she's still gone for another week or so.

I sit up, rubbing my eyes deeply to clear the sleep from them. I immediately regret leaving in my contacts when my eyes feel scratchy and crusted over. I twist my body to the side, scanning the room slowly, squinting through the dried lenses fixed to my irises.

"He left at seven," Rylee's voice informs me from the kitchen. I turn slowly, rising to my knees and leaning my stomach over the back of the couch so I can see her.

"I wasn't looking for him," I say quickly, stretching my back.

A pair of hands grab my ribs, scaring the daylights out of me. "Sure, you weren't."

"Dylan!" I yell, rubbing the skin he assaulted. A cool breeze enters the room from our open porch doors, bringing with it the smell of my brother's sweat. "Ew, take a shower. You reek."

Dylan reaches deep into the fridge, grabbing a water bottle from the stash I keep in the back so neither he nor my dad takes the last one and doesn't refill it. Naturally, since he figured out what I was doing, he *only* takes waters from the back, and not from the door where we keep them.

"You know, I bet if I were Jamie you'd want to bathe in my sweat." He points the bottle at me accusingly, raising his brows.

"Absolutely. Not. I don't care if it's Carson James' sweat, I'm not bathing—sorry. Old habits." I cringe, face burning bright when I realize what I've said.

"As long as you don't talk about the texture of his lips anymore, we're good," Rylee jokes, alluding to the first time I met him and made an utter fool of myself.

"*Deal.*"

"So, how was your nap time with Little Drummer Boy?" Dylan unravels a gross-looking, leftover wrap from Arby's that has been on the top shelf of our fridge for way too long to consider edible. A day is too long, in my opinion, much less however long that's been in there. Very few fast foods can be reheated days later, with the exception of Chick-fil-A's chicken nuggets, of course.

Rylee clamps the lid down on the blender she's been

dropping fruit into, ensuring it's well sealed. One time, a few years ago, she walked away while it was on, and the lid flew off. There's still a little pink goop on the ceiling from whatever the hell was in that thing.

"You two did look cozy," she advises, biting down on her bottom lip suggestively.

Color drains from my face, as does the air from my body. I don't even remember falling asleep. "What? No. No. Cozy? We were not... *cozy.*"

I suck in my cheeks, settling down on the arm of the couch, wondering what exactly that word entails. Cozy as in, on our own separate sides of the couch, under separate blankets, and using two different pillows... or cozy as in...

Don't think about it, don't think about it, don't think about it.

"Cozy how?" I ask, chewing my inner lip aggressively, a habit I thought I broke when I was thirteen.

"Couple cozy. Like you'd been making out all night and then fell asleep in one another's arms. Your head was on his chest, and I think you even got a little bit of drool on his—"

"Dylan, shut up," Rylee whips him with a dish towel, and he grabs it as she yanks it back, making him stumble. "He's lying, you were—"

Dylan flicks on the blender, drowning out whatever Rylee was about to say. "Sorry, what was that?"

She rolls her eyes, irritated. "I said—" Dylan turns on the blender again, and she closes her eyes, her way of collecting the last bit of patience she has left. The noise stops, and as she goes to speak, he presses the button once again. "Dylan, it's done!" she yells, yanking the plug from the wall. He puts his hands up in surrender, backing away slowly. "Jamie said he'd be back at ten to pick you up."

Dylan's head snaps up, then leans in toward Rylee, mumbling just loud enough for me to hear. "Does that sound like a date to you? It sounds like a date to me." Then his attention turns on me once again. "Golly gee, Tori, what are you going to wear?"

Rylee shoves him away, snorting at his cracking voice. "Don't wear heels, it's muddy outside."

I pick up my phone, using my thumbprint to unlock it. My eyes widen when I see the time. Nine-fifteen. Which only gives me forty-five minutes to get camera ready. Even though this isn't a planned publicity outing, I'm almost certain *someone* will catch sight of us and snap a picture. Better to be safe than sorry.

"Shit!" I breathe, launching myself from the couch, and skidding down the hallway, possibly stopping for a split second at the mirror to check my face for drool.

In my room, I find a pair of high-waisted jeans, shimmying into them and tripping on the side of my bed as I hop to my closet for a shirt. After five minutes of rummaging through everything I own, I sneak down to Rylee's room, closing the door quietly behind me. Since getting a real job and dating an international celebrity, her sense of style and expenses have risen considerably... great for her, and even better for me. My eyes are instantly snagged by a royal blue halter top that would match my blue Vans perfectly. It's not super cold today, so I can pair it with a cardigan, and hopefully sneak it back into her closet before she notices it's missing.

That was easier than I thought it would be. I step back, and bump the sliding door, causing her too-full shelf to shake, spilling the messy contents onto my head. Well, if she doesn't recognize her own shirt on me, she's going to notice this. Way to be stealthy, Tori.

I bend, quickly collecting a handful of the papers and t-shirts crumpled at my feet, throwing them back on the shelf. I squat for the second load and notice blue fabric sticking out from a small hatbox in the back corner of her closet. I scrunch my nose, knowing I shouldn't...

I rest my hand on the round, brown box, knowing I *really* shouldn't...

I really, really, really shouldn't...

Oh, what the hell? I wouldn't be having this internal argument if I didn't already know I was going to open it.

Sitting cross-legged on the carpet, I pull the box into my lap, removing the lid and peering inside.

Carson's infamous blue hat is the first thing I see, and I brush the material with my fingers. All the years I saw pictures of Carson wearing the one constant clothing item he never took off, and he hasn't worn it since the day he met my sister. And still, I've never actually seen it in person.

As a teenager, I would fantasize about him throwing it out into the crowd and landing in my hands. We'd lock eyes, and he would know. He would see me and know we were meant to be together. Sure, it sounds crazy, but I've always been a daydreamer. That's partly why I'm so miserable in real life—it will never measure up to how great things could be.

Below the hat are countless notes, all with the same handwriting, and a single picture with a note written on the back. I pull away the folded-up piece of paper so I can read the writing on the image first, a picture of Carson holding hands with a then-unidentified woman wearing his lucky blue hat. I still remember the exact moment I got the Twitter notification for it. Never in my life did I think it was my sister, or that it would turn into what it has.

Though it may be a bit unconventional, this was our first-ever picture together. It's still my favorite. Happy five months, Rylee. Thanks for brightening my world each and every day for the past 152.
I love you.

My gut clenches. I hadn't even realized I missed their anniversary. I shouldn't have. It has only been five months, not six, but it's still just as big of a deal—especially to my sister.

I thumb open the piece of paper, careful not to rip the tape attached. I scan the lines, recognizing what it must be. It's lyrics to a song dated January eighth.

And I can't go to sleep without the sound of your voice
On the end of the line after a long day
Distance may have us, and time may be brief
Before I met you, I didn't know what it meant
To need somebody

To need someone

I recognize the unfinished piece... it was the chorus to the first single they released for their upcoming album, called "Sincerely Me." I've loved it since the moment my ears were blessed with a Carson acoustic, but I'd never stopped to think about what the lyrics meant, or how coincidental the timing was.

It's such a beautiful song, of course it would be about my sister. "Rylee's coming up the stairs, if you want her to catch you snooping."

I jump a mile at Dylan's muffled voice through the door. Putting the box back where I found it, I snatch the blue shirt and thrust open her door, intentionally smacking Dylan with it. "How did you know I was in there?"

"Your room's empty." He shrugs. He touches my— *Rylee's*—shirt, and I snatch it away from him.

"Don't ever go in my room again," I hiss.

He coughs. "Hypocrite."

I give him a dirty look, crossing the hall to my own room where I will spend the next thirty minutes doing my hair and makeup. "Takes one to know one," I toss over my shoulder.

17

TORI

"Tori, Jamie's here!" Dylan yells like a doting housewife, as if I didn't hear the doorbell ring, or the front door creak open, or his necessarily loud greeting, *"Jamie! Hi, Jamie! Come on in, Jamie!"*

I swear, I'm going to murder him. It's not even a matter of when anymore, just where and how. I'm thinking somewhere he can yell since he seems to enjoy it so much.

Brushing through my loose curls, I twirl in the mirror and spray my favorite perfume from Bath & Body Works, spinning in a cloud of Pretty as a Peach. I bite my lip, assessing my bold eyes and bare-colored lipstick. I tried not to look too overdone since we're just going to a construction site... but knowing we're probably going to be photographed makes me kind of nervous. Can't we ever go somewhere in private? I'd much rather we watch a movie here instead...

That's not what you signed up for when you agreed to this.

"Coming!" I holler, grabbing my purse and taking one

last look in the mirror, flipping my hair for more volume. "Good as it's gonna get," I mumble, swallowing a gulp of water from the bottle on my dresser.

I start running down the stairs, but stop myself halfway, afraid of looking too excited.

How do you look too excited to go to a construction site? Honestly.

Taking a breath, I enter the kitchen where my siblings, Carson, and Jamie stand around the island. Each of their heads turn toward me, and I fight back the redness creeping across my cheeks.

"You sure you don't want us to come?" Carson offers, and my heart jumps at the idea. I would so much rather go with them than it be just the two of us.

Jamie shakes his head, and my hopes fall, causing my nerves to pick back up. "No. This is supposed to be your break. You've done enough to support me, no one will think anything of you not being there."

Carson clamps his hand down on his friend's shoulder. "I don't care how it looks. If you want me there, I'll be there. For you, not the cameras."

"I'm good, thanks," he holds out his hand, and the two of them do the cool-guy handshake. I roll my eyes. "Ready?"

It takes me a moment to realize he's talking to me. I nod my head quickly and wipe my sweaty hands down my jeans, giving him a—hopefully—convincing smile. "Let's go."

"Have fun!" Rylee smiles, catching my eye. "Jamie, you're coming back for dinner, right?"

Carson nods for him. "Yeah, I told him when you texted."

"Okay, sounds good."

Why is my sister suddenly taking on Dylan's role of interfering in matters that don't concern her? I already have to suffer through what is probably going to be an excruciating four-and-a-half-hour car ride with Jamie. I really don't want to sit through an awkward dinner, as well. I also love how Rylee is the one who told me how long the drive is when she popped her head in my room earlier. Had Jamie mentioned it last night, I'd have told him to just send me pictures.

We make our way to the front door with Dylan tailing us. Right away, I know this won't be good. He turns toward the stairs, and my chest releases. He's just going upstairs. Duh.

But then he looks back quickly, smiling like he's about to do me a huge favor. "Don't be afraid to get a little sweaty today, I hear Tori likes that."

"*Dylan*," I scold, glancing hurriedly at Jamie. "I don't," I assure him. "I mean, it's not that I'm opposed to sweat or anything, I just don't like it that much..." My words fall off, and I hold back the urge to bang my head off a wall. "It's an inside joke from earlier..."

Dylan cackles at the top of the stairs, happy that I've laid in the grave he dug me.

"Can we go?" I nod swiftly, pushing past him.

"Good idea," he breathes, grabbing the knob and holding the door open.

Jamie gets behind the wheel of his car, and I hesitate at

the door, recalling the last time the two of us were in a car together. He clicks his seatbelt, then shifts his attention to me, realizing I'm still standing on the street.

His hand extends toward me, and I hesitate before taking it, allowing him to pull me into the car. "I'm sober, I swear."

"You said that last time, too," I grumble, clicking my own seatbelt tightly into the buckle, then wiggling it just to be sure.

"You want to smell my breath?" He rolls his eyes, his hand clamping the steering wheel tightly.

"Just drive." I sigh, letting my head fall against the window. I mean, he wouldn't get drunk before going to the Foundation for the charity in his sister's name, right?

"So, what inspired the Mara LeMont Foundation?" I ask, then internally smack myself.

Seriously, Tori? Other than the fact that she's dead?!

"I—you know what I mean." I panic suddenly, worried that I said the wrong thing.

"Good publicity," he says bitterly, shaking his head. "The label wants me to get my head on straight, and their way of doing that is to use my sister's death for publicity and money that will be funneled back to them eventually."

"Couldn't you refuse?"

He laughs bitterly. "I would if they weren't right. The whole band is suffering because I can't get my act together. The world needs to see me healing, even if it's fake."

"And if this is only making you hurt more?" I ask before I can stop myself. He's doing this to please everyone else, and it's making him miserable. Mara's name is being exploited in order to clear his, and it seems like it's really eating him up inside. This is making him worse, not better, so what's the point? Does his health not matter? Is the way people perceive him in connection with the band more important than allowing him time to grieve?

Jamie bites his lip, shifting subtly in his seat. "I like that we're building homes for people in recovery who have lost everything to drugs... but I just wish it were for that reason only."

We fall into a deep silence for the rest of the drive, and the turn signal clicking is the only sound.

Jamie gets off the highway and turns down a dirt road overgrown by trees and weeds. It looks so peaceful I want to get out and walk the rest of the way, admiring nature and breathing in fresh air. My legs could use the circulation after the long drive, too, but I don't want to look like a hot mess when the paparazzi start hounding us, so I keep my mouth shut and let him drive up the winding path.

"Where are we?" I ask, loving the miles and miles of trees and land, houses so far from one another you'd think there was no one else on Earth. This is the polar opposite of our housing plan, where they're so close together you don't know where your lawn ends and the neighbor's begins. My sister is lucky, no one has bought the development on the left side of our house where her bedroom window is, but I wasn't so fortunate. I hardly ever open my curtains because the neighboring window looks directly into mine. It's uncomfortable.

"Eighty-Four," he smiles nostalgically. "I lived out here

a few years before I moved to L.A. to start pursuing my career. My dad's job caused us to move around a lot, so Mara and I never really felt at home anywhere, but this place was my favorite. We went to school here, which never happened because it was too hard to register when we knew we'd be leaving in a month or so. But we were here for seven months, I think, the longest we'd ever spent in one location. Mara loved it. She was in her element." His face breaks into a smile, reminiscing on his sister's happiness. "I was still in middle school, but she went to Silver Diamond High School, which is about ten miles from here, and joined so many clubs, and acted in the school musical... it was great."

We pull up next to a handful of trucks on the property. There are about a dozen men roaming around, hammering, digging, and building. "Is this the first time you've been back here?"

"That obvious?" he asks, hopping out of the car and jogging around to my side. I glide out when he opens my door, sliding my purse between the console and seat so it's hidden from view. I don't feel like carrying it with me the entire time, and if our last adventure together taught me anything, it's to travel light. Makes it easier to run.

A cool hand slides against mine, locking gingerly onto the tips of my fingers. I release a breath, relaxing my hand so it's not so stiff, and allow his fingers to tangle themselves with mine. Hand in hand, we walk up to the structure, keeping our heads low in case there are any photographers lurking beyond the trees.

Standing on the work-in-progress front porch is a tall,

slim man, smiling at Jamie like they've known each other forever.

"My man," he smiles, hopping down the steps to give Jamie a short hug. "It's been too long."

"How've you been?" Jamie pats him on the back and continues to the house.

The guy looks around, spreading his arms. "I'm no Jamie LeMont, but I'm making my way. When my old man died, he left me the company."

"I didn't realize, I'm so sorry." Jamie looks at him earnestly, leading us through the hole where the front door will go. "When was this?"

"Three years ago," he says, thinking hard, then adjusting his attention to me. "I'm Jackson." He smiles, extending a hand.

"Tori." I return his kind smile with my own, shaking his hand. "I'm the interior designer."

He raises his brows, glancing at Jamie who has taken to examining the structure. "I hear you're a little more than that."

Biting my lip, I prepare to change the subject so I won't be forced to lie about my relationship status to someone Jamie clearly used to be close to. I never anticipated having to discuss our status with the people in his life, I'd just assumed it would be a show for the media until they think he's getting better, then call it quits. I imagined the only people I'd be seeing would know the truth. Obviously, this man doesn't. "How much longer until I can have this place furnished?"

"Three weeks, maybe less if the weather permits, four

if it doesn't." Jackson takes off his construction hat, running a hand through his flattened hair, making it stick up every which way. "Have you seen the blueprints yet?"

I shake my head. "I'm newly hired."

"I see." He nods, looking at his feet. "Jamie, what do you think?"

"Exactly how I imagined," he calls back, a few rooms down. Jackson and I make our way across the house, twisting and turning around piles of wood sporadically placed throughout the structure.

We find Jamie in what I assume will be the living room, with a high ceiling and an open hole for a skylight in the center.

"How's Makayla?" Jamie asks, running his finger through a coating of sawdust on the windowsill. "You guys still talk?"

"Eight years strong." Jackson grins, cheeks turning rosy.

Jamie freezes in place, turning in shock, wonder struck across his face. "You're still together?"

"Since we were thirteen." He laughs, shaking his head. "Who would have thought my clumsy feet, tripping and knocking all her books out of her arms, would lead to this?" He pulls a silver band from his wallet, slipping it on his ring finger.

"You're welcome." Jamie winks, shoving his hands in his pockets.

Jackson looks at me, rolling his eyes. "When Jamie lived here, we went to middle school together, and I had the biggest crush on this girl, but was too afraid to talk to her. We walked by her locker every day after fifth period, and every day I'd say I was finally going to talk to her, then chickened out at the last minute. One day when we were passing by, this dumbass shoved me from behind, and I went flying into her so hard she dropped all her shit on the floor. She would have fallen, too, had I not caught my balance and grabbed ahold of her book bag."

"If it weren't for me, you never would have talked to her." Jamie smirks, thinking back on an easier time. "Remember Roy? He had the *biggest* crush on Mara."

"Oh shit, that's right!" Jackson replies, laughing hysterically. "He moved down south five or so years back, we kind of lost touch after that. Didn't he slide a Valentine's Day card in your book bag with her name on it?"

"Yep."

"Good times." Jackson's smile fades, his eyes finding Jamie's, probably realizing for the first time that it's real. Mara is gone. He clears his throat, running a hand down the scruff on his chin, and taking a drawn-out breath. "She's texted me every year on my birthday since."

"That's Mara for you." Jamie looks away, out toward the construction workers moving around busily, probably wishing he was out there instead of in here, suffocating in the thick fog of pain and remembrance.

"It was lonely this year. I didn't realize how much I looked forward to hearing from her until it was too late."

Jamie nods solemnly, far, far away from the conversation now.

"Did you see enough?" Jamie meets my eyes, giving me

a long look. I haven't, but the darkness in his expression says he needs me to have. So, I agree, reaching for his hand and giving it a squeeze.

"It was nice meeting you," I say to Jackson. He nods at me in understanding, mouthing an apology. I shake my head, making sure he knows it's not his fault. "If you're ever in Ambler, you should stop by for dinner."

"Mak would love that. She's been asking about you ever since she found out you hired me. And I'm sure she'd love to meet you, too." Jackson nods in my direction.

"Sounds great." I turn, tugging Jamie when he doesn't follow. He nods at his friend, then follows me down the dirt path where dozens of cameras block us from getting to the car. Jamie's hand tightens around mine when he sees them, so hard I can feel my bones cracking. I glance up at him, and right away I can tell he's holding himself together by a thread. A very thin, very taut thread.

I sigh heavily, looking for a way out. There isn't one. A few of the workers look up, shaking their heads apologetically. Someone must have tipped them off, or they've been here the whole time, waiting for us to come back out. It's common knowledge that Jamie is building a house here, so it makes sense the paparazzi would stick around. I wonder how often he gets to go out in peace, or if no matter where he goes, they never really leave.

It's sad that without Mara, Jamie feels completely lost and abandoned, yet realistically, with his crazy and chaotic life, he never truly gets a moment alone. Not even when he's at his worst.

18

TORI

"Jamie, is it true you're giving the house to rehabilitating drug addicts?" a short, stubby man asks, pushing his glasses so far up his nose they practically sit on his forehead.

Another reporter shoves her microphone in his face, yelling her questions over everyone else. "Have you visited your sister's grave recently?

"Victoria, did you start dating Jamie so you could get this job?"

"Are the rumors about the band breaking up true?"

"How long have you been dating?"

"Do you have an open relationship?"

"Victoria! Victoria! What do you think about his exes?"

"Kiss for the camera, would you?"

"Yeah, give her a kiss!"

"Aww, come on, show us some love!"

They each yell out, forcing their cameras into our

personal space. I push them away with my hands, but there are too many.

We're almost to the car. Yet, we're not close enough.

"I'm going to punch one of them," Jamie seethes under his breath, clenching his teeth tightly. His eyes are hard and glassy as he turns his shoulder, pushing through the crowd with extra force.

"Just one kiss!" a woman yells, shoving her way to the front of the group. Right about now, I'm wondering why the hell he doesn't travel with a security team. I suppose they want to feel some sort of normalcy, but having to deal with this on your own... it's a lot.

We reach the car, and Jamie opens my door for me, his knuckles white as a ghost. I reach my hand up, pulling his face down to mine without thinking or considering the mistake I'm making. My lips brush his tenderly, sending shivers up my spine.

It's just for the cameras.

"Don't give them what they want," I whisper against his soft mouth, pulling away and hopping into the car so I don't have to see his reaction. I'm an average height and weight, but I still have to put a lot of effort into getting my legs inside the small opening, with the paparazzi smashing up against Jamie as he closes it behind me, jogging around to the driver's side—thankfully not clotheslining any paparazzi along the way.

I breathe a sigh of relief when he's inside and shifting the vehicle into drive. He's silent as we race down the dirt path, going a lot faster than I'm comfortable with. I worry that he's mad at me, but I knew if I didn't do something he was going to attack someone again, and I don't know if he can charm his way out of another lawsuit.

"I'm sorry." I swallow. "I didn't know what else to do."

He doesn't say anything, just keeps driving down the road until we reach the entrance to a park I've never heard of, pulling halfway off the tiny road.

"Are you okay?" I ask when his head hits the steering wheel, dark hair falling into his face.

Jamie shakes his head back and forth but doesn't speak. I reach toward him, hesitating before resting a hand on his thigh.

"I don't know why I brought her up." He continuously shakes his head, squeezing his hands on the steering wheel. "It's like I couldn't help it. Like I *wanted* to torture myself."

I blink rapidly at the anger in his voice, not knowing what to do. I'm not good with my own emotions, let alone someone else's. When one of my friends would cry over a breakup in school, I'd just make a bad joke and hope they'd laugh. They always did... but this kind of pain isn't as easily forgotten with a dorky pun.

Jamie sits up after rubbing his eyes, and looks out the window, breathing rapidly. He's hurting so badly it kills me to watch.

"Sorry," he says shortly, apologizing for his own feelings. Feelings that I'm pretty sure he hasn't released until now—at least, not in front of anyone else, that is. His friends know he's hurting, but do they know how bad?

I squeeze his thigh where my hand rests. "Don't be."

He reaches for the gearshift, then drops his hand as his

head falls back against the seat in defeat. He closes his eyes, and a tear leaks out, falling down the light stubble on his cheeks.

"Jamie."

"I'm fine." He holds up his arm, keeping me away. "Just —I'm fine."

I grab onto it with both of mine, pulling him toward me.

"No, you're not." My voice cracks with emotion, or maybe fear of rejection. He doesn't resist. I don't think he has the strength to. His head falls onto my shoulder, and I squeeze my arms around him as his body writhes and shakes. My chest fills with a tight pain, squeezing me from the inside out. How could this happen to him? To Mara? I never met her, but from what I've heard, she was the sweetest, most kind-hearted person alive. She touched so many lives, and she's simply gone by the selfish act of a greedy pig. She wouldn't want this for her little brother any more than she'd want him to feel guilty for not saving her.

"It hurts so much," he whispers, burying his face in my neck. "All I feel is pain."

"I know," I rub his back, unsure of what else to say.

"This is what happens when I don't drink." His voice vibrates against me. "I'm not numb anymore."

I close my eyes, resting my chin on top of his head. "If you don't feel anything, you'll never get through it. You'll just keep pushing it down until it either eats you alive or... or you're dead, too."

"Maybe I should be," he says icily. "I wasn't there for her."

I push him off me, grabbing his face between my hands, withholding the urge to smack him upside the head—this is one situation I don't think that would help with. "Don't you *ever* think that. If she were here, she'd hate you for saying that, Jamie. She wanted more for you than to miss her so much you drink yourself away. You can't give up. You owe her more than that."

"There's nothing left," he says, eyes looking hollow and broken. "There's nothing without her."

I wipe the tears from his cheeks with my thumbs, shaking my head in disbelief. "You have *so* much. So many people who care about you, who love you, Jamie. So many."

"She was my best friend."

"And what would that do to Carson? Your other friends? Rylee? Dylan? Me? Then we'd be right where you are, hating ourselves because we couldn't save you. Because we weren't enough. Do you really want that?"

His head moves back and forth, and I know he'd never do that to us, but he's in such a bad place I'm scared of what he would do. "I just want the pain to stop."

"I know," is all I say, because what else can I? It's not my place to tell him it'll all be okay, because I don't know that. Eventually, it will get better, but that's not what he needs to hear. He needs to feel the present, the pain, not look forward to when it's gone. Nothing I say will make up for what he's lost or what he's going through.

It's so hard for me to imagine what it is he's feeling. If I ever lost Rylee or Dylan, I don't think I could live with myself either, so in a way, I understand. Being without one of them is unfathomable. As much as I complain about their bond and annoying habits, they mean so much more to me than words could ever express.

His deep brown eyes bore into mine, glassy and red, rimmed with sorrow and guilt. A part of me worries he's never going to get past this, and a feverish part of me really hopes he can. If for nothing else then so I can know the real Jamie LeMont.

His demeanor changes without warning, and he watches me closely as he speaks. "About that kiss..."

I bite my lip, thankful we're off the Mara subject, but wishing we could go back because I'm not equipped to deal with this conversation either. He's either going to tell me it was a mistake and can never happen again, or he's going to tell me it wasn't, and frankly, I'm not sure which answer I'm more worried to hear.

"Yeah, um..." I pucker my lips, looking down at my hands. He's still slightly leaned over the center console, and I find myself looking anywhere but in his dark eyes. "We should probably just pretend that never happened."

He nods slowly, eyes trailing down my face until they land on my lips. He looks back to my eyes, and then to my lips again, speaking softly, "Yeah, probably..."

He slides closer, his breath clouding my thoughts as his hand strokes my cheek. My lips slack, and I find myself moving toward him as well, holding my breath as panic settles in my chest. He kisses me gently, combing his long fingers through my hair, his calluses massaging into the base of my neck. I shift my knees onto the seat, finding his stomach with my hands, sliding them up his chest, then to his face, and into his messy hair. His hands roam down to my waistline, sliding beneath the fabric of my shirt, their coolness seeping into my skin as he slides them around my hips and up my back.

His hands slip beneath my thighs, and he begins pulling me onto his lap when I break contact, settling back in the seat. My fingers grip the door handle as we sit there, breathing heavily and avoiding one another's gaze.

My mind can't process what just happened, and my emotions are scattered in my head like the shards of a broken mirror. My eyes scan the brown sign in front of us reading *Mingo Park*, and thankfully, there's no one else around to scold us for blocking the tiny entryway, or to witness whatever the hell *that* just was.

Part of me wants to know why I stopped, because Lord knows I didn't want to, but I just couldn't bring myself to keep going. Not now, not when he's angry and upset over his sister.

"We should probably go," he says breathlessly, holding onto the steering wheel like a lifeline.

"Yeah, yeah." I nod, licking my lips. I grab my purse from between the seats and shove my hands in my lap once I notice how hard they're shaking. "Rylee's going to be starting dinner here in an hour or two. We don't want to be too late."

Jamie shifts gears and presses down on the gas, but instead of going forward, we shoot backward so fast he has to slam on the brakes before we hit a tree. He turns to me quickly, blinking away the fog in his eyes. "I'm not drunk. Just an idiot."

19

TORI

The two of us sit in uncomfortable silence the rest of the *four-and-a-half-hour* drive back to Ambler. He puts on the radio, but it's not enough to erase the awkward tension growing between us. I could slap myself for kissing him earlier. In fact, I wish someone would because then maybe I'd have some sense knocked into me not to do anything like that ever again.

He kissed you, too. I remind myself, unhelpfully.

The last thing I need is *that* thought rolling around in my brain, intercepting every logical one telling me it meant nothing, and it was nothing more than an in-the-moment thing.

Sure, sure, he kissed me back, but I opened that door. I opened a locked and forbidden door that should have stayed sealed shut from the inside. What was I thinking? We're fating. Now everything is going to be so weird because we're not dating, but we still have to pretend to fake date and hold hands and oh my God, oh my God, I'm freaking out. I bet Rylee didn't freak out like this when she and Carson first kissed. I bet she just fell right into the role of being his girlfriend like it was nothing, because they're the two most perfect people in the world, and put together, they're untouchable.

Breathe, Tori, breathe.

Living requires air, and I'm not getting much of that at the moment. The car is insufferable, and hot, and small. If I move any farther off this seat I'm going to be sitting on the road. I need to open the window, but if I do, that's going to draw attention to me and my internal freak-out, which is the last thing I could possibly want.

Luckily, we're almost to my house, but that makes me more anxious than sitting in the car with the guy I'm not dating, whom I kissed, who kissed me, that I no longer know how to talk to...

Oh Lord, Dylan is going to have a field day with this, I can already see it. I can hear his jokes and obnoxious cackling from five minutes away. *Five minutes.* Five. Minutes. Until I have to pretend I didn't just make out with Jamie LeMont in his late sister's car. I allow my mind to entertain the idea that it wasn't Mara's car, but the one I've seen pictures of him driving in *Teen Queen*—the sexy truck with big boy tires he owns back in L.A. The kind guys buy because they think it makes them look hard.

Please, please, please don't let them have seen our kiss on the news already. Honestly, don't these news stations have anything better to cover than my failing love life? Like, you know, *real* news that affects *real* people?

I'm finally starting to understand the downfall of fame

and being in the spotlight. It's awesome at first, but then you don't get a break. It never goes away. Even when this arrangement is over, it'll never really be over for me. Not only does Rylee still subject herself to the torment by dating Carson, but fating Jamie LeMont is probably going to haunt me for the rest of my life.

The second the tires roll onto my driveway, I hop out of the car, not giving Jamie a chance to get the door for me this time. I need air. I need space. I need to pull myself together.

What you need is to calm down.

Great, now I'm hearing voices of reason in my head, what else could go wrong?

Opening the front door slowly, I pray no one stops me before I reach the steps to my room. I can't handle harassment right now. I need to think.

What if he doesn't actually like me? I mean, he was upset, and I was there, and we all know Jamie is famous for getting it on in his truck... Granted, that was Mara's car and not the usual truck he's been photographed in with countless models back in L.A., but that doesn't change the fact that I'm now one of the girls he's made out with in a vehicle—oh my God. I'm officially one of the bimbos *Teen Queen* writes about whom I used to make fun of for not being good enough for him.

I've lost control. I'm spiraling. I don't know what I'm doing anymore.

"Hey, Tori!" Dylan hollers, peeking over the couch with a shit-eating grin on his face.

"Shut up, Dylan," I yell.

"I didn't even say anything yet!" he argues.

I hear Rylee giggling from upstairs, so I take off toward the sound. When I look back, Jamie's walking toward the living room and not following me, and I say a quick thanks to the Man Upstairs for that. I close the door the second I'm safe in my room, and collapse on the edge of my bed. My safe and warm and problem-free bed. Pulling out my phone, I click on Rylee's name.

Me: *My Room.*

She opens my message, and in a minute or two, I hear her and Carson in the hallway. "I'll see you downstairs. Can you check on the food?"

"'Course." I hear him kiss her and then bound down the stairs, greeting his bandmate. The boy I kissed roughly five hours ago. Twice.

"Tori?" Rylee calls through the door, knocking. I rush to open it, yank her in, then close it behind us.

"Have you seen the news? Have they said anything?" I pounce, pulling her onto my bed.

Her eyes widen, looking concerned. "No, you know I don't check Twitter as religiously as you. We've been watching a movie. What's going on?"

"Well, I—you see—" I bite my lip, scrunching my face in embarrassment. "I kissed Jamie," I breathe out in one, short sentence.

Her eyes grow even wider, jaw dropping open in amazement. "What? Tori, holy shit!"

"No, no, no, this is not a good thing. It's bad. So bad. So very, very bad."

"But it was *good?*"

"No! I mean, well, yeah, but no! Rylee, you're missing the point."

"Did he kiss you back?" she asks, way too amused by my love life.

I shake my head, trying to sort out my thoughts. "Sort of. Not really the first time, but in the car he did. I think. I don't know, it's all a little fuzzy right now."

"There were two kisses?" Rylee stands swiftly. "Dammit, I owe Dylan twenty bucks."

"Yes, and wait, you *bet* on my love life—or lack thereof?" It's my turn to stand in shock. "Rylee! This isn't a joke."

"Okay, okay, I'm sorry." She laughs, taking my hands, and sitting back on the bed. "And why is this so bad?"

I feel a strong urge to cry, but I push it away. There's no reason for me to break down right now. Rylee's right. I should be ecstatic. I've wanted to meet the band my entire life, and I just kissed the drummer. "He was upset about his sister, and I was comforting him. What if it was just an in-the-moment thing? We're just fake dating, that's why I kissed him the first time."

"So, the second time *he* kissed *you*?"

"Rylee, focus!" I whine, then lower my voice in case anyone can hear us downstairs. "I'm never like this. I date guys, then get bored and dump them. I've never in my life worried that a guy wouldn't want *me*, so why am I now?"

She shrugs, heaving a long sigh. "I don't know, maybe you really like him."

"What if it's just because of the circumstances?" I cringe at how self-absorbed that makes me sound.

"Have you once thought about how cool it would be to date a famous person?" she asks, then corrects herself. "Since you've started hanging out with him more, that is."

"No." I shake my head, taking a deep breath. "He's just a person, and he's going through so much. I don't want to start something with him just because I'm *here,* and he's sad."

My sister winks, wiping away the frustrating tear that's escaped. "I think that's your answer, then."

"But now it's awkward," I say, grabbing compressed powder from my vanity so I can touch up my makeup. "Why can't it be easy like you and Carson? You just loved each other, and it was enough."

"That's an understatement, and you know it," she cautions, easing back onto her elbows, examining her manicured toenails. "Things still aren't easy for us, but we make it work because we both want to. If one of us ever stopped... I don't even know what I'd do."

"You won't," I promise, knowing my assurance means nothing. Even still, it's the truth, and everyone knows it. The two of them were made for each other.

"You don't know that," Rylee continues, staring at her feet, looking small. She's always so brave and sure of herself that sometimes I forget she's only human, too. In fact, she's my little sister, and I should be helping her through these things, not the other way around. Except, I don't have any experiences to compare with hers or to use as advice.

"Everyone knows that but you, you idiot." I roll my eyes. "The two of you are sickeningly perfect for each other. Somehow you managed to find what some people search their whole lives for and never find. Love like yours and Carson's doesn't happen that often, though I wish it did."

Rylee gives me a side hug. "Thanks, Tori. I needed that. And back to you and Jamie, he's just—he's not Carson, and I don't mean that in a bad way. I just mean... they're different people, and so are we. Jamie deals with things differently than the rest of us and has a harder time letting go of his pain. His sister was everything to him, he can't just move on from that. You've got to help him get there. None of us have been able to break through to him, but maybe you can."

My little sister gets up and moves toward my door, brushing the natural waves styling her hair from her face. "Come on, let's go eat."

I stop her at the top of the steps, grabbing onto her wrist before she can break the barrier that is our privacy. Once we're downstairs, everything we say is fair game. "I just—I forgot how to be a sister to you. For a really long time, and I'm sorry for that. But I'm trying to be better. I am."

She smiles, pulling me into her arms. "I am, too."

"Oh, and Rylee?"

"Yeah?"

"Whatever you do, don't tell Dylan about the... you know."

She shrugs a shoulder. "Works for me, I get to keep my twenty."

20

TORI

Kris and Jer show up a little while later with Kirsten and Carmina, both looking stunning, as per usual. When everyone is finding a seat around the table, I try to sink down next to Rylee, but Dylan shoves me out of the way, so I'm forced to sit in the last remaining chair next to him... and also next to Jamie.

I sit down reluctantly, wishing I could pile a heaping mound of food onto my plate and disappear into my room for the night. Searching all the faces around me, I wonder if they all know, or if they even care.

Why do I?

Yeah, why do I? It was a simple kiss. We're fake dating, it's not completely ludicrous that we'd show a little affection in front of the paparazzi to sell our story. Except, I know deep down, *that* isn't the kiss that's bothering me— it's the one from after, when there were no witnesses, and no excuses other than it felt right.

"So, did everyone watch the news tonight?" Dylan tries

to make casual conversation. I kick his shin under the table with as much force as I can muster. "Jeez, I was just going to ask if anyone saw the weather." He bats his eyes at me innocently. He's anything, *anything* but innocent. "I was thinking of going golfing if it's in the fifties again."

"No, you weren't," I whisper, kicking him again. My brother ditches a fair amount, but he does have school every day, and he'd never skip to go golfing, of all things.

"Ow, what was that one for?" He bends, rubbing his shin with a pouting expression.

"That's for whatever you think of saying when I'm not around. Remember that, and then don't say it."

"Damn, you're scary after you've been kissed," he goads, clicking open his phone beneath the table.

"Dylan!" I snarl, flicking him in the ear.

He stands abruptly, always overdramatic. "This is abuse!" he yells, then stomps his way to the kitchen island for seconds of my sister's Parmesan potatoes. I shoot my eyes around the table to make sure no one else was listening, most of all, to make sure Jamie hasn't been listening. He's much too close to my malevolent brother for my liking. I'd prefer they lived on different continents.

"Rylee, this is amazing," Kirsten says through a mouthful of chicken cacciatore. Mom has made this recipe since we were kids, but I don't think any of us have ever figured out how to pronounce it.

"I can't take all the credit." She pinches Carson's cheek when she stands, heading for more. "He washed the chicken."

The whole table cracks up, and I cup my mouth to

keep my drink from spewing from my lips. Carson follows her to the island for seconds as well.

"Hey, if it weren't for me, all of this food I didn't help make would be burnt." He flicks her ponytail with his hand, grabbing her waist and planting a kiss on her temple. Rylee's elbows clutch to her sides to keep him from tickling her, and she focuses on getting the potatoes to her plate without jerking her arms and dropping them.

"They're so cute," Carmina coos, nudging Kirsten in the arm.

She grins, nodding her head in agreement. "In all the years I've known him, he's never looked this happy."

The two of them wrestle their way back to their seats, both losing several potatoes on the floor. It's times like these I wish we had a dog, because now someone's either going to tramp on them, or get roped into cleaning up. Probably me. On both accounts.

Once we're all filled up on second and third helpings, we pack what few leftovers we have into containers and stack them in the fridge for tomorrow night's dinner—that way neither Rylee nor I have to cook or eat frozen dinners again.

"Let's watch a movie," someone suggests once we're finished cleaning up and full on the dessert that Carson *did* help with. He was a little too eager to point that out, but it was still adorable.

Carmina plops down on the floor, right in the spot where we usually put the Christmas tree, and shakes her head. "No, it's only eight-thirty, let's play a game first."

I shrug, not caring either way. A game could be fun.

"Never Have I Ever," Dylan suggests, and Carmina nods vigorously. Suddenly, I'm thinking a movie might be more fun. Never Have I Ever is my least favorite party game, mostly because people always ask seriously invasive questions—though I suppose I'm just as guilty with that. My sophomore year of high school, my friends and I would intentionally target certain people to embarrass. It almost always ended with someone in tears. Sometimes it can be fun to expose people. Though, I know my brother, and I know if he's involved, *I'll* be the target of every one of his turns.

We all sit in a makeshift circle on the floor, and Carmina starts, since playing a game was her idea. "Hmmm, let's see." She puffs out her lips, stroking her chin in mock-thought. "Never have I ever... been famous."

"Come on," the guys groan, each putting down a finger.

"You, too, Rylee," Carmina nods at my sister. "You're famous by association."

She sucks in her cheeks, scrunching her nose. "Fine. But if I'm famous by association, so is Tori."

"What?" I gape as Carmina says, "Very well."

Now it's Rylee's turn, and she speaks without missing a beat. "Never have I ever been related to someone famous."

Carmina rolls her eyes, brushing her long, caramel-colored hair over a shoulder. "I deserve that."

"You do," she agrees, looking at me apologetically when she realizes I was a casualty of her war with Carmina. "Sorry, Tor."

Dylan stares straight at me when it's his turn to say something he's never done, his eyes looking like deep pits of evil and bad intentions. "Never have I ever kissed a celebrity."

"Damn." Kris *humphs*, folding down a finger. Jer sighs, dropping one as well. Carson follows, and Jamie's next. He looks at his hand curiously, then says, "I should probably put them all down on that one."

Kris laughs. "You have kissed a lot of famous women."

"They weren't all famous," Jamie defends, shoving his hands in his pockets. My cheeks heat, and I put down a finger while everyone else is distracted by Jamie's playboy tendencies.

"Most of them were," Jer intercedes. "You also have a thing for models. Oh, and—"

Jamie holds up a hand, interrupting his friend. "Can we get back to the game?"

"This is taking too long," Kris complains, looking at the TV longingly. "Can we just play with one hand instead of two?"

"In that case, I'm definitely out." Jamie removes himself from the circle, bumping my shoulder as he shifts backward.

After we go around a few more times, it's Dylan's turn again. He looks at me and raises an eyebrow. "Wait, you're out too? I thought we only got you on four. You should have one finger left."

I clench my teeth. He knows very well it was five because of the celebrity kiss round. But no one else caught that, and I'd like to keep it that way. "It was five."

"I could have sworn—"

"It was five, Dylan. Move on," I snap, and he shrinks into himself.

"Okay, okay." Only he, Carmina, and Rylee are left, both with one finger each. If he's vague enough, and smart enough, he can find something both of them have done and get them out at the same time. "Never have I ever secretly dated a celebrity for months, without telling anyone because I was scared my sister would fly into a jealous fit of rage and out me to the world if she found out."

"Dylan, what the hell?" I protest as Rylee yells, "You just intentionally targeted me!"

"How do you know that wasn't for Carmina?" he retorts, crossing his arms.

Rylee shoves him. "Because Carmina has one sibling. And it's Kris!"

Dylan quirks his lips. "My statement stands true."

"Why am I being dragged into this?" Kris whines, standing up and moving toward the couch for an escape. He looks around skeptically, picking up the remote and waving it in the air. "Movie, anyone, anyone?"

A few people agree, moving toward the living room area, eager to escape Rylee and Dylan's arguing.

"There's two of us left, who won then?" Dylan exasperates, gesturing between him and Carmina.

"It was about to be Carmina's turn. She would have won," Rylee explains.

"But she didn't take her turn."

"Dylan, she didn't have to, she would have gotten you out."

"You don't know that."

"Oh my God," Carmina stands, running a hand through her hair. "Never have I ever been a dumbass. There. I won. You're out, Dylan."

"Ha!" Rylee gloats, ruffling her hand through our brother's hair. "You lost."

"So did you," he mumbles, looking anything but happy. Dylan, God bless his heart, is way too competitive for his own good. He has a hard time accepting defeat with anything, including his grades in school. He likes to not only get an 'A' on every test, but to have the highest scoring percentage out of the entire class. It was not pretty when his then-girlfriend, Chloe, got a ninety-five, and he only received a ninety-two.

Now that the stupid game has ended, and Dylan and Rylee are no longer bickering, we adjust the furniture to clear a space for the small sofa Jer and Kris are carrying in from our entryway, so there's enough seats for everyone. Our couch is nice, but no more than four people can fit on it comfortably, and even then, we're shoulder to shoulder. However, the sofa can only fit two people, and our other two chairs can't fit more than one person each.

"I have a beanbag chair in my room," I offer up when it's clear we're one seat short. God, Mom is going to have a conniption when she gets home and finds her furniture slightly rearranged. It's not like she said we couldn't have friends over... I just think she underestimates the number of friends we have, or well, that Rylee has.

"That's perfect, thanks," Carmina exclaims, thankful

she won't have to sit on the floor since the couples have taken their spots next to one another on the couch, leaving the two living room chairs for Kris and Dylan. Jamie is leaning against the back of the sofa, and I pray that when I come back, Carmina will have sat next to him, so I can take the beanbag... preferably placed on the opposite side of the room where I can't see him, and he can't see me.

Dylan peeks up at Carmina, standing awkwardly as if she's not sure if she should take the last seat next to Jamie, or leave it for me when I get back. Then my brother says something I never would have anticipated, "I call the beanbag chair!"

Dylan despises beanbag chairs. Like, literally rues the day they were created. He's forever complaining that they're awkward and uncomfortable and give him neck cramps. And he just eagerly called dibs on mine, the very one he complains about the most. He stands, and Carmina seems to relax a little, settling down into his empty chair. Great. Now I'm definitely going to be next to Jamie—the little twit probably did that on purpose.

Other than Dylan, Jamie and I are the only ones left standing. I should say something to him, or at least try to ease the tension between us—I mean, it's not like we won't be forced to spend an unholy amount of time together in the next couple weeks. What's a little discomfort, right? Instead, though, I jump at the first chance I get to escape my own personal heaven and hell mashup, rushing upstairs to my room.

I shove open my closet doors, tossing the clothes I

normally pile on top of the chair carelessly to the center of the floor. Knowing me, I'll probably trip over them later. I yank the too-big-for-this-tiny-space chair from the grasps of my closet, and stumble backward, banging into something rock solid. I turn rapidly, wide-eyed and panting.

"*Shit,* don't do that," I gasp, clutching my fingers tighter around the material handle.

"I knocked," Jamie shrugs, biting his lip and backing away from me now that I'm on balanced feet.

Swallowing hard, I hold the chair between us as a buffer, as if it can stop him from wanting to kiss me again. Or maybe it's to keep me from pouncing on him like a cat. Yeah, it's probably the latter. "I was knee-deep in my closet, I didn't hear you."

"Can we talk?" he asks, sitting on my bed and wringing his hands between his knees. His eyes won't meet mine, which scares me even more than the thought of him wanting to kiss me again.

Dropping the chair, I take a seat next to him at the bottom of my small bed. Right about now, I wish I had a king-size mattress so I could be a lot farther away from him than my full size allows.

"Look, if you don't want to, we don't have to do anything," he says, then adds hastily, "About the kiss. It was a mistake."

"Oh. Uh, yeah," I say, sucking on my teeth, burning holes in the carpet with my stare.

We fall into a deafening silence, so thick I feel like I should clap my hands or something just to break it.

A few awkwardly quiet moments pass before he's the one to break it, breathing heavily and jerking toward me with obvious irritation. "Okay, why are you doing that?"

"Doing what?" I squeal defensively, locking eyes with him.

He shakes his head in exasperation. "Acting like I said something wrong. You kissed me and then I kissed you, and now you're freaking out."

"Freaking out? I never—I didn't. I don't freak out." Oh my God, what is wrong with me? "Okay, fine, I am, but you got all weird and closed off, too! You can't just put this on me."

"I have my reasons," he says, as if that should explain away his rotten attitude toward me after I held him in my arms while he cried.

I grunt in frustration, dropping my face into my open palms with a *smack*. Good, maybe it'll knock some sense into me. Not only is Jamie *Jamie*, but he's in mourning, and a total player, and, if I'm being honest, he's a borderline alcoholic. All of which I do not need complicating my life right now. "This is so messed up now."

This was supposed to be a nauseating arrangement orchestrated by my stupid little brother to make my life miserable. It was never supposed to end with me developing mixed feelings for this stupid-sexy asshole.

"Why does it have to be?" he questions seriously, placing his hand on my wrist, pulling it from my reddening face. I suck in a breath, trying to control my beating heart. "Because of me?"

I stand, pulling away from him so I have room to flail

my arms like the blabbering idiot I am. "No, because this —this was just a business arrangement. We were only fating, and then we fissed, and then we *rissed* and now things are rawkward!"

Jamie assesses me, blinking slowly like he's trying to see through a cloud of smoke. "What are you even saying right now? And why the hell are you talking like Scooby-Doo?"

I groan, tossing my head back frustratedly. He stands so he's looking down on me, waiting for an explanation. "I *said* we were *fake*-dating, and then we *fake*-kissed, and then we *real*-kissed, and now things are *real*-awkward!"

"Why didn't you just say that the first time?"

"I don't know!" I exasperate, arching my back so I can see his face looming above mine. "Why do *you* keep getting closer to me?"

"Because I want to," he murmurs, tucking my hair behind my ears. I must look like a mad, crazy mess. Jamie presses his hand to the small of my back to stop me from backing away, then closes the distance between us. My stomach flutters with nervous excitement, and a little bit of nausea. "You're cute when you're panicking."

Gee, then I must look like a newborn kitten right about now.

"Don't," I swallow when he leans in again. My heart can't handle this. His fingers find the back of my neck, sliding up and massaging the knots formed from hours of scouring Twitter and reading *Teen Queen* hunched over with a flashlight at two in the morning, when I should have been asleep. Yeah, that's right. Most kids snuck portable video games and phones into bed at night, but I smuggled celebrity gossip magazines.

"Why not, Tori?" he breathes, sucking in my air. More specifically, sucking the air out of my lungs. We're practically inhaling each other's oxygen right now, and I've decided it's not nervous excitement I feel. It's just anticipation. Anticipation so strong I think I might vomit.

"I don't know," I breathe in a whisper, moving my gaze from his lips to his eyes.

"Not good enough," he says, bending into me. I should stop him, I know I should, but as his lips are caressing mine, I become very aware of something I haven't wanted to admit to myself. I want this. The only thing standing between our lips is me, and if thirteen-year-old Tori ever found out twenty-one-year-old Tori turned away a kiss from Jamie Alexander LeMont... Well, let's just say she'd probably murder me in my sleep.

So, I let go, losing myself in the feeling of his lips moving against mine. Except the euphoria doesn't last as long as I wish it would, and my thoughts begin wandering to our moment in the car, and to his fragile state, and then to my past, which I can't seem to shake as of recently. With every good thing that happens to me, a bad memory is unearthed, halting my rush of excitement.

Jamie is oblivious to this, though, and he doesn't stop until my tears intermingle with our lips.

"What's wrong?" he pulls back so he can look at me, concern shining through his deep brown eyes.

Bringing my hands to my face, I turn away, trying to hide the tears and mascara stains, which is useless since he can see me in the giant mirror atop my vanity. "Look, I'm sorry if I pushed you. If you don't feel that way, and this is all a mis—"

"I fuck everything up. I can't—I don't want to fuck this up, too," I interrupt him, squeezing my eyes tight enough that I can pretend the world doesn't exist.

He pauses for a moment, and it occurs to me then what a perfect match we are. We're both so utterly messed up, and irreparably damaged, that we fit. "You won't."

"I always do. Every time."

Jamie collects me in his arms, resting his cheek against mine. I find myself staring at our reflection in the mirror. His gaze lingers on my face while mine stays put on us, scanning his strong arms and long torso that wrap around my slim body and adhere to me like a personally fitted Snuggie. We fit like the last two pieces of a puzzle, like the couple on a book cover gazing romantically into each other's eyes. We look picture-perfect. Except, we're both too messed up to stand a chance.

"If anyone fucks this up, it's going to be me, so don't worry about that." Jamie laughs to himself, kissing me softly on the cheek. "Besides, worrying about the future isn't going to help us right now."

"I thought you couldn't stand me." I lick my lips, placing my arms on top of the ones circling my stomach.

He looks to the side thoughtfully, his heartbeat pounding against my back. "Me too."

"Shut up." I shove his arms away, turning into him and

pulling him by the shirt, making a split-second decision that has the potential to light me like a fire or break me like a twig. "And kiss me."

His eyes grow playfully wide. "Demanding."

I smirk, dangerously. "You have no idea."

21

___

TORI

Jamie and I spent the remainder of the night curled up on my bed, watching uncountable hours of TV. And kissing—there was some of that. Okay, a lot.

And as much as I love, love, *love* that, a huge part of me keeps whispering that this is... wrong. Not a bad wrong, but a this-is-going-to-end-painfully kind of wrong. And if I'm being one-hundred percent honest with myself, I'm scared of hurting him. And not just by breaking his heart. His sister is gone, and I can't help but worry he's either using me to fill a void, or is going to somehow end up devastated by something I do. Because something always, always, *always* goes wrong.

It's my love life, how could it not?

I woke up this morning, probably earlier than I ever have in my life, with a smile on my face. I looked at Jamie adoringly for way too long to be normal, and ever since, I've laid here waiting for his brown eyes to open.

His chest rises softly, matching the rhythm of his

breathing, and I can't help but try to memorize every crevice of his face, from his thick brows, to his warm skin and ever-present stubble. He's kind of breathtaking.

"Let's go out today," his voice interrupts the silence, scaring me half to death.

I clutch my chest, willing the shock to subside. I lift my eyes from where they were lingering on his full lips, and we lock eyes. I roll my eyes, flipping onto my back and tucking my cold hands under my arms. Then I say, sarcastically, "'Morning."

He props himself up on his arm, moving away the strands of hair across my face. Jamie bends over me, kissing me gently, electrifying every nerve in my body.

"'Morning." He stares at me for so long it makes me uncomfortable in my skin. "What? You can stare all morning, but I can't for five seconds?"

I shove my hands against his chest, knocking him backward. "You were awake that whole time?"

He shrugs, and I have my answer. "I'm serious, though. We should do something today."

"Like what?" I sit up, adjusting my tangled sweatpants and running a hand through my matted hair.

He pulls me back down, under his arm. His heat spreads through me like a fire catching. "I don't know, but I'll figure it out."

I drape my own arm across his stomach, playing with the hem of his gray t-shirt. Never did I think yesterday morning that I'd be waking up next to *this* today. My phone buzzes, and I groan, rolling away from Jamie to silence it. "It's my mom. She's called a few times. I should call her back."

Jamie pouts cutely, almost making me take back my words. "I've got to get to the hotel and shower anyway. We're supposed to actually write songs today instead of sitting and arguing over what flavor of Ben & Jerry's is the best."

"You're kidding."

"I wish I was." He rolls off my bed, kneeling on the floor before standing up. I follow him to the hallway, where he stops and turns to me. "I'll call you when we're done, and we can catch a movie or get dinner or something?"

"Yeah, that sounds good." I smile, standing on my tiptoes as he bends down to kiss me. The way he offered up plans was kind of cute in a bashful, nervous sort of way. As if I wouldn't want to spend more time with him after last night. "Bye."

He bites his lip, giving me a heart-stopping wink before disappearing down the stairs. I wait for a minute before I follow to ensure he's gone, then make my way to the kitchen to find Rylee and Carson lip-locked on the island stools.

I clear my throat loudly, making them jump. Rylee turns, eyes growing wide, shifting between me and the door Jamie just left through.

"Hey, Tori..." She smirks, turning back to Carson with raised brows.

Carson returns her surprised look, trying to act casual. "We uh, didn't realize Jamie was still here."

Rylee and Carson are both staring at me, mouths wide open, and enjoying this way too much. I guess it would be more fun to be on the other side of this, though I don't bother reminding Rylee I never got that chance, because I know it'll just sound petty.

"He's not," I respond, ducking my head and shuffling to the fridge for an almond yogurt. That's *technically* true. Jamie's not here anymore... so he's not *still here.* I turn back around, gripping the small container in my hand so hard the sealed tab starts to rip off. "Okay, but like, don't tell Dylan."

Rylee puts her hands up in surrender, eyes crinkling in the corners from her excitement. I can tell she wants to press for information but keeps her questions minimal since we're not alone—as if I don't know she tells Carson everything we say anyway. "Are you guys...?"

"I don't know." I breathe out heavily, deciding against the yogurt, and instead, moving to the freezer for some frozen waffles. "We're hanging out later."

"Cool," she says, biting through the shit-eating grin on her face. Her subtlety is clearly lacking.

I quirk my lips unsurely, worried about what exactly this means. We're not Carson and Rylee. If this is just a phase or a way for him to pass the time while he's in Ambler, things will be so awkward when it ends. With that dreary thought on my mind, I untwist the waffle bag and pop two in the toaster.

"Well, I should probably get back to the hotel, we're *writing songs* again today." Carson rolls his eyes, kissing my sister slowly. "Love you."

"Love you." She twirls a piece of hair between her fingers, following him with her eyes like I did Jamie when he walked down the stairs earlier.

When the door snaps closed, we both look at each other and just *squeal.*

"Tell me everything," she insists, as she's on the edge of her seat, literally.

"Well, there were a lot of doubts—mostly mine—and a little bit of crying—me again—but I think we're going to try to make this work?" I twist my hands in and out of my long-sleeve shirt, giddy and terrified as anything. "He wants to do something later, but I'm worried. We haven't been officially anything when we were photographed before, it was all platonic. And even with the lack of privacy part aside, now there's going to be more pressure..."

"As far as the media knows, this is no different," she reminds me. "And just because things have internally changed between you two, doesn't mean anyone will think anything different. The only pressure being put on you is by *you.*" She looks at me knowingly, and I suppose she's right. I am the only one making things complicated by overthinking them in my jumbled brain. "Oh, and Mom called me earlier. Said you didn't pick up."

"Shoot, I meant to call her back. I got... distracted." I shrug, puckering my lips.

Rylee rolls her eyes, then scrunches her nose a little. "I'm sure you did. She, uh... she saw the pictures from yesterday."

"What did she say?" I gape, completely forgetting that

my parents have access to the Internet and social media—especially now that they claim it's the only way to find out anything about us.

"Uh, I believe it was something about another one of her daughters keeping crucial, life-altering events from her...? I don't know, but if it makes you feel better, she seemed just as mad at me. So, thanks for reminding her about *that* wonderful time."

"I aim to please." I sigh, leaning against the counter. Mom was not happy with Rylee for how often she lied about where she was and who she was with during the month she started dating Carson. I have no doubt the fact that I didn't tell her about the arrangement with Jamie right away reminded her of just that. "Has Dylan seen the kiss?"

She nods her head, *yes*. I assumed as much after his comments at dinner and during Never Have I Ever. "He thinks it was a publicity thing, though. He doesn't know you kissed about thirty times after that."

"And it's going to stay that way," I warn, a small part of me loving that I can keep him in the dark the way he did me.

"No," she shakes her head. "No. We are not doing this again, Tori."

"Hey, you started it," I argue. "It's only fair I get my turn, too."

"Fine. But if he outright asks me, I won't lie. Not anymore."

"Deal."

22

TORI

Carson picks Rylee up around four to take her to dinner. I'd think it was super sweet if I wasn't bored out of my mind already. The two of us have been sitting on the couch doing nothing all day, and when Dylan got home from school, it became the three of us. I'd be lying if I said I haven't been patiently—more like obsessively—waiting for Jamie's call. I'd also be lying if I said the lack of communication hasn't been driving me up a wall. I get that they were in a band meeting, but Carson has been texting Rylee twenty-four-seven—no, no, no, *twenty-five-eight*, and my phone has been quieter today than it ever has. Normally, Megan and Quinn would be texting me, but even they're radio silent. I suppose I deserve that since I never told them I was seeing Jamie, and they had to find out from Twitter of all things. Huh, maybe I'm more like my sister than I thought.

Anyway, I keep telling myself to stop worrying, but that's easier said than done when my mind is going through every Godforsaken possible explanation as to why Jamie hasn't reached out once since he left this morning. The most common, and personal least favorite, theory that keeps running through my mind is that he can't stand me, and never wants to see me again. Then there's the ever-persistent idea in my head that after a little time to think, he's decided I'm of no interest to him. The list could go on for days.

What's worse is I've never gotten like this over a guy before. Normally, I don't worry about these kinds of things because I do the breaking up and keep tabs on my exes at all times—my friends were kind of like a cult and would report their every move to me—or at least, that's how it was my sophomore year of high school. That's the year my friends refer to as, "the year Tori had more boyfriends than final exams." Which is not at all true... okay, maybe it's a little true.

I'll admit, I was a bit bold back then, especially more so than I feel when I'm around Jamie, but I've moved on, and turned over a new leaf. Never again will I date seven boys in one school year, i.e., nine months.

Eh, I had fun, that's all that really counts. Plus, do relationships even count when you're only fifteen? Looking back, I can't imagine a single relationship I had being serious. Take Dylan and his ex-girlfriend. They dated for two years of their lives, and yet, were never in a *real* relationship. I don't think either of them cared about the other at the end of the day, it was just about the title. About being able to say you were in a "relationship."

After America's Most Adorable Couple is gone, I'm left

staring at the shredded holes in my jeans, alone in the living room with my little brother. I'm not sure why, but Dylan frightens me. Not in a scary, horror movie way, though I suppose that could qualify in the right circumstances...

You never know what he's thinking or concocting in that dangerously messed-up head of his. I feel like everything he says has an endgame, and I have to answer exactly right to keep him from seeing into my soul. And somehow, annoyingly, he knows *everything*. Sometimes even before I do. Where Rylee waits for me to admit my feelings and open up to her, Dylan pries me open like an elevator door.

"Why are you staring at me like that?" He squints at me, then widens his eyes, feeling around on his forehead. "Oh shit, did my third eye grow back again? Dammit, the doctor said this ointment would work!"

A laugh erupts from deep in my belly, forcing me to cover my mouth to contain it. "You have so many issues."

"Maybe you just don't have enough—wait, never mind."

I shake my head in amusement. I consider myself a fairly humorous individual. Rylee, too. Dylan takes the cake, though. That kid can turn anything into a comedy show.

"Ha. Ha." I feign boredom. We both know he can do better than point out that I have plenty of issues.

I'm afraid he's just going to harass me further, but to my surprise he changes the subject.

"So, how's the fating going?"

...spoke too soon.

Can I even call it fating anymore? Aren't we technically *rating?* "It's an experience," I assure him honestly. "I never really knew what Rylee meant about the media until I experienced it for myself."

"I never want to know. Thank God none of them are female." He sighs, though I'm sure being best friends with Kris qualifies as somewhat similar to what we're going through. Maybe not, though. I suppose the media only freaks out when one of them is seen with an unknown pretty girl. I applaud Rylee for keeping her cover for so long, I have no idea how that's even doable.

"Carmina is," I smirk, raising a brow. "And she's cute."

Dylan blinks slowly, not used to being on the receiving side of harassments, much less ones that change the conversation to him and a girl. "Wait a minute, you just Dylan-ed me!"

"And you just Tori-ed the conversation!" I point out his deflection. "Say something! I know you like her." I plead with him, holding my palms together in prayer.

"She's all right." He refuses to acknowledge the truth.

I suck on my teeth, hitting him with my best stare. "Oh, come on, don't bullshit me. Remember, you can't deceive the deceiver."

His eyes grow wide and challenging. "Okay, then, what about you and Jamie? Do you have feelings for *him?*"

"Hmm, that'd be a great question if this conversation was about *me*. But it's not." I flick the center of his forehead, mind flitting back to his third-eye joke.

"Fine, okay, she's cute, and snarky, and kind of perfect,

but she has a boyfriend, and I don't have a shot anyway," he huffs, angrily crunching up a water bottle on his thigh. I don't think he realizes there's still some water in it.

"What do you mean? Any girl would be crazy not to want you, Dyl."

"Oh, I know." He raises his hands in surrender, assuring me that his confidence is not at all wavering— because how awful would that be? "But she's the sister of a famous person. She would probably never stoop to peasant level."

My brother is either the most intelligent or idiotic human being alive. There's no in-between. "You do realize your older sister is dating the lead singer of the same world-famous boy band, right? The same singer who is best friends with your world-famous, bass-playing best friend? The one you hang out with more than your own family? Who is also best friends with my current fake boyfriend that I'm only with to help *his* appearance?"

"When you put it like that—"

"You sound stupid?" I offer up, receiving a sour look in return. "Besides, if she does think that way, you have two options. Either you forget about her because that's a really bitchy thing to think about someone, let alone your brother's best friend..."

Dylan peers up at me through dark, thick lashes. "Or?"

I smirk, loving the fact that I've cracked the impenetrable Dylan Green. "Or you have the whole summer to change her mind."

"She's Kris' sister, though. Isn't there some kind of

code?" The glimmer of hope in his eyes is replaced with tempting uncertainty.

"Just don't cheat on or dump her, and you won't have a problem," I say, as if it's actually that easy.

"And what about you?" He cocks an eyebrow, assuming a lazy position in the armchair.

I clear my throat, feigning innocence. "What about me?"

I'm not sure why I don't answer him outright, because I know exactly what he's asking me, and he knows I know that, too. I didn't want to tell him anything, but I suppose he already knows, so there's no point in lying. Still, if I'm going to spill my guts to him, the least he can do is work for them.

"You and Jamie. I saw the kiss."

Sucking my lips between my teeth, I cringe. One of our few intimate moments—not to mention the very first— has been projected on every platform in the world. Is it wrong of me to wish it was for my eyes only?

At this, I purse my lips, and I think Dylan realizes I'm not quite ready to talk about it, because he drops the subject. And after one of the most civil conversations I think we've ever had, we fall into comfortable silence, flipping through channels and watching half of a movie before Dylan gets bored and skips on to the next one.

As annoying as it is, I can't get mad at him because I'm too worried about not hearing from Jamie to pay attention to anything he puts on anyway. He promised to call this morning, and I know they're out of their meeting by now because Carson was already here. So why is he avoiding me?

Maybe he's just busy.

Right, right. Something may have come up. I mean, he's a pop star, for crying out loud, he has quite the life.

Still, a text, no matter how blowoff-y, would have been nice. It *is* only five-thirty, though. Maybe later meant, like, *later,* and he knew he'd have some stuff to do before we hung out and I'm just overanalyzing for absolutely no reason.

Not once do my eyes leave the bottom left corner of our TV screen, where the current time is always displayed in small block letters, except for when I check my phone for a notification—even though I'm pretty sure the ringer is turned up as loud as an iPhone allows. I'm tempted to ask Dylan for the remote so I can change the time setting, but then he'll wonder why, and I don't feel like spelling out my overbearing mind to him at the moment.

When it hits nine, I eventually give up hope, sinking farther into the couch, and curling up with the fuzzy throw blanket that always seems to be here when I need it. I'd lost most of my faith in Jamie around six or seven, while still holding out a little optimism that he'd call with a reasonable explanation that I couldn't be mad at. He didn't. Not even a text.

I try not to let the disappointment in my heart burrow too deep because we were only a potential-couple for one night, even though my feelings for him have been a long time coming.

See, this is what happens when I let people in. I'm

guarded and careful, forever holding everyone at an arm's length until they give me enough reason to trust them. Then, I open up. I reveal myself. And soon after, I get let down. There hasn't been a time in my life where I wasn't. Is it possible I set my expectations too high? Or maybe I just have too much faith in humanity. Maybe it's just me.

"You okay? You seem quieter than usual," Dylan asks earnestly, eyeing me with a troubled guise. I nod my head, mumbling a response, and burying my nose beneath my shield from the world—a fuzzy blanket. "Is it about yesterday?"

"I said I'm fine." I shimmy farther under the covers, trying to hide my expression. I thought yesterday was the start of something, and it turns out it was nothing more than the beginning of the end. Maybe I'm being stupid and overdramatic, but he said he wanted to go out, to do something, and I thought that meant he wanted to spend time with me, to get to know me. Was that just a typical-guy empty promise? The kind they make as if they mean it, as if you're important, but don't actually intend on keeping? I'll never understand the point of that. Why say something you don't at all mean or intend to follow through with when you could simply say nothing? He didn't have to ask me out, he could have said goodbye and left. But he didn't. He made a big show out of spending the night with me and wanting to hang out again later. Why? What was the point in leading me on that way?

Dylan reaches over the chair he's molded his ass print into, and tugs on the tail of my blanket, narrowly missing my ticklish feet. "You've been checking your phone every five seconds, and you haven't sent a single Snapchat to anyone all night."

I raise my eyebrows.

Dylan looks down guiltily. "I checked your Snap score."

"I'm fine," I insist, mumbling into the fuzz. I feel his weight at my feet as the couch shifts, and he rests a hand on my ankles.

"What'd he do?" he asks tenderly.

I don't want to tell him, or talk about it, or even *think* about how mortified I feel, but Rylee's not here, and as much as I'd love to avoid the topic, I also desperately need to get it off my chest. I just feel so naïve. I should have known better. I've been through this before. Hell, I've *done* this to guys before. Maybe not the exact thing, and not with a rock star, but I've ghosted my share of uninteresting boys. Never once did I think I'd turn into said uninteresting girl.

Licking my lips, I pick the fuzzies off my tongue from talking into the blanket. "Jamie was supposed to call me after their meeting, and we were going to go out."

"Like a real date, or some publicity stunt?" Dylan's voice raises an octave when he realizes I might have been stood up.

Not might have—I *have* been stood up.

"We kissed."

"The whole world saw that, Tor, that's not news."

I shake my head, peeking above the blanket. Dylan's staring at the TV intently, though he's not watching it. There's a look of pure disgust on his face, and as upset as I am, the thought of him caring about my feelings is enough to warm my frozen heart just a little. He doesn't only care about Rylee. He cares about me too.

"I know. I meant... *after* that. And then after *that*. We fell asleep watching a movie last night. He didn't leave until this morning when he promised we'd do something today." My chest tightens, and I force it to release. I'm completely overreacting, and I'm sure Dylan's going to tell me so any minute.

It doesn't feel right talking about this with my brother, anyway, so I don't say anything further. Rylee gets it. Hell, she's been through it. Dylan couldn't possibly understand.

When he finally opens his mouth to speak, his phone pings, drawing his attention away from our conversation. I'm not sure what's stronger: my annoyance, or the gratitude I feel toward whoever has distracted him.

"Uh, Tori," he says slowly, unsurely. His Adam's apple bobs as he swallows, and he sets aside his phone, clicking pause on our movie and putting on the regular news. "You might want to see this."

I glance up at the flat-screen, jaw dropping at what I see.

"Turn it up!" I scold him, unsure of when he turned it down to begin with.

"In other news, Jamie LeMont was seen tonight entering the apartment of Stacy Gonzales, who is rumored to have arrived in Philadelphia early this morning. Does this mean the end is near for Jamie and his fleeting relationship with Victoria Green, the older sister of Rylee Green, who has been dating none other than Carson

James for just over five months? And what does Carson think of Jamie fraternizing with his ex?

"A few hours before the pair were seen together, Jamie was spotted at the Down Philly nightclub, looking like he'd had quite a few drinks. Sources say this is where he ran into Ms. Gonzales. She later tweeted 'How bittersweet it is to reconnect with old friends.' with the tongue and eggplant emoji, not leaving much to our imaginations. Then the pair was seen entering her apartment not long after." A picture of Stacy touching his hand as they walked inside appears on the screen, and vomit rises in my throat. "After the death of his s—"

"Turn it off." I rub my eyes, checking my phone in one last pathetic hope that he texted or called or recognizes my existence. Nothing.

"Where are you going?" Dylan asks, concern etched in his face when I stand from the couch with a new purpose.

I don't bother changing or touching up my worn makeup from a day of sitting around like some pathetic loser. I slide a pair of flip-flops on my feet and grab my purse from the table next to the door. "I'm going to kill him."

"You sure that's a good idea?"

"Don't worry. I'll frame Stacy," I call over my shoulder, not caring at all that this officially counts as premeditated murder. He did this to himself. When Dylan doesn't look happy with my response, I say, "We're supposed to be dating to help his image. Personal feelings aside, yeah, it's a good idea. How am I supposed to keep up this charade if he's caught shacking up with some blonde bimbo who's a one-night-stand away from being a stripper?"

"Fine, but I'm coming." Dylan runs upstairs to grab his coat, then rushes back down, slipping on his high-tops. "When the cops ask, I knew nothing of this."

"I'll tell them you buried the body for me."

"And you think I'm twisted?" He shudders, pushing past me into the cool night air.

23

TORI

The elevator is in use when I stab the up arrow fifty times with my thumb just in case it stuck the first time. So, instead of waiting for who knows how many people to get off and on, I take the stairs. Two at a time. Granted, by the time I get to the top floor, the elevator will probably have picked up Dylan and reached it at the same time as me—minus the hyperventilation—but I'm not thinking that far ahead. I can't just sit in an elevator and ponder what I'm about to do, because chances are, I'll chicken out. I need to keep moving, keep my mind busy until I can sink my fist into that sexy-smooth mouth of his.

Dylan's name appears on my phone, and I roll my eyes, trying not to sound out of breath when I answer. "What?"

"If you would have waited two seconds, you'd be here by now with your lungs fully prepared to yell," he informs me unhelpfully.

I hang up at his smug comment, walking casually to the suite doors as if I'm not plotting a murder in my head, that way, if anyone sees me, they won't think I have ill intentions.

I tell Dylan to wait outside, but naturally, he doesn't listen. He's probably just hoping Kris is here with his sister.

Knocking on the door, I absentmindedly fix my hair, then remember I'm not here to impress anyone, least of all Jamie. I pull my hands away and rough it up a little, then worry it makes me look like a crazed serial killer. But before I can fix it again, the door swings open.

It takes me a moment to adjust my eyes, lifting them from the chest in front of me, up to Jer's face. I always forget how tall he is.

He opens his mouth, then closes it upon realizing he has nothing to say, so he just gives me an apologetic smile.

"Come in, Tori," he says, opening the door just enough for me and my brother to squeeze through.

Kris and Carson are talking in hushed whispers in the living room but stop when they see me.

"Where are you going?"

I look at Kris, as if that's really the question he's asking me right now. "I'm going to kill him."

He puts his arms out, stopping me before I can reach Jamie's door. He regards me carefully, glancing at Carson and Jer for backup. "He's really messed up, Tori."

My eyes narrow, and I take a step toward him, leveling our eyes. "I'll kill you too."

"After you!" he enthuses, steering clear of my wrath.

I slam open Jamie's door, steam pouring from my ears. "What the hell is wrong with you?"

Jamie's lying on his bed, no shirt, and unbuckled jeans hanging loosely on his hips, holding what looks to be an icepack to his cheek. He glances past me, a look of pure indignation on his face. "Way to go, Kris. I asked you to do *one thing.*"

"It was our friendship or my life, man. And I wanna live." Kris exits the room, but not before giving me an apologetic look and a halfhearted thumbs up. As soon as the door closes, I'm suddenly wishing he'd stayed. Suddenly wishing I could rewind the clock and go back to before I knew where Jamie was all day. Because now that I'm here, I have no idea what it was I was planning to say to him, because let's be honest, I could never do anything to mess up that pretty face of his.

Jamie stares at me for a long while, then closes his eyes, letting the icepack fall from his face.

I try my best to hide my reaction, but the deep purple bruise forming around his cheekbone, right below his eye, steals a sharp breath from my lungs. "Did you run head-first into Stacy's door?" I shake my head, not feeling at all sympathetic despite my concerned tone.

"Carson punched me."

I bite my lip, suddenly it all makes sense. Carson used to date Stacy, the actress Jamie was seen with tonight, and now Jamie's bringing her back into their lives. Dick move. "Can't say I blame him."

"Spare me the lecture." He winces, grabbing his stomach, which makes me worry he's going to throw up everything he drank tonight. Drank. Oh my God, he's sick because he's drunk. I thought he was doing better.

"Clearly you need one," I remark, looking around his room for hiding places, and mostly trying to find something else to occupy my eyes other than his ripped stomach. "I can smell the smoke on you from here. Where are they?"

"Where are what?" he groans, reaching for the garbage can next to his bed. "Tori, you need to leave."

"The cigarettes you keep stashed in here. Where are they?"

"Why?"

I roll my eyes in disgust. "Because I want to smoke them," I spat dubiously. "I'm going to throw them away, you idiot, now where are they?"

Jamie refuses to answer me, resulting in a fresh wave of rage to burn its way up my neck and to my cheeks. My anger takes over, and I start opening his dresser drawers one by one, digging through everything he owns, determined not to stop until I find every cigarette pack and bottle of alcohol in this room.

"You'll never find them all," he warns. I ignore him, collecting them from under the furniture, in his pants pockets—I'm pretty sure he has a pack for every outfit he owns—and in his bathroom cabinets.

I even find a travel-sized bottle of bourbon... behind his shampoo bottles?

Honestly, what the actual hell?

After I'm sure the bathroom is clean, I head back into his room to finish dissecting his drawers. I yank out a pair of faded jeans, shoving my hand into each pocket until it wraps around something in the front left one. I pull it out, examining at least a dozen condoms that spill over my fingers.

Raising my eyebrows, I hold them up, looking at him doubtfully. "Someone's a little too self-assured."

"They're not mine," he stammers, face going red. He shifts awkwardly on his back but continues to stare directly through me.

"Right." I scrunch my face, tossing them in the trashcan next to his bed.

"This morning was great," he says, and I hear him shifting on his bed again. Then he bends over the garbage can, emptying his stomach all over the condoms.

Serves him right.

He leans back up, pressing his hands against his bare stomach, continuing as if he didn't just upchuck while inadvertently confessing his feelings to me. "You... and us. I was happy."

Anger flares in my chest at his words, though I can't be sure if they're truly his, or a side effect of all the alcohol in his system. Either way, how can he sit here after what he's done and say these things? I meant what I told Dylan earlier. Regardless of how I may or may not potentially feel about the mess in front of me, I'm supposed to be dating him for the media. What does that say about me when the guy I'm seeing is caught shacking up with an A-list celebrity, and I stay with him like I have no self-respect? How does that make me look? He didn't once think about me. Not in a professional manner, and certainly not a personal one.

"Poor thing," I scoff, prolonging my search to hear what else he has to say. Yes, I'm weak. I hate it.

"Then I got here, saw today's date, and realized that I was having the best day I've allowed myself in five months... and it's her birthday. I forgot. I actually forgot my sister's birthday. Her first birthday since she passed." His voice cracks, and I could slap myself for feeling just a little bit bad.

I bite my lip, keeping the angry edge to my voice. I can't let him know he's getting to me, so I continue collecting cigarettes and lighters—honestly, how many do you really need?—pretending his words aren't causing me to melt at his feet.

"You make it really hard to be pissed at you," is all I say. I will not give him the satisfaction of pulling him into my arms like he hasn't made me want to cry all day, even if he sort of does have a good reason for blowing me off. Still, he could have made up *some* excuse, not waste himself away and lead me to believe I meant nothing to him.

I get it, I do. Mara means *everything* to him. She is his entire world, and I would never expect him to entertain me on a day like today. That doesn't change the fact that, despite his excuse, I'm still a little hurt. He didn't just get wasted. He got wasted with another woman.

He sucks on his teeth. "You're managing just fine, I see."

A pang of guilt nags at me, but I push it down, reminding myself that I'm not all wrong for being upset.

Satisfied that I've gotten most, if not all, of his addictive substances, I stand, staring at his miserable face. "We're going to finish this arrangement because I made a promise to Elizabeth to see it through, but after that we are done."

"I didn't sleep with her." Jamie looks sincere for the first time since I walked in here, and yet I'm still incapable of trusting anything he says right now. I waited on him all day, so excited to see him again, and this is what I get? A piss-ass drunk who looks about five seconds away from retching again? He may be shirtless, but this isn't at all the night I had in mind. "You've gotta believe me, Tori. I wouldn't throw away what we have."

"We never *had* anything." I take a breath, willing the shaking in my hands to go away along with the voice that reminds me I'm lying to, not only him, but myself. One of the cigarette packs falls from my grasp and I bend to pick it up, finding another bottle of whiskey stashed behind his bedpost. "You know, for a *second* I thought maybe you were worth it. That was my mistake."

I turn my back on him, struggling to hold all the bad habits of his I'm juggling.

"Told you I'd be the one to fuck it up."

His words send icy shivers down my spine, releasing a few of the tears I've been shoving down for the past several hours.

Stay strong. He's not good for you.

"Well, I'm so glad you managed to get some satisfaction out of this, Jamie. Congratulations. You were right." I let the door slam hard enough to shake the entire building.

I make it halfway through the living room before I stop to take a breath, noticing for the first time that I'm not alone. I search the faces staring at me until I find my brother's. "Dylan, can we go?"

"Yeah." he punches Kris in the arm. "I'll see you tomorrow."

Kris nods somberly, looking tired and worn down. His energetic eyes are much sadder than usual. "Bye, Tori."

I'm almost to the door, almost away from their pitiful eyes, when someone stops me, right as I'm twisting the doorknob. I jump, and turn toward the hand gripping my arm, so lost in my thoughts I hadn't heard anyone behind me.

"He'll work through this," Jer says lowly, his eyes are much more assuring than all my fears are, and what I know to be true. "It won't be easy, but he really needs you. Jamie's a tough one to crack, but I think you'll like the man you find when you do."

I shrug him off, forcing back the tears welling in my eyes. Jamie needs me? Yeah, right. He has a plethora of girls just waiting for the opportunity to take care of him. He doesn't need me, of all people.

"It's whatever," I choke, biting my lip anxiously, trying to look the least bit put together. I'm not sure why, but I'm desperate to make Jamie think this will roll right off my back—yet another chink in my armor. "It's not like we were really together. It was just publicity."

Jer purses his lips, looking like he doesn't believe me, but he doesn't push the subject.

I look past him at Carson, who's staring absentmindedly at the door behind me. "Where's Rylee?" I ask, remembering the two of them were supposed to be on a date.

He blinks a few times before my words register. "I dropped her at my parents' house. Jer called about Jamie mid-dinner, and I didn't have time to take her home. I would have brought her here, but she didn't need to see all of... this. She's dealt with enough of our crap."

I nod once, understanding. "I'll pick her up."

Rylee's lucky he cares enough to keep her out of the drama. If she were here, I'm sure Carson never would have punched Jamie.

I just wish I wasn't the one smack dab in the middle of it.

24

JAMIE

"Where is she?" I stumble out of my room, half bent over and wobbling on my feet. Someone grabs my arm to keep my balance, but all I can see is the broken look on her face —the image of her disappointed eyes, her lips pulled tight with emotion she tried desperately to hide beneath sarcasm and subtle digs.

I didn't just mess things up, I hurt her. I made her cry —well, not in front of me, but there's no doubt in my mind she shed a few tears before making it downstairs. Or maybe she didn't, because one thing I've learned in the time I've known her is to never underestimate that woman.

I never wanted this, to hurt Tori, to turn our arrangement into one so uncomfortable she'll probably back out tomorrow—I just wanted her, and it's taken losing her for me to finally have the courage to admit that to myself.

"She's gone," Carson says, watching me with stony eyes.

"No," I slur, stumbling into the couch. I didn't realize just how drunk I was until I stood up from my bed in a rush to follow her. "I've gotta go after her."

"I wouldn't," Jer says from the entryway, half of his face shadowed over. "You'll only make it worse if you puke on her shoes."

"She's never going to forgive me, is she?" I push away the hands on my back, which must belong to Kris since he's the only one I don't see.

"You really screwed up this time, man," Kris says, patting me on the back. And that's when I know just how royally I messed things up with her. I let my own self-pity get in the way of my feelings for Tori. When I'm with her, all my problems fade away... mostly drowned out by her constant bickering and snarky mouth, but that's what I love about her. She's not afraid to tell me how she feels, or what she thinks. You don't find honesty like that anymore. The Green sisters are a special make of woman for today's societal standards, and I'll never forgive myself if I lose out on someone as special as Tori. There's just something about her I can't shake. Before her, I didn't care about anything except my next drink or cigarette. Victoria Green was the wakeup call I never knew I needed. I've known her for months, but in these past few days, I've actually started getting to know her, seeing her as more than the horrible sister she can be to Rylee. And when she's busy distracting me with her ridiculous comments and rude insults, I forget just how miserable I've felt every waking moment since my sister died.

Carson shakes his head, disappointment gleaming in his eyes. "Let her go, Jamie. She doesn't need this."

"I can't. I can't let her go." I breathe, struggling against Kris, but not getting anywhere.

"I didn't sleep with her," I say, because I need them to believe me, need them to understand. "I didn't sleep with Stacy."

That bitch is going to get an earful if I ever see her again. She caught me when I was drunk, and lured me with threats of blackmail. I knew if Carson found out, he'd hate me, but she had this all planned out perfectly. She knew the cameraman would be there when we got to her apartment. She knew what it would look like if she got me back to her place. She knew exactly how the media would spin it. And I was too out of it to know any better.

"Like you didn't sleep with her in Dallas?" Carson asks, spreading his arms wide.

I point at him accusingly, stumbling forward when I try to move. "Hey, I didn't tell you that so you could throw it in my face."

Stacy has been using that against me for years, blackmailing me with it, and tonight, drunk off my ass, I finally had enough. I finally told Carson, so now she can't hold it over my head like she's been doing for the past few years, so what she did tonight won't ever happen again. She doesn't own me anymore.

Two years ago in Dallas, Texas, I was out at a party and ran into her. I don't remember how it happened or why I ever would have given her the time of day, but I woke up the next morning, confused and hungover, and next to Stacy Gonzales. I panicked. I was mortified. She was Carson's girlfriend. Afterward, I made her swear she'd never tell Carson what happened. I should have known better than to think she'd keep her mouth shut without a price, using me whenever she needed something. But I dealt with it. I never thought she'd go this far to blackmail me, or that she would want to hurt my reputation. I knew as soon as I saw the pictures that I'd lost Tori, and decided that this would be the last time I'd ever let Stacy use me. So, I came clean. I told Carson. He punched me. Now she has nothing over us. Next time she asks me for a favor, I can just tell her no. Sure, she could go to the tabloids, scream it from the rooftop, *really* ruin my reputation, but it was never about that. I only ever cared about what Carson thought. The media is going to say what they want to, no matter how much of it is the truth.

"You slept with my ex-girlfriend while I was still dating her. That doesn't just go away," Carson fumes, eyes fiery and hurt. Almost nine years of friendship, and I've never seen him so upset.

"I was drunk! Plus, you never really liked her anyway," I defend, raising my hands in surrender, as if that makes sleeping with your best friend's girlfriend okay.

"And what about Rylee? She tells me about your subtle comments to her, but I gave you a pass because your sister had just died. Is it a mission of yours to fall in love with every girl I date?" Carson's anger ricochets off the penthouse walls. The room goes still. Jer and Kris exchange a look, as if asking one another if they knew, not at all expecting that. They probably had no idea. Until three seconds ago, even I had no clue Carson knew.

Tension builds in the silence, getting stronger as time goes by and I'm unable to formulate a response. "I was never in love with Rylee, I just—she was there for me. Mara loved her, and when she was gone, Rylee made me feel closer to her somehow. She has the same light in her eyes that I used to see in Mara's. In my grief, I mistook that for more than it was." I drop my head, massaging my temples to rid this splitting headache I have. "I'm sorry," I say again, or maybe for the first time. I'm not entirely sure. All I do know is that I need to sober up, and I need to talk to Tori. I have to prove to her that I'm not the loser she thinks I am. She's the first person in a long time who sees me, and I'm not about to let that slip away. "How do I make things right?"

No one says anything for the longest time. They just stare at me, at the disappointment that I am, until Carson finally speaks up, voice thick with emotion. "You can't."

He can't bring himself to look at me.

Hell, I don't think I can even look at myself.

25

TORI

Three days. That's how long I go without leaving the house—except for one time because I had to—without putting on makeup. Without changing out of my pajamas. Without answering my phone. Not only am I disappointed, but I'm *humiliated* all the same. The media won't stop knocking on our door or trying to snap pictures through the windows, which I'm not convinced is legal. They're a frenzy of bobcats waiting to pounce.

The only way for me to avoid being photographed is to hibernate. Or at least, that's what I convince myself. It's certainly not because I feel like my hopes and dreams have been sliced in half and run over by a dump truck. Mom and Dad weren't particularly happy about coming home to a lawn full of reporters... *again*. When they found out why, though, they were a little more sympathetic. Or at least, Mom was. Dad just wants to go to work without worrying about running over someone in our driveway.

A plate appears in front of me as I'm watching the

latest news coverage on my train wreck of a life, and I glance fleetingly at the shadow looming over me. I smile weakly, taking three warm chocolate chip cookies from the dish. One of the biggest benefits of my parents being home is my mom's heavenly baking. "Thanks, Mom."

"You have to leave the house eventually." She laughs, placing her skinny bottom on the arm of the couch next to me. "You know, when I was seventeen, this wretched kid, Robert Brown, cheated on me. Two months, and he decided I 'wasn't what he wanted.' Or at least, that was his excuse when I confronted him. Personally, I just don't think he had the capability to keep it in his pants."

"*Mom.*" I scrunch my face, wishing I were anywhere but part of this conversation.

She laughs lightly, placing a kiss on the top of my head. "My point is that you'll realize in the end that he wasn't worth the time you spent wishing he'd change his mind and show up with flowers and a sweet smile. They never admit they've made a mistake, not even to themselves, but eventually, they always realize they let go of something worth holding on to."

"Jamie and I weren't even dating," I exasperate, knowing I shouldn't be thinking that much into any of this. We were sort of together for maybe twelve hours. If even. And I use the word 'together' very loosely. "It was all fake. Besides, I just don't want my picture taken."

Mom rolls her eyes, and in that one gesture, I see so much of Dylan staring back at me. "I'm sure."

"I'm serious," I say, a little surprised that Dylan got every quality I hate about him from our mother—his eye roll, his knowing smile, his impeccable intuition. "It was just for publicity, and yet he still managed to humiliate me."

Mom plops a cookie in her mouth, blowing at the strands of hair hanging down her forehead. "Do you take me for a fool?" She pauses, then, "Never mind. Don't answer that."

The doorbell rings, and my stomach drops down a fifteen-story building. That sound is never a good one anymore. Carson doesn't knock because Rylee unlocks the door for him when she knows he's coming, and it's not too often we have surprise visitors.

Mom glances up at the door longingly, then at the oven timer counting down fifteen seconds. "You can, however, answer that." She smiles, heading back to the kitchen where she slides a thick pair of oven mitts onto her slender fingers.

I walk gingerly to the door, fully prepared to curse out whoever it is that wants to know Lord knows what about me or my sister's personal lives. Just how far these imbeciles are willing to go for a scandalous story is ridiculous, and I refuse to feed into it.

"Oh, you've got to be kidding me," I say, closing the door just as quickly as I yanked it open. His hand shoots out, sliding through the opening at the last second.

"Hear me out," he pleads, holding up a small bundle of flowers, an apology brimming in his eyes.

"I've heard enough." I stand in the door, holding the knob with my hand, ready to slam it shut any second.

"Please. I made a mistake. Several. I know that, but—"

"Bye, Jamie." I close the door more slowly this time, never taking my eyes away from his pleading face. Part of me worries that pushing him away isn't going to help him get better, but I can't subject myself to heartache just to make sure he doesn't do something stupid. That's how your kindness gets manipulated and used against you.

"I'm horrible at being honest." His voice is muffled through the door. I should already be walking back to the living room. I should be sitting on the couch, turning off the news, and putting on a good movie to occupy my mind. Yet, I don't move. "I don't mean that I lie, I just suck at expressing how I feel. My whole life, I've gone along with what everyone else wanted at the cost of my own happiness. My selfishness has ruined relationships, hurt the ones I care about, and hurt me, too, because I didn't know how to be myself. I didn't know how to express what I wanted. I've never been okay with *me*. But I'm—I'm trying to figure it out."

Unaware of which direction to turn, I stand frozen in our entryway like a deer caught in headlights. I wish I had better judgment, or a voice of reason in my head telling me what to do. Instead, I'm stuck with the unreliable voice in my head that begs me for one thing but warns that I should do another.

"Tori, please. I screwed up." There's a thud on the door that I imagine is his head. My gut wrenches, feeling as if it's being twisted and squeezed and rung out by uncontrollable emotions. "Give me a chance."

I turn the knob unsurely, standing face to face with the earnest eyes of a man I'm not sure I should trust. I suck in my cheeks, breathing hollowly through my nose. "You won't get another one."

He shakes his head, reaching for me. "I won't need it."

His hand is just shy of touching my face when I stop it, shoving away his touch. "Uh-uh. It's not that easy."

"Come look at a property with me. It's twenty-five minutes away. Jackson suggested it would be a great spot for another house." Jamie takes my hands, not letting me pull away. "Let me make this right."

"Just business," I maintain, pinning him with a glare.

He nods once, looking down. "Just business."

"I'll get my purse."

Running up the stairs, I change into nicer clothes and grab my go-to gray purse with silver studs around the exterior edges. I take a breath, reminding myself I'm doing the right thing, then turn to find Rylee standing in my doorway, leaning casually against the frame. Judging by her attire, it looks like she's going out. "You going with him?"

"Am I stupid?" I blurt, then curse myself. I can't rely on Rylee to be my conscience for everything. I've got to learn to do things on my own. Make my own mistakes without holding anyone else accountable. Still, hearing her thoughts might ease my own.

She shrugs, biting her lip. "I don't think he slept with Stacy," she admits as her gaze falls to the carpet. "I think she manipulated him like she does, using his past as ammunition, somehow thinking it would get Carson's attention, so he'd reach out and they'd reconnect."

"That's despicable. To hurt Jamie over that, too? After

what he's been through?" I shake away my disgusted thoughts, because I know my sister, and I know she's not done yet. "But...?"

Rylee sighs, folding in her lips. "But... Jamie—God, I don't even know—he has a lot going on in his head. He needs someone like you. Oddly enough, I think you're sort of good for him, but that's also a huge burden to put on your shoulders. And he may not have slept with Stacy last night, but he *has* slept with her before."

"Okay, but I'm sure that was before she was with—" I stop at her expression, my mouth half open in shock. "Oh. Wow."

I know I should be repulsed by this information, but all I can think about is that now even Carson, the person who has had Jamie's back through everything, is probably at odds with him, too. All because of this stupid, manipulatively seductive girl. Now Carson punching him makes complete sense.

Rylee folds her arms across her chest, looking as lost as I feel. "Jamie has a good heart. He's just really hurting right now."

"You never answered my question, though," I remind her, then quickly reword my earlier question. I already know this is stupid. "Am I doing the right thing?"

My hopes crash along with her falling expression.

"I don't know," she says honestly. "Only you can answer that. Just follow your gut."

If Rylee Green doesn't know what the right choice is—my Little Miss Perfect, annoyingly, yet wickedly smart sister—then how in the hell should I?

26

TORI

"Are you gonna talk to me at all?" Jamie asks after fifteen minutes of excruciating silence. I figured since he's the one who has to mend things then he should also be the one who makes conversation. I wasn't about to ask him how his day is going. Still, silence isn't a setting I find comfortable, unless it's with one of my siblings. Then it's serenity.

I cock my jaw, gazing out the window at the rapidly moving horizon—green trees and cute little houses flashing by before I can take them all in. "I wasn't really planning on it."

Jamie heaves a sigh, drumming his fingers on the wheel to the low volume of the radio. Nothing drives me crazier than a radio that's on, but so low you can't hear it. It's like the nuisance of a repetitive sound in a quiet room while you're trying to study—completely irritating. Either the music is up loud enough to sing along to, or it's not on at all. Though, I suppose obsessing needlessly over the volume of the radio is keeping me distracted from the real issues at hand. I'm grateful for that, yet I know I should be thinking up excuses to remind myself why feeling something—*anything*—for Jamie is a bad, bad idea. Except, it seems like every time I look into his dark brown eyes, all reason and logical sense fly from my head.

The car rumbles into an empty dirt lot, and my heart leaps at the possibility of being out of this suffocating vehicle, because the tension is weighing on me more than I anticipated. At least we'll be in the open and around other people. Heat bubbles in the air around us, mingling with my anxieties and making me want to forgive him for the sole purpose of ridding the strain on the remainder of our time spent together.

Right. The *remainder* of our time together. As if once this arrangement is over, I'll never see him again. He may not come around as much, but so long as Rylee's dating Carson and Dylan is friends with Kris, Jamie will always be part of my life. It's practically unavoidable.

I cringe at the thought of this feeling becoming a permanence every time I'm around the people I've idolized for almost the entirety of my life. I've loved 13 Days of December *almost* as long as I've been alive. A few more years and I will have been obsessed with them for over half of my life. I still remember hearing "London Hotel" on the radio for the first time.

Hopping out of the car, I take in the terrain. Dirt and trees and... dirt and trees. Blinking nervously, I turn in a circle, looking for more signs of life other than the animals lurking in the woods. No materials, no vehicles, no workers... no one but us.

"Jamie?" I ask, trying to keep my anger from bursting me open at the seams. "Where are all the other people?"

"I just wanted to talk to you without prying ears and cameras," he says, rounding the car with a large duffel bag. I widen my eyes.

"Talk or murder?" I look around at the large wooded area, populated with nothing but miles of grave-worthy land, and trees large enough to hide several bodies within.

He ignores my comment, motioning for me to follow him to the center of the clearing. "The deal isn't official for the land yet, so no one would think to look for us here."

"So murder, then." I breathe, twisting to look at the tops of the trees, which seem to spread so far above my head I'd need a plane to reach them.

It truly is a great place to build a house—secluded, lots of room, beautiful scenery—but I was under the impression it would already be in *progress*.

"Tori," Jamie pleads, setting down his bag, and taking my reluctant hands.

"Gimme the keys," I brush him off, holding out my hand. "I came to help you, and you took advantage of my trust. I won't make that mistake again."

His eyebrows raise a few inches as he fumbles through his jeans pockets until he settles on the right one. "These keys?" he mocks, chucking them as far as possible into the trees.

"What the hell?" I yell, lifting my hands and thrusting him backward, before raising an arm and slapping his face. He purses his lips, snuffing out his growing smirk.

I wish he didn't enjoy it so much. It takes all the fun out of being pissed.

"I played baseball in middle school. Pitcher." He shrugs, nodding in the direction he threw the keys. "And I see you took up the art of jaw-rattling slapping? What do they call it? Ju-slap-su?"

"You're hilarious." I tighten my lips in a strained smile, huffing in defeat. I've already gotten dirt on my favorite gray sneakers, I'm not about to chase the keys into sketchy woods so thick the sun can't reach through. Jamie threw them, he can get them. I just need to annoy him so much he wants to leave.

He opens the bag he carried over, smoothing out a large flannel blanket onto the dirt. Rummaging through a second, smaller cooler I hadn't noticed before, he pulls out what looks to be a McDonald's bag. I don't have to see inside the thin paper to know it's a grilled chicken sandwich with medium fries and a Dr. Pepper. I can smell it from here. Though, I bet he didn't know to ask for extra pickles.

"Extra pickles," he reads my mind, holding out the bag as a peace offering.

I step forward, my love for greasy fast food outweighing any doubts I have in his character. "How did you—Rylee. That sneaky bitch."

My sister must have told him to get me extra pickles. Only she would know since she always gives me her neglected ones. Just the smell of them makes her gag.

Though, I highly doubt she knew he'd ambush me with a picnic.

Or maybe it was Dylan. He's always looking for an excuse to put me in the most uncomfortable situation humanly possible.

Reaching out, I take the bag, collapsing a safe distance away from where Jamie sits, unraveling his own bag.

A part of me claims I'm being overdramatic, and I'm highly sure that part is right, but is it so wrong for him to work for my attention? So many guys just expect girls to fall at their feet and beg for any morsel of acknowledgment. It can't be a crime to weed them out by checking their loyalty and commitment. Lord knows none of my other boyfriends would have ever done this much to win me over. They never cared enough. If my parents taught me anything, it's that the people who truly care about you will make an effort. Everyone else is just along for the ride.

"I ruined any chance I had with you, didn't I?"

I shrug off his sad stare, hating the guilty feeling accompanying his soft-spoken words.

"I truly didn't—" Jamie sighs, probably tired of explaining himself over and over, reciting the same five words to prove his case—*I didn't sleep with Stacy*. "Stacy and I were together once, years ago, and it was a mistake. I knew that the moment it happened, but I swear to you nothing happened yesterday. She was blackmailing me. She thought Carson's thing with Rylee was a fleeting lapse of judgment, and now she's panicking, so she wanted me to drive a wedge between them. Her exact words were,

'You've slept with one of his girlfriends before, what's one more?'" His jaw clenches, teeth biting his inner lip raw. "Clearly, she doesn't know your sister. But I didn't want Carson to find out about what happened all those years ago because I was ashamed. He's done so much for me, and I slept with his girlfriend."

There is a cool spring breeze in the air, so I wrap my cardigan tighter, crossing my legs for warmth. "Why are you telling me this?"

What I really want to do is yell, *"Why do you think I care?!"* but I refrain. I can exhibit self-control on sparring occasions.

"Because I need someone to understand. I can't explain what I did back then, but I can be honest about what I've done now." His fingers shove the bag toward me. "I also brought cupcakes. Kirsten made them."

I slowly pull the lid away from the plastic container, bending half of my nails in the process. Skimming through the cupcakes, I finally settle on one with vanilla dough and a pretty pink heart designed atop white furls of icing.

I'll give it to the girl, she's talented in the kitchen. The art is so intricate it could be professionally done. Hell, if I didn't know any better, I'd think it was. Placing the container back in the bag, I begin zipping the compartment when I notice a small container sticking from within one of the interior pockets. I reach in with my free hand, pulling out a bent plastic box of slightly used candles with remnants of chocolate icing caked to the bottom.

"Where's your lighter?" I prod, thumbing the edges of the plastic packaging until I manage to pull it apart without dropping my cupcake.

"Wh-I don't—" he starts to defend, as if I'm naïve enough to think he doesn't have one on him in case he needs an emergency cig.

"Just give it to me." I pull out a candle while he's running to the car, and shove the box back where I found it.

He tosses the silver lighter next to my thigh, then drops back down closer than before—smooth bastard. Carefully, I place the candle in the center of the craftily designed dessert, then apply pressure to the spark wheel. It takes a few tries—most likely running low on lighter fluid—but after a few attempts, I finally have a bright flame. I hold it to the candle until it's lit, then raise the cupcake between us.

"What are you doing?" Jamie wonders, looking lost. He tucks a piece of long hair behind his ear, shifting uncertainly, as if at any second, I might tip the candle and light his shirt on fire.

I reach for his hand, then let both his and mine hover between us. I give him a small smile and quickly squeeze his fingers. "Happy birthday, Mara," I whisper, feeling a nervous spark somewhere in my stomach, worrying this might upset him, instead of bringing him comfort. I didn't exactly think this through.

Jamie stares at me like I'm some foreign being the world never knew existed, then finally he repeats my words, voice tight with emotion. He watches the flame for what feels like eons before clearing his throat. "Should we blow it out?"

When he speaks, a gentle breeze wafts by, strong and willful, snuffing out the tiny blaze.

"I guess not." I blink, staring at the candle wondrously, pulling my arms closer to me and out of his reach, wrapping them around my stomach.

Jamie squeezes his eyelids to hide the boiling pain deep inside that's swimming to the surface. "Do you think she knows? Does she know how sorry I am?"

"I'm not sure." I sound a little helpless when I speak, like the question he's asking is far beyond anything I could ever comprehend. "But she knows you love her. I think that's enough."

He nods once, then looks up toward the sky, eyes shimmering brightly. "I hope so."

27

TORI

Windows down, we zoom across the winding backroads until I'm just nauseous enough that I don't feel carsick anymore. I reluctantly took Jamie's jacket when he offered, since my knitted sleeves and ripped jeans weren't doing much for warmth. It's fifty degrees today, warmer than it's been over the past few days, but still not warm enough to be outside for long periods of time without some source of heat. I'll never understand how the weather goes from a hot, summer-like day to a cold one the next.

I can deal with the chill, though, if it means the windows are down. Wind threading through my hair and slapping across my face is a feeling no other can compare to. For a moment, I can close my eyes, and everything goes away but the numbing sensation of freedom. It vibrates across my skin and deep into my core, clawing away all the problems and worries rising to the surface.

A quick glance at the speedometer tells me we're nearing eighty-five, and I find an odd type of solace watching the numbers climb. At first, I tried to act like I didn't condone how fast we were going, telling him so on more than one occasion, but we both knew what I really meant was 'you're not going fast enough.' I love the thrill, the danger, the unknown. If I can still see the shape of the trees as we pass—and not just a blur of motion—then we're going too slow.

Except, driving at this speed means less time on the highway, and we make it back to my house in half the time it took us to get to the property. Before I know it, I feel the slow deceleration of the tires as we get off the exit, turning down my road.

"I think Carson's here," Jamie speaks the first words either of us have said in fifteen minutes as we pull into the driveway.

Carson normally parks farther away so no one recognizes his vehicle, but Jamie, on the other hand, doesn't seem to care at all about the paparazzi. He hates them, but in some ways, I think he's accepted that they became a part of his life the moment he chose this path. He knew very well what he was getting into.

"Would he be anywhere else?" I joke, picking up the cupcake wrappers from the floor, and the fries I have left over from our picnic. I know Jamie wants me to wait for him to get the door, but I'm just not there yet, so I get out before he has the chance.

He pauses halfway around the car, hands in his pockets. "You live to make me frustrated, don't you?"

"You can close it," I offer, biting away my smirk. Once inside, I contemplate shutting the door in his face, but figure that'd be too far. Jamie must expect me to do the same because he pauses just before the entryway. I don't acknowledge this, though, and I also don't bother inviting him in, instead grabbing the small bundle of daisies he brought me earlier and taking them into the kitchen. They're not overly priced, showy, vibrant, or tied with bows and glitter. They're an earthy collection of flowers bundled together with a rubber band that could easily have been handpicked from a field. I don't know why, but the idea of him putting more than money into a small bouquet—like time, thought, and consideration—warms my soul a little.

"You're back!" Mom cranes her neck over the couch in greeting, then does a double take when she realizes I'm far from alone.

"Mom, this is Jamie," I breathe through the words, having forgotten that my parents are home again, and that I can't bring boys into the house freely without drawing unwanted attention.

"Hello, Mrs. Green," he says, taking two long strides forward and extending his hand to her.

"It's a pleasure." Mom smiles sweetly, shooting me an incredulous look. "Daisies?" She stands, taking them from my hands, and examining the pretty flowers. Her brows raise along with the grin splayed across her thin lips. "How thoughtful."

Mom eyes him interestedly, glancing between the two of us with intense curiosity. I hardly blame her. There's no denying Jamie LeMont is one sexy piece of man. You'd have to be blind not to give him a once-over, no matter who you are. I'd always thought he was gorgeous on posters and in filtered Instagram pictures, but if I'm being honest, the real him is beyond comparison. Comparing him to a digital image is an insult to the man standing beside me. He's a vision in tight jeans and a long-sleeve white shirt that hugs him in all the right places. The only reason I'd accepted his leather jacket was because he'd already had it halfway off, and I was not going to deny myself the pleasure of scrutinizing his biceps. And *normally,* I don't like guys with his length of hair either. Carson's messy curls are more my speed, but somehow, Jamie manages to take the long length to an extraterrestrial level.

"How long will you boys be in town?" she asks, filling a small blue vase with water. Mom tucks her hair behind her ears, looking like a teenage girl for a split second. "I never got a chance to ask Rylee before she scampered off."

Jamie shoves his hands in his pockets, coming up behind me, close enough to make me want to move away, but not so close that it looks like we're together. As if anyone else in the room is dissecting the distance he's standing from me. "Just for the month, probably, then we're going to head down to Carson's beach house for the summer."

I love how I'm thinking of these things while my mom is asking innocent questions.

"It must be nice to get some time off." She sighs, dragging her forearm across her cheek to remove a few pesky hairs, knowing all too well the taxing struggle of a demanding job.

Before he can respond, I cut in, wanting this awkward introduction to end. "Where's Rylee?"

"She and Carson are upstairs." She quirks her lips down in disapproval. She forgets that we had the house to ourselves for half a month.

Before leading Jamie upstairs, because he's clearly not leaving, I add one final thought, mostly because I can't help myself. "Mom, if they were gonna do it, I assure you it wouldn't be while you're home."

"Just... go upstairs." Mom shoos us away, shaking her head as if to rid herself of a bad thought. "I apologize for my daughter."

Jamie smiles knowingly. "At least someone feels my pain."

"Shut up," I snark, sliding past him to the hallway.

He bumps my wrist when we reach the stairs, and I turn expectantly, waiting for whatever he has to say.

"Are we good?" he asks, the fingers that touched my wrist are slowly moving down my hand to the side of my palm where they linger.

"I guess." I sigh, biting my lip nervously. "I'm sorry I went all Godzilla on you."

Jamie reaches for my face, smoothing his thumb across my cheekbone affectionately. "I deserved it."

I tilt my neck, resting my cheek in his hand, and look up into his eyes. My stomach churns nervously as I inspect how the different shades catch the light, reflecting specks of caramel and green. "You kind of did."

Jamie shifts his weight to bring himself closer to me, and on instinct, I back away, tripping on the steps behind me. "We should—" I start, grabbing the railing to keep from hitting the ground, but don't get to finish because Dylan comes bounding down from upstairs. For the very first time in the sixteen long and tortuous years he's been alive, I'm beyond ecstatic that Dylan has inserted himself into the equation.

Except for the first time *in literal history,* he has nothing to say but, "Hey, Tori," and then. Keeps. Walking.

What. The actual. Hell?

It is official. He was born with the sole purpose of making my life miserable. One day someone decided that the first-born child of the Green family needed a cute little hazel-eyed devil to destroy the ground she walks on.

The one time—*the one time*—I want him to crack a joke, or insult me, or try to turn my face the color of a tomato, he lets me down. If I weren't so embarrassed, I'd have stormed after him and tackled him to the floor.

Instead, I'm stuck standing awkwardly with Jamie staring at me like he got all the signals wrong. I don't want him to think it's his fault, but it kind of is. He technically didn't do anything, but had he been stronger, he wouldn't have ended up at that club to begin with.

My stomach clenches, and a wave of guilt rolls through me. *If he'd been stronger.* What is wrong with me? How could I even think that? He's grieving the death and birthday of his sister all while struggling with the need to drown his sorrows in alcohol, and I have the audacity to think he should have been *stronger?*

Heat spreads across my cheeks, and I press my hands to them to hide my reaction. God, I'm such an idiot.

Jamie purses his lip, eyes narrowed in uncertainty. "You know, I should probably go. I've got a thing. In the morning. So, uh, I'll see ya."

When I open my mouth to respond, his back is already to me, lifting his leather jacket from the seat I dumped it on when we walked in, knowing he'd have to come in to get it. No, I didn't slam the door in his face, or invite him in, I goaded him in because I didn't know how to do it otherwise.

"Jamie—" I start, but he just raises a hand in acknowledgment as the door closes behind him.

Slumping against the wall, I rid myself of all the voices telling me I should run after him. Do I even want to? A paranoid part of me worries I'm only attracted to him because of a lifelong infatuation, but I know that isn't true. If it were, I wouldn't have spent so much time trying to convince myself there was nothing between us, that I didn't feel anything for him. But I do. He spent the entire, perfectly planned day, trying to win me back. And it worked. It really did. So, I don't know why I shied away from him like that.

Self-preservation. That's why.

The fear of being let down again is so much stronger than the pain of giving up on a good thing too soon. I suppose I'd rather lose him now, rather than risk having my heart broken. How messed up is that? To give up on something without trying because you're scared?

Now tomorrow, or in an hour, when I realize what a horrible mistake I've made, how can I expect him to simply let it go? Because now *he's* going to be scared of getting hurt again, and it's all my fault. I shouldn't have leaned into his hand like that. If I hadn't, if I hadn't let my guard down, then maybe he wouldn't have made a move, and we could have played out this friends' territory a little longer.

"Dammit," I hiss, knocking the back of my head against the wall.

Dylan saunters back down the hallway with a bowl of cereal and an oatmeal cookie in hand, two ice-cold waters sticking out either side of his sweatpants.

"Jamie leave?" he asks, looking indifferent.

I finally understand why he didn't make a joke. He saw the news. He saw me yesterday. No wonder he wasn't up to the task of making relationship jokes or sarcastic comments about my attraction to Jamie. He was trying to protect me. For once in his life, my brother actually tried to do something nice for me.

I glare at Dylan, yanking a flip-flop from the shoe cubby and chucking it at his head. *"You had one freaking job!"*

I let my shoulders fall, dropping my forehead in my hand, leaving Dylan to wonder why in the world I'm mad at him for finally doing what I've always asked: leaving me be.

28

JAMIE

Am I an idiot?

Did I misread the signs? Did I try too hard, lean in too soon? Other than the misunderstanding with Stacy, what's changed since two nights ago? Because I know, even mad, if I'd made it to Tori before she got in her car yesterday after she stormed out of the hotel, if I had kissed her, she would have kissed me back. I can't be the only one who felt it, who feels it. She has to feel it, too. I know she does.

I bang my head on the arm of the chair three times before Kris sets aside his laptop, folding his hands in his lap like a therapist. "Tell me, Jamie, what's on your mind?"

"You, cutie." I wink, reciting the line one of our fans used on him a few years back in a meet and greet. He'd asked her what she wanted to do—meaning what kind of pose did she want for her picture—and that was her exact response. I've got to hand it to her, we've heard a lot—and I mean a *lot*—of crazy things, between the fans, the media, and our own collective humor, but that rendered us all speechless.

"Stop it." He scrunches his nose and swats his hand.

Even in my immense state of depression, I can't help but laugh at his ridiculousness.

"Girl troubles?" he teases.

My infatuation with Tori is anything but a secret around our suite. In fact, the guys harassed me about her before even I considered the possibility of there being something more than an acquaintance there, way before the idea of fake dating was ever a possibility. Besides, at the time, I was still into Rylee. I hate myself for it, but I lied when I told Carson my feelings for her were a misconception... I'm not entirely sure they were. I felt something for her. No matter how fleeting, it was there. But I stomped down those emotions a while ago, and since meeting Tori, they haven't resurfaced.

"I thought we were on the same page," I tell him, uncommitted to the conversation. If I keep it light, then maybe it won't weigh so heavily on my shoulders. "We're not."

"Just to be clear," Kris leans lazily on the couch cushions, staring off into space, "who rejected who?"

Dumbass. He already knows the answer to that question, he just asked it to get under my skin. I should consider myself lucky he's talking to me at all, although I'm pretty sure it's only out of pity since Jer is still unhappy with me, and Carson is giving me the cold shoulder.

He hasn't spoken to me in two days, and we haven't

gone a day without talking, or at least texting, since I was thirteen years old. None of us have. Unlike a lot of boy bands, we actually get along. We chose each other. We weren't put together or forced in by a contract. We chose one another and have continued to for the past eight years.

Carson walks into the suite, as if on cue, and I gnaw at my lip, staring at the floor. I'm only willing to apologize so many times before it becomes his problem instead of mine. I'm ashamed enough as it is without begging on my knees.

"Guess who got rejected?" Kris blurts in an attempt to get Carson talking. I'll admit, yelling or making fun of me would be better than this. I just want something, some sort of acknowledgment. I want him to scream at me—even punching me again would be better than not speaking at all. This is so unlike Carson. It's a territory I don't know how to navigate, despite my best efforts.

Carson doesn't flinch. "Don't care."

Kris watches him walk down the hall to his room. "He just needs time."

With nothing else to say, I nod my head, reminiscing on all the times Carson's had my back. More so than ever after Mara died. One mistake took that all away.

I don't want to tell this to Kris, but I'm afraid no amount of time will mend us now.

I've always been wild, my time with Stacy was no exception of that, but this is different. This is reckless.

I've been drinking since I was fifteen, but it was only for fun until Mara died five months ago—then it became my remedy. I have no excuses for what I did, other than I was drunk. But that can only account for the first time… if Carson knew about the others…

"Are you going to fix things with Tori?"

His words strike a funny feeling inside me. I thought that was what I was doing, but somehow it backfired. That's never happened to me before. I've never given this much thought to a girl who wants nothing to do with me. Until Victoria Green. "Nah, I'm just going to give her space from now on."

He's quiet for a moment before he says, "Are you sure that's what she wants?"

My gut screams 'no', but maybe that's just my head projecting my own desires onto her again.

My foot taps the carpeted floor in distress, so forcefully Carson has to press his hand to my knee to stop it from shaking the entire row of chairs. We are pressed so close together I'm practically sitting on Jer's lap. I know for a fact I must be sweating on him.

"It'll be over soon. Just take a breath." Carson squeezes my shoulder, reminding me to breathe. A knot unfolds in my chest, but not enough to detangle my nerves or rid me of the apprehension I've felt since a week ago, when we finally decided on a date.

Still, I won't look up. I won't look at her casket. I won't smile at the people coming in to pay their respects who never knew her. That don't care. That are only here because of social obligation. Personally, I wouldn't have blamed them for not coming. In a way, I think staying home would have been the respectful thing to do, as opposed to shedding fake tears over the body of a girl they couldn't care less about, other than the fact that what happened to her was tragic.

Tragic.

If I have to hear that word one more time, coming from some rich snob who couldn't give a rat's ass about my sister, I might just lose my thinning patience.

The people who did care about Mara, who care about me, aren't so insensitive. They don't have to tell me they're sorry because they know me, and they know words mean nothing. Words don't mend a broken heart or return life to a lost soul. Sometimes they provide relief, but not here. Not like this. Besides, most of, if not the only people who cared about my sister, are sitting right here with me.

My parents have been stationed by the door, claiming it's necessary to greet everyone as they come in. I know better. They just can't stand being in the same room as her body. One wrong flick of the eye, one wrong turn in the direction of a coming voice, and you'll see her. Lying there like a plastic doll. The dress she wears isn't one she'd have been caught dead in while she was alive, but it covers the gunshot wound just fine— or so the funeral director told us. When we first walked in here, I almost threw up. I still might. And that was before her body was appropriately positioned in a designer casket at the front of the room for everyone to pout and shed their fake tears over.

An elderly couple shuffles their way to me, and the wife extends a hand. I stand to be polite, wobbling on my feet a little. She wraps an arm around me as her husband pats my back in a form of support, as if that simple gesture makes me feel more at ease, as if a pat on the back can take away the trauma etched in my heart.

"We were so sorry to hear about Mara, son," the husband says, and I vaguely recognize him as one of my old neighbors from when I lived in Pennsylvania, but I could be wrong. I was just a kid then. My parents make a point to keep in contact with our old friends from different places—personally, I couldn't care less.

The woman nods as her husband speaks, filling in the silence that accompanies what should have been my response. I'd be lying if I said I didn't notice her brief intake of air and widening eyes when she smelled the fifth of whiskey I downed before the car picked us up. I reek of alcohol, and everybody who gets close enough to me knows it. "If you ever need anything, no matter how far away you are, you just let us know, okay, hon?"

"That means a lot, thank you for being here tod—"

Whatever I might have said next is cut off by the strangling sounds that erupt from my throat. I clench my fists at my side, staring through blurred vision. I feel Carson stiffen behind me, and the clutches of his fingers as they try to latch on to my suit jacket before I storm toward the door, ready to smash in the face of the man smiling at my mother.

"You have some nerve showing up here," I growl, thundering across the room with Carson not far behind.

"Jamie?" Mom asks worriedly, glancing between me and Dad, and then back up at the stranger—well, stranger to her. Not to me.

"He's not welcome here, Mom," I grit, stepping in front of her.

"Do you know who this is?" she asks Dad under her breath.

As far as I know, they've only seen Danny, my sister's abusive ex, in a handful of pictures. When she first came to me, claiming he hurt her, she'd said she didn't tell our parents yet. And once she was settled, and landed on her feet again, she didn't feel like revisiting the past, so she never told them.

"Hey, I loved your sister," Danny spits, puffing his chest as if he could take me. Not in this universe or the next could his scrawny ass beat me in a fight. "She's the bitch who ended things."

"Okay," Carson intervenes then, knowing the next words flying from Danny's mouth will be when I punch him so hard his voice strangles in his throat. "Jamie's right, you need to go."

Carson doesn't wait for him to oblige, just pulls me down the hall to an empty room, closing and locking the door behind us.

"I should kill him," I swear, pacing up and down the floor. If it weren't for him, Mara may never have started self-medicating. He's the reason she turned to drugs in the first place. He should consider himself lucky he's still breathing.

"You should do no such thing."

"My sister is dead, and that piece of scum is still alive! It's not right!"

There's a soft knock on the door, followed by Rylee's soft voice, "He's gone, guys. Your dads got rid of him."

My muscles release at that, and I nod my head, even though she can't see me. Carson's dad must have stepped in, too —God bless him.

After giving Carson a nod, indicating I'm okay, and that there will be no more skull crushing for the rest of today, I twist the doorknob, but not before he pierces me with his stare. He is possibly the only one whose words mean more to me than silence.

"It'll take time, a lot of it, but you'll get past this. We all will. But today, it's okay to hurt."

29

TORI

"Oh no, what happened?" Rylee calls from her open bedroom door as I stomp unnecessarily loudly into mine.

Carson left shortly after Jamie, and I'd still been slouched on the floor, trying to figure out how many times I must have been dropped on my head as a child to be so foolish that I pushed away Jamie LeMont.

"I happened," I exasperate, throwing my hands up as if to ask the world, 'Why?'

Why am I like this?

She shifts in her bed, probably propping her head toward the end so she can hear me better. We used to do that all the time as kids when we were too lazy to move from the comfort of our mattresses. "Wanna talk about it?"

Flopping back on my own bed, I slam a pillow over my face. "Not particularly."

"Huh?"

I remove the pillow, raising my voice a little, "Not particularly!"

"Okay, then," she sasses, and I imagine her eyes growing wide like they often do when she's being sarcastic or humorous.

Flipping to my stomach, I pull out my phone, click on Twitter, and then exit out of it just as fast, hating the reflex and constant need to be connected. I toss my phone to the floor. The last possible thing I need is to see what the world is saying about last night, or see some out-of-context pictures of me and Jamie from today. For a quick second, I entertain the idea of them having snapped a picture of us lighting the candle for Mara's birthday. From afar, it probably looked like we were having some ritualistic séance. The thought makes my lips upturn a little. Not a lot, but enough to ease the tension in my shoulders.

You know what? If things with Jamie are meant to work out, they will. And if he leans in again, which is doubtful now that I humiliated him and practically fell over to get away from him, I won't pull away. I won't force him away anymore. I'll be stronger than that. Until that day comes, I'll be his friend. I'll work with him. I'll continue to fate him. And if it turns into more, great. And if it doesn't, well, then so be it.

Please turn into more, please *turn into more.*

"Tori, where's your phone?" Rylee calls out, making me jump from my thoughts.

I glance over at the black screen on my carpet where I threw it a little while ago, before I was lost in Fantasy Land. "Why?"

"Um. Jamie's outside."

"What?" I panic, absentmindedly grabbing at my hair.

"He just texted me," she continues, making me wonder what time it is and how long it's been since he left. Maybe an hour? Possibly two?

"You're kidding." I lunge across the room, turning on my phone to find three missed texts, all from Jamie. "What do I do?"

There's a long pause before my sister answers, and I know in my gut it's because she has to get her laughter under control. "You could answer the door?"

"Right." I breathe, nodding to myself. "Just, get the door, Tori. Why didn't I think of that?"

I reach the entryway in seconds, bracing myself for whatever I'm about to find on the other side. A quick glance at the clock explains why he didn't knock. It's eleven-fifteen at night. I hadn't paid attention to how much of the evening went by while I was slumped on the floor in misery.

Upon opening the door, I find Jamie in the same outfit as earlier—leather jacket, white shirt, and dark gray jeans hanging low on his hips. I'd like to say my eyes don't travel up and down him twice before they find his face, but they totally do. Without shame.

"Hey." Unease rolls through me, as does leftover embarrassment from earlier.

He swallows, seeming uncertain as to why he's here, putting himself through more awkward quality time with the girl who would rather fall over than kiss him. "Can we talk?"

Can we talk.

Oh dear. Even outside of relationship parameters those

words strike ice to my core. That phrase should be banned from conversation, because nothing good in the history of the world has ever come from those three little words.

"Yeah, come in." I rotate to the side, but he stretches his neck, admiring the stars above. "Let's walk?"

Nodding, I grab Rylee's coat from the rack to my right, so I don't have to make him wait for me to dig one out of my closet. I then throw on a pair of purple Nikes that don't match my outfit one bit. In retrospect, I should have gone to get my own coat so I wouldn't be walking in thirty-degree weather in night shorts and a baggy t-shirt that Rylee's jacket is almost longer than, but desperate times call for desperate fashion choices.

The two of us walk side by side, shoulders brushing occasionally as we stroll across the small slab of concrete that can hardly be considered a sidewalk. Occasionally, I bump into Jamie to avoid stepping in a pothole and snapping my ankle.

Feeling like someone needs to break the dense air strangling us, I decide to swallow my pride and speak up first. "About earlier..." I start, not sure where I intended to go with this topic. Except, I brought it up, so I can't chicken out now. "I really didn't mean to—"

"What if we're just friends?" he offers quickly, cutting me off.

I halt in place. After a few paces, Jamie turns back when he notices I'm not beside him anymore.

"Friends," I repeat.

"Yeah." His hands find his pockets on impulse, burying themselves inside. "Let's be friends."

"Friends," I repeat again, dumbly.

He nods once.

"Are you trying to kill me?" I blurt, then clamp my hand over my mouth just as quickly as the words spilled out.

His words say one thing, but the way his eyes trail across my face says something entirely different, but for his sake, and the sake of our little business arrangement, I concede. "Um. Sure. That sounds like a... smart idea."

"Yeah?"

"Yeah," I avoid eye contact, despite him still searching my face. "Friends."

"Friends."

We fall into a rhythm, walking staggered enough so our coats don't brush anymore, because when our coats brush, so do our hands, and that's a recipe for disaster.

"You're wearing shorts," he says after a moment, causing me to raise my eyebrows. My eyes fall to his jeans, shredded, and halfway tucked into his ratty combat boots with white socks visible between the rim and holes.

Laughing softly, I roll my eyes at his wardrobe—he can't be much warmer. "You're the one who wanted to walk."

"We can go back if you're cold."

His offer is tempting, and a good *friend* would turn around for the sake of the other not getting hypothermia. But... I don't want to. I am absolutely freezing, but with so much else on my mind, I hardly notice the cold.

"I'm fine," I tell him, shivering a little beneath my coat, suddenly aware of the thousands of goosebumps building mini mountains on my legs. The slight breeze also doesn't help, though I can't complain. It could be snowing. "How are things with you and Carson?"

Jamie's jaw tightens at the mention of his name, and that alone tells me they're not good. Jamie and Carson being at odds is just so... strange. It has been the two of them against the world for a good chunk of their lives, and to think something could sever them is insane.

"They've been better," he answers regretfully. "Kris has come around, though I think he just feels bad for me. Jer is still pissed about the Stacy rumors, because now the label is cracking down on us. I was supposed to be getting my life together, and now it's all spiraling out of control, thanks to her."

I raise my eyebrows, pinning him with a stare.

"All right, it's a little my fault, too," he admits, dipping his chin and smiling sheepishly at me from the corner of his mouth. "Carson, though... he can't look at me without disgust in his eyes. I mean, I don't blame him. Stacy cheated on him with me, and if that wasn't bad enough, they dated for another year and a half after that, and I never told him. And if she got me, his closest friend, to keep quiet..."

"Who knows how many other guys she was fooling around with," I finish, nodding.

He grunts, frustrated at his self-made predicament. "I knew telling him would only hurt him—and our friendship—so that's why I didn't. But looking back now, I think he would have preferred knowing the truth instead of staying with her all that time. The band still hadn't *made it* yet, and I was afraid of sabotaging everything we spent our lives working for. Instead, I knowingly let him date a girl who gave more attention to her side pieces than she did her own boyfriend. He deserved more than that."

Not to mention, if he had told Carson back then, it'd probably be water under the bridge by now. Or maybe Jamie's right, and telling him could have jeopardized their success. I suppose none of that matters now, but it sure makes you wonder how different things would be if he had come clean. That one event could have meant the difference between Rylee finding Carson, or me and Jamie. Dylan and his friendship with Kris. The possibility of that one minuscule thing, four words, *'I slept with Stacy,'* could have meant the difference between where we are now, and my siblings never meeting them to begin with.

Though, a stupid, naïve, and cliché part of me likes to think that no matter what, Rylee and Carson would have found each other regardless, but the realist in me knows that's not how the world works. There's no such thing as soulmates or fate or destiny. Things just *are.*

"Have you tried talking to him again?"

Jamie stops, shifting the gray beanie he's been wearing since I'm still holding his green one captive, revealing a deep purple bruise above his eye. The discoloration is still visible on his cheekbone, but it's healing much better than the part he has hidden. "No. The last time he punched me."

I've been wanting to ask *how* exactly that happened, but bringing it up would inadvertently address the night I tore apart his room and threw his condoms in the trash.

Not my finest moment, but hey, it looks like he got past it, so...

"He's got quite the right hook." I assess the blotches of red mingled in with the wonky black and purple marks. We slow as we reach the end of my neighborhood, pausing long enough for me to lift my fingers, brushing them over the swollen skin. Jamie winces slightly but doesn't pull away.

His own fingers find my neck, pressing into a small indent I have in the skin just above my collarbone. "Since we're comparing battle scars, where'd you get that?"

My lips stretch thin, thinking back on the memory. I suppose not all scars are reminders of horrific events, though I could still kill my brother for putting me in the hospital. "When Dylan was seven, he used to ride his skateboard more than he used his own two feet. And it was awful, not only because he'd fly around us in circles like a gnat, but he'd also try to bend down and snatch our stuff and zoom off with it. Well, one time, while I was jump roping, he thought he'd try to steal my new MP3 player, but he got too close, and the jump rope caught on his arm. He didn't realize at first, and kept skating, but it knocked me backward into a chair, and I tripped, falling, and scraping my neck off the corner of this wooden table my dad built. He'd just made it as a storage desk for his tools in the garage, but he hadn't finished sanding it down yet. It cut me open, and they had to remove a bunch of splinters and gave me four stitches."

"That is awful luck." He chuckles, bumping into my shoulder as we continue our walk back to my house.

"It is, though," I exclaim, laughing at how ridiculous it sounds. What are the chances? Really? "I've sworn since the day that kid was born, he was only put on this Earth to torture me."

When he only laughs, I can't help the words I say next. I'm not sure if it's the dark night or my nerves, or the inexplicable feeling that I can tell Jamie anything without judgment, but I just want to talk. "He and I are so different. I don't know. Sometimes I wish I was more like Rylee, because maybe then he'd care about me like he does her."

Jamie looks at me, then, and in his eyes, I can tell that admission makes him see me differently. Suddenly, I regret splaying my feelings on the sidewalk for us to stomp over. "I'm sorry. I-I don't know why I said that. It was stupid," I retract my words, as if now he can forget I said them.

Instead, he asks, "Why do you always compare yourself to her?"

I suck on my bottom lip, even though doing so is going to give me chapped lips tomorrow from the cold air. "I don't, I just—"

"But you do," he interrupts, pointing out the truth I'm unwilling to admit. "You always compare yourself to her, and her relationship with Carson. It's okay that you're not your sister."

"Everyone expects me to be," I admit, digging further into a hole that's only going to collapse on me before I can climb out. "She's everything that I'm not, and I was mean to her because of it. For years, I tormented her, tried to turn people against her for my own gain, all because I wasn't her. It's like I wanted people to see her true colors, except she wasn't pretending to be anyone else, so there was nothing left to reveal. She's charming, and funny, and genuinely nice to people even when she can't stand them. I'm the oldest, and yet I've never been able to measure up to her standards. Even Dylan has it better than me."

"Tori, if people don't accept you for who you are, then that's their loss because they're missing out on a fantastic person. No, you're not Rylee, and yeah, she's borderline perfect, but... not everyone wants perfect. Some people prefer messy." His teeth gnaw on the corner of his lip as his eyes trace the border separating where we stand from my driveway, as if crossing it breaks some kind of invisible barrier we built during our walk. Out here, we're safe. We're away from the car where we first kissed, and the door just beyond the place where I pushed him away, only a few feet from where we had our first sleepover, and first-ever *real* conversation on my living room couch —at least, our first-ever conversation that was more than sly insults and curt exchanges. Like I said, it's safer out here.

I smirk deviously, torquing my chin so the hair falls away from my face. "Is that your offhanded way of telling me I'm a mess?"

He scoffs. "I don't have the right to award that title to anyone. No one's a bigger mess than me."

I think back to when I was close enough to touch his bruise, and then scroll through the last half hour in my mind. Not once did I get a whiff of his usual cigarette and whiskey musk. "But you haven't drank anything today, have you?"

He grimaces, going a little pale. "Not since the other day. But the night is still young."

"Don't even joke about that," I warn, toeing my shoe into the gravel. He shifts awkwardly as well, and we both stare at the line in the concrete.

"So, friends, then?" Standing between my porch and his car, Jamie quirks an eyebrow, the right side of his mouth rising with it. The glow of the streetlamp illumines half of his face, reflecting off his brown eyes that, in this lighting, almost look a deep golden color.

I nod. "Friends," I recite numbly, which seems to be all I'm capable of saying on the topic. I don't have the guts to say more, to yell that *no, I indeed do not want to be just friends.*

I could kick myself for having those thoughts earlier in the night. They must have been like a virus, jumping from my mind to his, and filling it with stupid, ridiculous, and unfathomable ideas.

Jamie turns to walk away, pocketing his hands once again, and I revel in the sight of him, shoulders back, cocky grin, challenging eyes. He's doing this for my benefit, but it's almost like he wants me to give in. I can't blame him. I want me to give in.

"But..." I start, cheeks heating with a blush. I take a step toward him, following my thumb as it trails the collar of his sleek leather jacket. "Before we're *just friends.*"

Rising on my tiptoes, I pull his face toward mine, molding our lips together, and breathing in his warm scent, almost like pumpkin or cinnamon, matching the sweetness I taste on his lips.

"Just so you know." I bite my lip, hoping I didn't just make a huge mistake.

He watches me, bewildered, and I know I'm probably sending him Bat-Signals from across the country right now, but I don't care. I needed him to know I didn't *want* to pull away from him, it just happened.

I need him to know that whatever *was* happening between us wasn't a mistake or one-sided. Not for me, at least. Maybe I'm wrong, but I can't shake the feeling that the friends proposal was just his way of easing the tension after how I reacted to him earlier tonight.

"Goodnight, Jamie," I whisper, glancing at the ground before I turn away, jogging up the front steps and into the sweet-smelling warmth of my home. But no matter how many cinnamon spice candles sit out, or loaves of pumpkin bread my mom makes, it could never compare to the way the scent radiates from his skin. I don't think I'll ever quite enjoy a cinnamon latte again, not when he tastes so much sweeter.

30

TORI

"Don't hate me," are the first words I hear at eight in the morning when my ringing phone wakes me from a restless sleep.

After I kissed Jamie, I had a really hard time calming my mind long enough to fall asleep. I couldn't stop wondering whether I'd made a mistake. He extended an olive branch—no, a *friend* branch, and I took it and then I spit it back at him like an olive pit.

Is it impossible for me to leave well enough alone?

"Why would I hate you?" I grumble, smashing my morning face back into the pillow, hidden away from the world. The only time in my life I've woken up on time was in December, when I was tirelessly trying to map out where the band might go and beat them there. Needless to say, I haven't worried about an alarm clock since then. Because of my boy band obsession, I seriously neglected the winter/summer job I usually come home to during breaks from college and was fired. I haven't felt like looking for a new one, so I'm planning to get one on campus when I go back in the fall. For now, though, at least the money I'm making working for Jamie is more than enough to meet my most basic needs.

The silence on the other end of the line makes me uneasy, and I sit up, running a hand through my mangled strands of hair, puffing out a long, exhausted breath.

Jamie moans, seeming to dread breaking this news to me as much as I dread hearing it. "My parents are flying into town."

"And?" I question when he doesn't say anything else. "What does that have to do with me?"

"Well..." he draws out the word, voice raising a few octaves.

"Jamie."

"They don't know we're not really dating," he admits, causing my stomach to drop like a ton of bricks. "And they want to meet you."

If I thought my stomach dropped before... "What? Why the hell haven't you told them?"

His voice drops low, shame lingering in the spaces between his words. "It wouldn't kill them to think I'm getting my life together."

How is it that he manages to make me feel guilty every time I want to throttle him? It must be some kind of psychic power.

"Jamie, I'm not going to lie to your parents!" I exclaim, dropping my voice to a whisper. "You need to tell them the truth."

"I know, I know. Just not today? They flew in from

California to see me, and they won't take well to finding out my first serious relationship is a sham to fool the media. They're already concerned enough about my drinking without having to worry about me living a lie. They're honest people, Tori. They've never belonged in L.A."

"And you're sure you're their son?"

"Funny. You're hilarious," he deadpans, not sounding at all amused.

"Really?" I ask, shocked. "Not even a smirk?"

"Will you help me or not? Because otherwise, it's going to be a long drive back from the airport after I tell them this is all a ruse." Jamie sounds desperate, and I can't exactly blame him for not wanting to disappoint his parents. It's like an instinct. No matter how high you are, how successful, your parents always have the power to bring you back to Earth. They remind you of reality, and who you really are. As much as I don't feel comfortable doing this, I know if I had different parents, or a different homelife, I'd ask him to do the same thing.

I groan, flopping back on my pillow. "Ugh, okay, fine. But do not oversell it, do you hear me? No overdoing it or being extra... I don't know, cute, or whatever. No needless touching or affection. We need to convince them we're together, not that we're planning a wedding."

"All right, I understand. We'll keep it plain, simple, and boring."

Gnawing on my inner lip, I pray he's capable of doing that, because the desperation I heard in his voice moments ago tells me he's willing to do anything to sell our relationship, and another day up close and personal with Jamie LeMont will not be good for my heart.

"See you soon, friend," he mocks. "Oh, and try to remember not to kiss me."

The way his voice arcs on the word *friend* makes me want to crawl out of my skin. I should have known better than to think I have the right to ask him to keep his distance when I planted one on him in the driveway last night. It's official, kissing him was a monumental mistake, and I hate the way I love the way it makes my heart flutter.

I roll my eyes, hovering my thumb over the screen. "Screw off."

I spend the next hour and a half tearing my closet to shreds, and applying, washing off, then reapplying my makeup at least three times, if not more. At first, I do a bold look with bright eyeshadow and peach lipstick, but then I thought about how Jamie said his parents are honest. Then I looked in the mirror again and decided I resembled a hooker, so I tried a no-makeup makeup look, which turned out to be a complete and utter disaster. And by disaster, I mean, I looked like a washed-out raccoon with no eyeballs.

I finally settle on a medium look. Light foundation, nude eyes with a thin trace of eyeliner around their shape. It's enough to make me look like a functioning person, but not too much to make me look like a nightclub stripper— or at least, those are Dylan's words.

"I did not look like a nightclub stripper." I cringe, tracing my lips with a light liner before applying a clear layer of lip gloss.

Dylan's made himself at home on my beanbag chair— the one he hates sitting on—eating metaphorical popcorn while he watches me trip around my room in search of my favorite earrings. "I mean, throw on a pair of leather shorts and a slinky top... you were there."

"Don't you have anything better to do?" My stomach growls loudly, yearning for something to satisfy my increasing hunger. Normally, I eat as soon as I wake up, but Jamie's news threw me for a loop.

He smiles darkly. "Nope. This chair is horribly uncomfortable, by the way."

"Leave." I kick the seat, pushing the top in an attempt to dump him out of it.

He grunts in annoyance, standing and kicking it toward me. "Happy?"

"Very," I reply sinisterly as he closes my door.

Peace at last.

While I wait for the minutes to tick by, I pull out my phone and scroll through the dozens of missed texts and calls I have from Megan and Quinn. My gut clenches when I realize I haven't spoken to them since my birthday. Since I started fating Jamie. I hadn't heard from them after the news broke about our "relationship," but once he was seen with Stacy, they suddenly became interested. As much as I'd love to say I've been too busy to respond, I've mostly been avoiding the incessant questions I know are coming my way. I don't want to lie, and it's not as if I signed a contract stating I am forbidden from disclosing the truth to friends and family, but I know I can't tell them it's all a sham.

I'm not sure why, but the idea of admitting the truth is mortifying. They won't understand. They'll think I'm being used—I mean, I am, but no more than Jamie is in this circumstance—or that I'm pathetic—no comment—or that I'm so desperate to date a member of my favorite band, I settled for a platonic relationship. They'll think I'm a joke. Maybe I am, but at least I know what I feel isn't a decade-old infatuation. I wasn't attracted to Jamie until the moment I kissed him—or at least, that's when I finally admitted it to myself. He constantly irritated me with his cigarettes and bad attitude, I never knew there could be more than that beneath the surface of my indignation. If I had ulterior motives, I wouldn't have tried to avoid him. I wouldn't be actively pushing him away to preserve my heart.

Releasing a long breath, I click on the video call button at the top of our group chat, praying for a painless conversation.

"Wow," Megan sasses when her face appears on the screen. "Little Miss Too-Good-For-Us has finally called."

"Ha, Ha." I fake laugh, trying to hide my annoyance. "I've been busy."

"Oh, we've seen," Quinn pipes up, raising her eyebrows challengingly. "We've seen it all."

"Yeah, from the news and *Teen Queen*. Because *someone* couldn't be bothered to tell us," Megan adds, shaking her head. It's hard to tell if she's genuinely mad at me, or just messing around. She's not usually the type to get all up in arms over something like this. She's generally a pretty carefree person, and doesn't give a crap about anything but booze and boys.

I struggle with a response, wishing I'd have rehearsed my excuses before I rushed into this last-minute phone call. "It's not like it was a secret."

"Seems like it was from us." Megan averts her eyes. So, genuinely mad it is.

"Okay, but for real, how the hell did you pull this one off?" Quinn asks, shaking her head in disbelief. She doesn't seem personally offended like Megan does. "Did you have to hypnotize him?"

Megan rolls her eyes before I get the chance to answer. "Come on, Tori's gotten every guy she's ever wanted. Who were we to assume celebrities would be any different? Although, keeping him seems to be a bit tricky..."

Quinn bites her lip, looking as if she's not buying it. "But Jamie LeMont? I mean, with his sister dead, I guess now is as good a time as any to slide in while he's feeling charitable."

My jaw drops, my annoyance replaced with the sudden urge to defend myself. It almost feels like I'm eavesdropping on a private conversation not meant for my ears. "You seriously think I'd take advantage of him like that?"

I don't miss their hesitation, neither girl saying a word until Megan finally speaks up. "I guess it wouldn't be the worst thing you've ever done. And it *is* kind of genius."

"No, it's disgusting." My lips fold in on themselves, and

I try to keep the anger burning in my chest from heating my face. "The fact that you would even insinuate that is repulsive."

Quinn scratches around her nose piercing, twisting the gem a little. "Really, though, did your sister set you two up? How did it happen?"

Staring at my palms, I trace the lines with my eyes, trying to come up with something to make them jealous. It's not like I have a backstory prepared, and at this point, it's starting to feel like I have to explain myself for having a boyfriend. Maybe I was right to keep the truth from them.

Is this how I made people feel in high school? Like they weren't good enough, like they were silently judged for being who they are?

Clearing my throat, I bring my eyes back to their expecting faces, licking my lips, and twisting a piece of hair around my fingers to give them something to do. "It wasn't Rylee," I say, which is technically true. This whole nightmare started with Dylan's idea. "I've gotten to spend a lot of time around the band in the last few months, and Jamie and I really hit it off."

"I thought you felt left out?" Megan states the obvious.

"Not by him." This is technically true, as well. When no one else noticed I was there, Jamie always made an effort to acknowledge me, even if it was only to be an ass or get under my skin. This whole time, he's been the only one I felt like myself around. Still, I have told the girls several times since December that I don't feel like I'm part of the group. I'm there, but on the outskirts, watching their well-oiled machine run flawlessly without me inserting myself and jamming it.

"Even when he's with his side piece?" she asks, obviously referring to the rumors about Jamie's time with Stacy Gonzales. I suppose I should be grateful she considers Stacy the side piece and not me.

"Hey, now you can give your sister a run for her money," Quinn says, obviously sensing the growing tension. Megan used to know better than to push my buttons, but apparently, I've gone soft, and she's starting to notice. She used to stick up for me, not question me. I hate the small part of me itching to put her in her place, to show her I'm still in charge so she'll shut those ruby lips of hers and worship the ground I walk on. Except, I'm not sure how I ever had the energy for that sort of thing. The idea of it isn't as enticing as it used to be, anyway.

I suck on my cheek, dropping the piece of hair that's now standing out from the rest of my well-placed curls. Little does Quinn know, I've let go of my jealousy—mostly. I think there's a small piece of me that will always be a little covetous of Rylee, but I can learn to accept that. I have to if I want to be a part of her life. "I don't care about that anymore. Rylee's been there for me a lot recently."

Meg rolls her eyes at the same time as Quinn, a gesture that's significantly annoying me this morning. "Yes, because you have so many problems. You have, like, the easiest life of anyone I've ever met."

Just then, the doorbell rings, and I silently thank the powers that be for ending this conversation, because it's going to be the last one I have with them for a while. A very long while.

"I've gotta go, Jamie's here." I stand, biting my lip to hold back a satisfied smirk. "He wants me to meet his parents."

I end the call as their jaws are unhinging.

I take a deep breath. Plain, simple, and boring. What could go wrong?

31

TORI

"Hey, babe." Jamie leans in quickly, putting a hand on my waist, and bending to kiss the skin below my cheekbone. "I really am sorry for this," he mumbles quietly, for only me to hear.

I force a smile, stepping back to meet the eyes that tell me he's not sorry at all. He loves unraveling my patience.

I turn my attention to the couple behind him, both looking exhausted after such a long flight. At least they managed to fly into Philly instead of having to drive in from the Pittsburgh airport.

"Mom, Dad, this is Tori." He nods awkwardly in my direction, shifting on his feet as his parents take me in.

His mom smiles with large, white teeth. "I'm Dawn."

"Rick." His dad nods, extending a hand. "I'd love to say I've heard all about you, but that would just be from the media." He gives his son a pointed look, placing his hands in his pockets.

The resemblance between the two is uncanny. Same

dark hair, strong build, hard eyes. Jamie's mom, on the other hand, is the spitting image of Mara, except with raven black hair instead of blonde. If I remember correctly, Mara used to dye her hair a lot, so it's possible her natural color matched Dawn's.

Both of his parents are undeniably young, and incredibly good-looking. If I had any questions about where his good looks come from, I don't anymore. The proof is standing before me.

"It's really great to meet you." I return his father's handshake.

"And have you heard anything about us?" His father raises a dark brow at his son, though his words are directed at me.

Of course, he hasn't told either one of us about the other, we're not even dating!

I swallow. "Tons."

"Is that so?" He's not one bit convinced. "What's my favorite drink?"

I blink absurdly, bouncing from Jamie to his father. Jamie just shrugs a little, looking embarrassed. No, more than embarrassed. He looks like he wishes he could disown his parents and move to Switzerland.

I groan inwardly, not only hating the third-degree questioning, but also the undeniable need I have to pass his dad's test.

"Bourbon," I guess, sounding surer than I feel. It's all I've seen Jamie drink, so I'm hoping he got the taste for it from his father.

Rick nods once, not quite looking satisfied, but accepts

my answer, nonetheless. The relief displayed on Jamie's face matches how I feel—like I've just outsmarted a lie detector test.

"Are your parents' home, Tori?" Dawn smiles kindly at me, dimples digging deep into her freckled cheeks.

I shake my head. "They're at work today, but they really wanted to be here."

"Well, I'm sure this won't be the last chance we get to meet them." Her smile deepens, making her look even younger than she already does. If I were to guess, she's probably in her early to mid-forties, which means she must have had Mara straight after high school, and Jamie not long after.

If my mother was here, no way in hell would she be okay with this little charade we're putting on. She'd have told them the truth the second they walked through the door. And my dad... well, he's not exactly thrilled with our arrangement to begin with. In fact, he's hardly spoken to me since he found out. He thinks I'm ridiculous for putting myself through this for nothing. It doesn't feel like that to me.

"Did you guys eat?" I ask, hoping they want food, because I'm famished. "I haven't had breakfast yet."

"Oh, we should go to that little place you pointed out to us in town, Jamie." Dawn nods toward her son, already reopening the front door.

"Abyss Coffee?" I ask, knowing there's no other place memorable enough to mention.

Jamie's mom holds the door for us as we file out, and

Jamie's hand finds mine when we pass through, giving it a gentle squeeze.

"How did you know?" she wonders, bending to fix the gray socks peeking out of her combat boots.

"Um, because your son wouldn't know that place existed if it weren't for me." I shove my shoulder into Jamie as he chuckles. I told him about Abyss months ago, but I had no idea he'd actually gone. Quinn and I used to meet Megan there before school almost every morning. The owners considered us regulars, and we always, *always*, sat at the same tiny table in the back, by the big window where we couldn't be heard gossiping.

"So, Tori," Rick speaks up once we're in Jamie's car, me in the passenger seat, per his mom's insistence. "We hear you're interested in interior design?"

"I am." I nod, glancing sideways at Jamie, who must have filled them in a little during their drive. "I just changed my major from business to that, actually. I've already taken most of the basic required credits so I can still graduate on time. I've also started taking some online courses in real estate."

"Oh, that's right," Dawn expresses, tapping the back of my seat in thought. "You've been helping Jamie with the Foundation."

Biting my lip, I nod, shooting another nervous glance at his frame. He's stiff. Uncomfortable. He hasn't said a single word since the introductions at my house.

"I just want you to know that your involvement really means a lot to us. We might not agree with the public angle Jamie's manager has chosen, but regardless, the cause is one we all strongly believe in. My baby deserved better than what happened to her."

Rick places a hand on her knee, squeezing it tightly as she stares out the window. His face matches her pained one, and for a moment, I see a million little pieces of Jamie in their expressions. Dark, lost, haunted. I wonder if they were happy before this, and if they'll ever be totally happy again. Rylee told me once that Jamie's parents knew very little about what Mara was going through. I think they knew about her multiple rehab trips, but they had no idea how in debt she was to the man who killed her.

Jamie whips the car into a parking space, jumping out the second he pulls the keys out of the ignition.

His parents glance at me, confused at his rude and anxious behavior. "We'll grab a table and meet you inside." I hop out after him and retrace his steps to the side of the building.

I find him leaning against the building, fumbling with his lighter and a cigarette. I sigh, yanking it from his hand and stomping it into the loose gravel.

"This is why I didn't want them here." His jaw clenches.

I touch his face with my hand, lingering my fingers on his five o'clock shadow. "Hey, hey, look at me. Look at me."

He does so eventually, dropping his head so his temple rests against the red brick, watching me. "They make me remember."

"And you want to forget." I nod in understanding. His parents remind him of growing up, of Mara, and all he wants is to forget what that felt like. "Come here."

I draw him in, and he lets his forehead fall to my shoulder, resting his arms on my hips. His head rotates back and forth, hair getting caught on my chapped lips. "I'm such a mess."

My arms tighten around his shoulders, holding him close. "At least you're not the only one."

He laughs at this, straightening and smoothing out the pieces of my curls he messed up. "Yeah, you are pretty screwed up."

I punch him in the arm, cracking a smile. "You didn't have to agree with me, jerk."

"How'd we end up like this?" he wonders aloud, running a hand through his hair.

"The world's a dark place." I shrug, as if that explains it.

Jamie nudges my chin with his thumb, and I tuck it to my chest with a goofy smirk. "At least there's still a little good left in it."

I memorize his face, the way he looks at me, his heavy breathing. I take in the way his eyes stare right through me, into me, and how his lips fold over on themselves quickly, before he looks away, realizing that I, too, am staring. "Yeah. There is."

His eyes trail beyond me before he can respond, and he pockets his lighter quickly, clearing his throat. "Mom."

"Is everything all right?" Her eyes dance between us worriedly, and I wonder how long she's been standing there. How much of our conversation did she hear? "You guys have been gone for a while, and your father wants to order."

Jamie's eyes trail back to me longingly, lingering on my lips before his attention returns to his mother. "We're good. Let's go eat before he raids the kitchen looking for sausage links."

She throws her head back, laughter bouncing off the building. "My boy." She squeezes his arm through a layered hoodie. "I missed you."

"Missed you, too, Mom." He shoots his gaze to where I follow behind them, motioning for me to catch up. When I do, he slings an arm across my shoulders, keeping me at his side as the three of us walk into the café together.

We find his dad staring hungrily over his menu at the table diagonal to ours, eyeing a plate of large strawberry pancakes with sides of sausage, bacon, and hash browns.

"It's about time," he grumbles, slamming it closed and placing it to his left. "You guys better know what you want."

Jamie and I exchange an amused look.

"I'm ready whenever you are," I say, pushing my menu aside as well.

Jamie agrees with me as his mom says, pointing to the same table his father was just sizing up, "I want whatever they're having."

32

TORI

The four of us burst through the door, a dozen bags in each hand—all mine and Dawn's, of course. Turns out, she's a worse shopaholic than me, if that's possible. I've never met a single person who could match pace with me in the mall. She did. In fact, she gave *me* a run for my money.

"I *love* that hat," she gushes, tilting the burnt orange beanie I bought to accent the brown shirt I'm wearing.

"Does that mean you can finally give me back my green one?" Jamie asks, gazing at me beneath his long lashes.

I rise on my tiptoes, pushing the hood off his head, revealing messy strands of hair. "Nope!"

He gives me a playful shove as we travel in a pack toward the living room, and I stumble over my feet, almost ramming into the wall.

"You're back." Rylee bounces down the stairs, greeting Mr. and Mrs. LeMont, whom I assume she's met before.

"How's your new job?" Dawn inquires, raising her eyebrows, irises wide.

Rylee bites her lip, popping the lid open on the leftover smoothie she made for breakfast. "You know, I think Elizabeth likes me. She's not in town right now, so everything she has me doing is online, but either way, it's my senior year, and I only have three classes thanks to her, so…"

At this, Dawn laughs, and I can't help the resentment simmering in my chest at the way the two of them talk so easily. But I stomp it down. There's no need to be jealous of Rylee. It's a waste of energy.

"Are you guys staying for dinner?" Rylee asks, leading us the rest of the way to the living room.

"We'd love to," Rick starts, giving her a kiss on the cheek in greeting. "But I'm exhausted. These two ran us into the ground this afternoon."

"Shopping's good for the soul." I smirk, shrugging my shoulders.

"Amen," Dawn agrees brightly.

Rylee falls into conversation with Jamie's dad like they're long-lost friends. I watch them talk, wishing I could be as confident and conversational as Rylee always seems to be. If it's not anger or sarcasm, sometimes I'm not sure how else to talk to people.

I startle when I feel a small hand on my wrist.

"Can we go for a walk?" Dawn tilts her head toward the back door that leads to our lawn.

My stomach does somersaults. "Sure."

Once outside, Dawn walks along the grass in her bare

feet, and I stand like a statue on the concrete deck, watching her as she turns slowly, staring fondly at our surroundings.

"This is such a nice little town," she remarks, eyes glowing. "I'd have loved to bring the kids up somewhere like this, but I'm afraid Rick's job didn't allow it."

"Jamie told me you guys used to travel a lot. He said he loved living in Eighty-Four."

"We all did. It was a sad day when we had to leave."

"I bet."

She watches me for a long moment, eyeing me up and down as if trying to decipher a math problem in her head, until finally, she opens her mouth. "Can you be honest with me, Tori?"

I gulp, hating that I've been anything but. "Of course."

"Woman to woman... is he okay?"

I blink rapidly, not at all expecting to have this conversation the day I meet his mother. I consider her carefully before deciding, with all the lies and deception, I can give her this. I can be honest with a mother who loves her son unconditionally. "No."

She sighs, nodding shortly as though that's what she expected me to say. "Should I stick around? Or, I don't know, visit more often?"

"He loves you, but I don't think that's what he needs right now. I'm sure he'd love to see you more, though." I cross my arms over my stomach, dipping my fingers inside the oversized sleeves of my shirt.

"Gosh, I wish it were easier with him. Mara was never necessarily open with us, but she was my daughter, things were... simpler. She could talk to me about stuff Jamie won't talk to anyone about. In fact, he *doesn't* talk to anyone. He keeps it all buried inside until it eats him up, and I don't know how to make it better. I just wish I knew how to help him."

"Me too." I sigh, leaning against a pillar with a sconce atop it. It won't be long until the dark completely settles, and they turn on.

"But you do." She shakes her head. "He's at ease around you. I've never seen him look at anyone like that but Mara."

"Like what?" I swallow, anxieties suddenly creeping up my throat, making my tongue feel heavy in my mouth.

"With appreciation. With love. I may not see my son often, but he's still just that, and I know him, even when he tries to hide himself from me."

I can't take it any longer. The lies. Dawn is so nice, and I can't stand that she's thinking these things about the girl her son is only dating for show. "You know we're not—" My words fall short. After all of that, all of her admissions, I can't bring myself to say it. She's opening up to me, and I can't bring myself to tell her the truth.

She holds up a hand, her features hardening. "I figured this was one of Elizabeth's concoctions. I can't stand that woman."

"You and me both." The guilt clamping my chest lessens a bit, and a weight lifts from my tiny shoulders. "I'm sorry we didn't tell you sooner."

"I just wish he didn't feel like he needed to lie to me

about it." She presses a finger to her lip, lost in thought. "Still, he trusts you. And my son doesn't trust anyone."

"I don't think you understand," I say cautiously. "Jamie and I aren't really dating. I'm just helping him clean up his image. And to be his friend when he needs me."

Friend. Ugh, I'm really starting to despise that word.

"Precisely." She points a finger. "That's not part of the job description, now, is it?"

"No, I guess not. But it's not like that. We don't feel that way about—"

"Let me stop you right there," she interrupts, holding a hand between us as if to get her point across. "Everyone in the history of the world who has fake dated has developed real feelings at some point."

"Is that so?"

"Yes!" she exasperates. Her expression changes, a fond look relaxing her features. "I fake dated someone once."

"Wait, really?"

"Yep. My best friend. We only did it to make my ex-boyfriend jealous. He'd always been suspicious of us, so we decided to get a little payback after he dumped me for this other girl, and then wouldn't stop begging me to come back. But I knew there was always more than a fake relationship between us."

"What happened?"

"I got pregnant." My jaw drops to the grass. "But Rick had already proposed before that happened. Mara was just a happy accident. She also pushed up the wedding and made it a hell of a lot cheaper than the big fancy one we were planning to have in a year. Except for the dress—I had to pay extra for one that hid my baby bump."

I watch her, speechless. Dawn married the man she fake dated to make another man jealous.

"My point is that you mean a lot to my son, and I don't know you very well—though I'd like to—but I think he means quite a bit to you, too."

Jamie appears at the sliding glass door, peeking his head out. "Dad's ready to go."

Dawn nods, squeezing me in a hug. "He needs you," she whispers before meeting her son on the deck, hugging him next.

"Don't you want me to take you home?" he asks, mirroring my thoughts.

She pats his cheek affectionately, placing a kiss on his forehead. "I already called for an Uber. I'll see you in the morning, baby."

"'Night, Mom."

"Goodnight."

Once she's inside, Jamie lets out a hefty puff of air, collapsing into a lawn chair, and rubbing his temples like he's trying to massage away a headache.

"Your parents seem nice." I sit across from him, propping my feet on the table and staring at the polka-dotted socks.

"They're good people," he agrees. "It's just, being with them used to be an event. At a certain point in my career, I was traveling all the time and doing so much that it wasn't worth them coming along with us. Mara stuck with me for a while, but even she couldn't take the jet lag any longer. So, whenever they came to visit, and we were all together, it was like that feeling on Christmas morning, when you're excited to unwrap the presents, even though you already know what's inside because you snooped the night before. Without her here, it doesn't feel right."

While he talks, I can't help thinking back to what his mom told me, about him trusting me. This, right now, him telling me any of this, means that he trusts me enough to be honest. I think deep down he just needs someone to listen. Not to try and understand or to compare tragedies or tell him it'll be okay. He needs me to listen.

"God, I'm sorry. I just keep laying all this heavy stuff on you. You didn't sign up for this." Jamie squeezes his eyes shut, dropping his forehead into his palm.

I nudge his knee with my foot. Once. Twice. "You don't have to apologize for being sad." I nudge him again, and this time, he grabs my ankle, pulling it into his lap.

"I know." He shifts his body so he can reach for my shin, pulling my other foot onto his thighs, and holding them hostage by the ankle. "Just... distract me. Talk about something else, please."

I pretend to think really hard, scrunching my face in thought. "Okay, hmm... uh, you mentioned yesterday that the label is cracking down on you. How so?"

"Really? That's what you choose?"

"You put me on the spot," I defend, rolling my hands into the sleeves of my brown sweater, looking to the ground sheepishly.

Jamie drags his fingers along his scalp, rustling the

strands of his hair a little. "The label wants me to cut my hair."

"You can't." My jaw drops. "I-I just mean that it's your signature look. You're known for your long hair."

I blink dumbly, trying to comprehend how him cutting his hair is going to make him seem more put together. If anything, it'll look even more like he's going through a crisis if he chops off the one thing he's recognized for... other than his music, of course.

His eyes squint, and he stifles a laugh, looking up at the stars as if they hold all the answers. "What you're saying is, I'd be devastating a lot of people if I got it cut off?"

"Absolutely. Lots and lots of poor souls would rue the day you chopped away a piece of your identity," I reason. "Cutting your hair would be like selling your soul to the devil. It's career suicide."

"You're really selling this," he jokes. "Also, I love that you think my career is contingent on the styling of my hair."

"Good." I blink. "For your fans. 'Cause, you know, I'm always looking out for them." I swallow my tongue, sucking in my cheeks to keep them from flapping any longer.

I might as well have just said, *'Don't cut off your hair before I get the chance to run my fingers through it again!'* Because it's what we're both thinking.

"Not that I care. 'Cause I don't." I scoff, then shrink back into my chair.

Shut up, shut up, shut up!

The back porch sconces flick on, and reflect off of his eyes, lighting them in a glow as he tries to catch up with the words spouting from my lips.

"I'm just going to point out that you picked this topic." He bites his lip, holding back a smirk.

Desperate to change the subject, I come up with the safest topic I can think of. Work. "Did you get the design layout I sent you?"

"Yeah, it should stack up well with our plans so far. I really like the furniture you picked, too. It fits the style."

"And it's pretty cheap. I was thinking we could paint the entry walls white and hang some art going up the stairs. I've been researching galleries and found a few that donate to local charities for addiction recovery. I figured if we're going to spend all this money, we might as well buy from the right places."

"I didn't realize people did that," he muses, looking pleased with my results.

When Jamie sent me pictures of the house's work-in-progress interior, I was shocked. Though, I suppose when you have thirty-some people working on a house, it gets done quicker than usual—not to mention his name and influence, which I'm sure has the construction workers trying even harder to make it perfect. Especially since the charity is planning to build many more. Still, after seeing the foundation that day we visited, I thought for sure it would be four more months until I got a true idea of what I'm working with, despite the timeline Jackson gave me.

"There's still some good people left in the world," I

muse, eyes tracing the lines on my palms as I remember our conversation before breakfast.

"I should head home," he releases my feet, and I pull them back, feeling a rush of cold air where his hands rested. "Carson mentioned having a writing session tonight, and the lack of his presence here means he meant it. I shouldn't piss him off any more than I already have."

"He'll get over it," I assure him, standing when he does.

Jamie squeezes the back of his neck, exhaling a long, exaggerated breath—or maybe not exaggerated. Tired. Sad. Worried. "We'll see."

"He will," I say firmly. I don't know that for sure but agreeing and installing more doubt in his mind won't help anyone. "Now, go write some number-one hits for me, okay?" I pause. "Also, as your number one, and most certifiably insane fan, I expect to get a first listen of the album before it's released."

"And every pre-released single," he promises, crossing his heart. He drops his eyes, glancing up at me through his lashes. "In a few weeks we have to go to a movie premiere, show our faces, walk the red carpet, the usual... I don't really want to, but the label thinks it'll be good to get us all together for an event—for publicity. You should come."

I nod unsurely, searching his expression. "Yeah, it'd probably be good for the fans to see us together, and not just *sneaking* around." I emphasize *sneaking,* because as much as we've made it look like we are, almost every outing we've had has been to drum up attention on Jamie's thriving love life.

"Of course," he nods. "That's exactly what I was thinking."

Jamie pockets his hands, twisting his shoulders a little before he turns, glancing back at me. "You should know, I didn't want to make things right with you just so you'd continue our arrangement."

"Then, why did you?" I can't help myself.

He gnaws on his cheek. "Is it so hard to believe maybe I just want you in my life?"

I giggle. "Kinda."

"Goodnight, Tori," he rolls his eyes, sliding open the glass door.

"'Night." I lean back on the chair with a *thump,* tucking my feet beneath me. Never in my life have I felt so in over my head.

33

TORI

The next few weeks fly by in blinding colors. And I mean *blinding*. Between neon paint samples that border as an eye sore, accent colors, aesthetic photography, and decorations, I don't think I've ever seen so many colors in my life. That's not to mention the blur of emotions that burn in my chest whenever Jamie's around. That is a whole different array of colors, and I can't seem to decide which ones are brighter.

The house isn't *quite* where we wanted it to be for the grand opening, but nonetheless, it's this afternoon. People are traveling from all over for the unveiling, which translates to Media Circus. If Elizabeth wants relationship exposure, this is her time to shine. Maybe that's why she decided to make the trip this weekend. Or it's possible she feels lonely after several weeks without belittling others.

Oh, and my once-in-a-lifetime opportunity to walk down a red carpet with 13 Days of December is one day away. *One*. I've never been so excited to get dressed up for an event in my life. Even *prom.* Ask anyone, and they will tell you the same thing—prom was the highlight of my life, the moment I waited for since I was ten years old and watching the prom scene in *High School Musical 3.* Prom, for lack of better words, was my *everything.*

This beats that night and its nine-year buildup of excitement by miles. If only I could go back and tell ten-year-old me what she should really be saving her hopes for, because a sweaty dance floor with fake friends and an absentee date isn't exactly what I'd had in mind. I'll never forgive that boy for texting me two hours beforehand that he was *sick* and *couldn't make it,* only to see pictures of him at a golf club with Caroline Phillips—a girl from a neighboring high school—hours later. If it weren't the end of our senior year, I'd have made his life a living nightmare. I heard he married her, though, so good for him, I guess.

No, I still hope he's miserable. I suppose I'll never completely be rid of my selfish ways. All in all, self-preservation isn't the worst defense mechanism. It keeps me sane, at least.

Speaking of sanity, riding in Rylee's stifling car isn't doing much to keep mine intact. Carson and Jamie have yet to speak to one another, and I'm not just talking about during the drive. For some reason, Jamie has it in his head that he's apologized enough times, and that it's on Carson to forgive him... except what he did isn't something that's fixable with words. It takes time. God knows if Rylee ever showed a *sliver* of interest in a guy I was into, I'd never let her live it down, so I see where

Carson's coming from. Honestly, I think their situation has been harder on Rylee than it has either of them, mostly because she's stuck in the middle. She's on Carson's side—obviously—but she's Jamie's friend, too. She can't exactly treat him any differently. But being his friend is almost like a slap in the face to Carson, so she's just been keeping her distance until this blows over, which explains why Carson hasn't been around the house as often when Jamie's there. Whenever they're together, it's at a mutual location. At a certain point, I think things got out of hand, and instead of being hurt, it's turned into a pissing contest of who can stay mad the longest. Well, I think we all know who would win if I were involved.

Regardless of all that, silence makes for one long-ass car ride.

Carson loves driving, so Rylee let him take the wheel. Her car was the only one that could fit all of us—Carson, Jamie, Rylee, Kris, Jer, Kirsten, Dylan, and me. Some of the boys' siblings are in a car behind us. Jamie begged to go with them instead, but Elizabeth put her foot down, claiming the band needs to look united. Jamie's parents went home a week ago, but to say they're proud would be an understatement. In fact, I think they're prouder of him for this than his outstanding music career.

"So, how's the songwriting going?" Rylee attempts to break the ice, closing the book she's been reading, and turning her attention on the boys.

"Decent," Jamie says, which is followed by Carson's response of, "Awful."

"What they mean is, 'We don't have shit,'" Jer translates, shaking his head.

Kirsten quirks her lips to the side, resting a hand on his knee. "You'll figure it out."

"We always do," Kris continues her thought, shoving Jer's head from where he sits in the very back, squished between Dylan and Jamie. Rylee's in the passenger seat, next to Carson, and I'm in the middle with Jer and Kirsten. It seems the unspoken goal when piling into the car was to put as many people between Carson and Jamie as possible.

Other than the tension between the band, things with Jamie and me have been steady the past few weeks. We've both held up our ends of the 'just friends' agreement, and so far, nothing else drastic has come between us. He's also three weeks sober, which is the longest he's managed since it became a problem, and especially commendable given all the stress he's under.

I talked with Rylee the other night about the boys and their *predicament,* and she said Carson hates pushing Jamie away, but doesn't know how to let him back in either. He's afraid of being the one to push him over the edge. But he's hurt. He trusted Jamie unconditionally, and he stabbed him in the back, then lied about it to his face.

"What if you guys release a greatest hits album? Take the pressure off your deadline?" I suggest.

Rylee rolls her eyes, and for a second, I'm worried my idea is dumb. "Tried that. It was *Elizabeth-ed.*"

"Elizabeth-ed?" I laugh, raising my brows questioningly.

Kirsten smirks. "You know, when someone shoots down a good idea because it wasn't theirs and they have to be in charge?"

Kris pipes up proudly, "Rylee and I coined the term."

"How very creative." I flutter my eyes sarcastically.

"You're just mad you didn't think of it," Ry teases, twisting in her seat since her boyfriend isn't doing much to hold casual conversation.

"Dude." Jer turns in his seat as well. "Tori just *Elizabeth-ed* your term."

"Rude." Kris crosses his arms, looking out the window dramatically. Except, he's in the middle so he's basically craning his neck to see around Jamie's hair. "The lack of respect in today's generation is astounding."

"Shut up," Rylee sasses, facing the front again.

Everyone else keeps talking, but I tune them out as Rylee says something under her breath, taking advantage of the bickering in the backseat over who *Elizabeths* things the most. I think the current vote is on Kris.

Carson takes his eyes from the road, smiling softly at Rylee, and laces their fingers between them on the center console. He says something I can't hear, making this the first time he's spoken the entire ride.

I lower my voice as I lean forward, inserting myself between them. Rylee elbows me in the shoulder playfully. "We're good."

I scoff. "I know that." Sighing, I scoot a little more forward just in case there are any prying ears in the back. "I'm going to tell you what a very wise man once told me when I was too stubborn to forgive the person I love most in this world."

"What's that?" Carson smiles easily, seeming relieved that I'm not going to yell at him.

I bite my lip. "He's trying. And if you keep pushing him away, you're really going to lose him."

Rylee looks impressed as she allows her head to fall against mine. "And who told you that?"

"Our brother," I snort, and the three of us fall into a fit of laughter. "I'm serious, though. The kid gives good advice when he's not being a little snot."

"Hear, hear." Rylee holds up her water bottle, taking a swig.

Carson almost misses his turn, so he slams on the brakes, swerving and causing everyone to fall to the right side of the car.

"Sorry," he mumbles, receiving several looks of disapproval from his passengers, including me.

"Thank God." Kirsten stretches once we're parked, tripping out of the car. Jer grabs her wrist before she falls face-first into the door.

"I got you." He kisses her cheek, and she laughs, swatting him away.

"I hope you're all camera ready," Kris says, fixing his hair in the window. Instinctively, I reach for mine as well.

Dozens of photographers bound up to the car, spreading out evenly so they can snag pictures of us all, including Carmina, Justice and Jax—Jer's siblings—who just got out of the vehicle behind us. Though, it's clear most of their attention is on the band, specifically Carson.

Jamie appears behind me, finding my hand beneath the long sleeves of my oversized sweater. I didn't want a bulky coat weighing me down, so I opted for a stylish sweater I could layer instead, though my thighs are freezing through the gaping holes in my blue jeans. I'd have chosen a different pair, but they're all equally as ripped up. What can I say? I like them like that.

I'd normally be freaking out at the thought of holding Jamie's hand, but honestly, I'm just grateful for the extra warmth.

I watch as security forces the paparazzi aside, creating a walkway to the front of the house—which looks like an entirely different building than the one I visited. Carson leads the way, with Rylee at his side, and I watch as Kirsten locks onto Jer's arm, so easy, as if they're a puzzle piece that clicks together. Like missing halves.

"Remind me again why I stopped drinking?" Jamie mumbles beneath his breath. I squeeze his hand, moving so my inner arm lines up with his. For warmth, of course. No other reason.

"Because if you—" my words fall short when my eyes land on a familiar-looking, lanky girl wearing heels that accentuate her toned legs and long torso, champagne blonde hair brushing the edges of her model hips. She stands a few feet from the front porch, watching us carefully as we near the house.

I glance at Jamie, expecting him to be waiting for me to finish my thought, but he, too, is captivated by the girl whose diamond eyes sparkle like the sun, practically oozing money. Fame.

Her eyes are on Carson, but when he doesn't notice her, or maybe just refuses to look, she settles on the boy holding my hand, licking her lips tauntingly.

"Hi, Jamie," her silky voice coos as her lashes move up and down, taking him in like a drink of water on a ninety-degree day.

"Stacy." He nods in acknowledgment, swallowing hard and eyeing the paparazzi around us—no, not the paparazzi. He's looking for Carson. I only realize this when he finds him, because his posture stiffens when the two of them lock eyes, exchanging unspoken words. To say the least, neither of them look particularly happy about her presence.

Stacy Gonzales. She's not just a part of Hollywood. She *is* Hollywood. Stacy embodies everything girls dream of being when they grow up. Except, what the rest of the world doesn't seem to know is that she's a backstabbing snob, but I don't think those headlines will ever make the news. There were photos of her circulating on the Internet for weeks after she and Carson split, already hooking up with a new guy. The media painted him as broken-hearted and desperate for love, whereas she was the brave, strong girl who could handle heartbreak like a pro. That was one of the only times someone one-upped Carson with bad press. She's a literal goddess, and if I thought she was pretty in the movies—*she has a freaking action movie franchise*—then words can't describe her in real life. As much as I'd love to stand here gawking at how perfect she is, and how I could never measure up, her wandering gaze on my boyfriend—*fake boyfriend*—seems to show her in a different light. One that's not so appealing to me.

As far as the world is concerned, Jamie's with me, and the fact that her eyes are stuck to his ass like Velcro doesn't sit well with me

She may be America's Sweetheart, but from what I've heard, her personality sucks every attractive quality from her body. After all, she has been blackmailing Jamie for years. And just because she has a pretty face doesn't mean I'd hesitate to add a little black and blue to those high cheekbones.

"Thank you all so much for coming today," Jamie speaks, cutting through the loud chatter of the crowd. I hadn't noticed him let go of my hand and make his way to the stage. "As you know, this cause is one that's important to me, as I wish someone would have done something like this for my sister. The Mara LeMont Foundation is donating this beautiful home, designed and built by Jackson Building Company—" Jamie, nods toward Jackson, standing beside a small girl wearing a large smile, whom I assume to be his wife Makayla, "—that has been breathtakingly decorated and fully furnished by someone with an eye for design and passion for the cause, Victoria Green." There are a few 'awws' in the audience at the mention of my name, and at that, Jamie smirks a little, finding my gaze among hundreds of others.

I don't hear the remainder of his speech because my attention is fully on Stacy, dabbing at her eyes as Jamie mentions Mara again. I roll my eyes, resisting the urge to yell 'fake!' and then cower in the crowd where no one can see me.

Everyone claps as Jamie cuts the ribbon with unnecessarily large scissors, and makes his way back down the steps, shaking several hands along the way, smiling, and engaging in business-oriented conversation before he directs them inside for a more in-depth tour. I find Carmina at the edge of the crowd, and I'm relieved to escape the cameras for a breather.

"He's good, isn't he?" She shakes her head, watching while he laughs lightheartedly, as if he's not hollow inside.

I shake my head as well. "I don't know how he got up there and talked about her at all."

"Did you see Stacy? Eyeing them both like a snack." She nods in Carson's direction this time, sucking in her cheeks. A sour expression replaces the usually angelic one she wears. "You haven't always been around, but that girl has done some serious damage to Carson. Even now, when he's happy and moved on, she still managed to gut punch him. And Jamie doesn't need this. Why is she even here? This is almost as bad as when Mara's abusive ex-boyfriend showed up at the funeral."

"What?" My eyes grow wide. Okay, I guess I'm still in the dark about more than I thought. Mara had an abusive ex? He went to the funeral?

"Oh, shit. No one was supposed to know that, *including me.* Jamie only told the guys about how he treated her, but, well, you know Kris."

"My lips are sealed. Besides, if Kris knows, so does Dylan. I'll just blame him."

She holds her hands up in prayer. "Thank you."

Carmina makes her way to her brother, intercepting before the paparazzi can bother him for another interview. That's the thing about an event such as this, it's harder to avoid the cameras. They have to give interviews, unlike when they're walking from dinner or the grocery store.

"You've done well," Elizabeth says, scrutinizing Jamie's every move. "It appears he's gotten his life together."

"But he hasn't," I point out, against my better judgment.

She raises thinly waxed eyebrows. "Excuse me?"

"He's not better," I state. "Actually, having your shit together and looking like you do are two totally different things. He needs more than what public photographs can offer him. He needs real help, and less pressure from you."

I don't mean to sound accusatory, but it definitely comes off that way. And Elizabeth doesn't take it well.

She levels her eyes, cheekbones poking from her thin face, lips in a hard line. "I highly advise you to stay out of business you can't possibly understand."

"Oh, so the label isn't trying to make Jamie perfect despite his sister dying five months ago? They don't want him to cut his hair to look more *together?*" Swallowing dryly, I plaster on a smile as pictures are snapped in our general direction. The last thing I need is to be headline news again. I can see it now, *'Jamie's girlfriend had resting bitch face at charity donation supporting alcohol and drug abuse victims.'*

"This is a serious matter, Tori. One I don't expect you

to understand, but we only have Jamie's best interest at heart. We're doing everything we can for him."

"I'm sure you are," I respond dryly, walking away before she can further make me want to scream at her in public. She has done *nothing*. She forced Jamie to fate me and then gallivanted off to enjoy a boy-band-free vacation. She doesn't know what it means to help someone, to care about them, much less someone in such a fragile state. As much as I hate to say it, Jamie isn't going to stay clean for long with the way they're pushing him. His life on a normal day is utter hell, let alone at a time like this.

How many more smiles can he fake before they are permanently broken?

"Everything okay?" Jamie touches my shoulder, and I jump. "Sorry."

"I thought you were a reporter," I say breathlessly, tucking a short strand of hair behind my ears, glancing around at the eyes on us. Most of them have already talked to Jamie and are moving on to Carson and the other boys. And my sister.

Jamie raises his eyebrows, looking around at all the people desperately trying to get a word in with the band. "Nah, I saw you talking with Elizabeth, and remembered the first conversation she had with Rylee. Got paranoid."

"Didn't she basically threaten to reveal her identity?"

"Not in so many words, but yeah."

"Don't worry. She wasn't the one doing the threatening," I quip, squinting up at the sky.

Jamie just watches me.

"I told her she should be less concerned about your

image and more concerned about you." I suck in my cheeks, realizing that was a bold thing of me to say, especially since Jamie and I aren't truly together. "Too much?"

"A little." He blinks quickly, looking torn. "Why do you think I need someone to hold my hand?"

"That's not what I meant," I explain, feeling oddly defensive. "I was just saying she's concerned about the wrong things. Her priorities are off."

"And she has a reason to be concerned about me?" he retorts, face tight in... anger? Annoyance? I'm not sure which, and I'm even more unclear on the why.

"Why are you getting so mad? She works for you. You should be a priority."

"The band is her priority. And by helping them, she's helping me. I don't need you to—"

"Jamie." A slender hand clutches his shoulder and slides down his arm affectionately, pausing at his fingertips. Her body wedges itself between us, just enough so that I'm compelled to take a step back. "Your speech was brilliant. I was hanging on to every word."

"Ugh, me too," I mock her, batting my lashes. "I even teared up a little."

"Right?!" Stacy says, not bothering to acknowledge me, instead acting as if I'm a disembodied voice in the air. "That was so brave of you. Mara would be proud."

Jamie looks unimpressed, his eyes still heated and on me. He's not nearly ready to let go of our conversation, and Stacy interrupting only further sours his mood. Maybe I overstepped, but does that necessarily mean I was wrong?

If he was rightly getting better, it wouldn't be so hard to fake it for publicity, essentially making Elizabeth's life easier.

When Jamie refuses to grant Stacy his attention, she releases his limp fingers and tries a different tactic. Like a mask, I see the sweet, innocent façade she puts on slip a little as she replaces it with a replica. Except this one isn't so kind and giving, and you can see the malice beneath her flawless skin. "Where's your little girlfriend?"

My lips press in a small line. As if she doesn't know who I am.

Jamie grunts, finally removing his eyes from me, and looking for a distraction in the surrounding people who couldn't be more uninterested. The one time he wants to be bombarded by people to rip him away from the conversation he's in. He hardly looks at her when he gestures in my direction. "Stacy, this is Tori."

She pops her gum, clamping it between smiling teeth. This time she does look at me before returning her attention to Jamie, and seeing her full profile this close only confirms my suspicions. Every single thing about Stacy Gonzales screams snob. "No, no, the one you *wish* you were with. Carson's girl. What's her name again? Raelynn? Renae...?"

I could slap her just for coming here to torture Jamie. And Carson. *And* my sister. This is an event for Mara, and Stacy is doing everything in her power to turn it into a media frenzy. Not to mention trying to create drama by shooting out accusations that are completely and utterly absurd. If anyone overhears her, Rylee will make the front page of every magazine for a year.

"No wonder you won't leave him alone." I match her smirk with my eyes, moving so she has to look at me. "With that attitude, I doubt you have anyone else charitable enough to be around you."

She levels her lips and clenches her jaw tight. I suppose where she's from no one questions her. Too bad I don't live in 'Stacy's World' like the rest of the nation. "You know he's only with you because you're second best, right? He can't have your sister, so he's settling for her understudy." She tosses a grin at Jamie, touching his triceps. "I get it, I do. She's the closest to Rylee Green that you'll ever get." Stacy's eyes flutter to me and back. "I wouldn't tell Carson, though. I mean, I'm assuming you told him about *us,* considering he can hardly stand to look at you. If he found out about your feelings for Rylee..."

"He already knows," Jamie spits, stepping close to her, his words stabbing me in the gut. "There's nothing you can do to get between us anymore, Stacy. You should leave."

I'm torn between pulling him back, playing the mediator like always, or swapping to Team Stacy.

She doesn't bother saying more. This was what she wanted. A confession. That is, after all, the only reason she came today. To ruin Jamie for telling Carson the truth about their little affair, because now he'll never forgive her —not that he would have anyway, but somewhere in her delusional mind I'm sure she convinced herself she still had a chance, and that my sister was a mere obstacle.

The only thing that keeps me from turning on Jamie is

the satisfaction it would bring her. Well, that, and my pride. This is not the place to cause a scene. Plus, I meant what I said. Today is about Mara and the good he can do in her name. Not me. Not Stacy. And it certainly is not about her vendetta against Carson and my sister. She played Jamie and is here to collect her reward. She, just like the rest of the world, thinks that Jamie and I are really an item, and by telling me that he has feelings for my sister, she's ruining his happiness like he did hers by coming clean to his best friend.

"So long as we're all on the same page," she says finally, giving me a small wink and flashing her pearly teeth. "It was great seeing you, Jamie, though I really do miss our nights together."

"Go home," Jamie replies, already seeking me with his hands. Damage control, I presume.

Stacy smirks, glancing down at her toes and then back up seductively, before she sashays away, happy with the mess she's made of an already impossible situation.

Nights. She said *nights*. Plural. Not one drunken party mistake. But multiple.

"Tori," Jamie's voice sounds strangled, explanations and excuses rolling up his throat like a tidal wave, ready to fall from the tip of his tongue.

I press my hand to his chest, gritting my teeth. "Not. Here."

34

TORI

"Tori, I can explain," Jamie chases me into the house after an excruciatingly long car ride home. Not only were the two of us silent, but everyone else was *happy*. They talked and laughed and congratulated Jamie, made plans for dinner, and discussed the premiere tomorrow. The premiere that it doesn't look like I'll be attending now that Jamie and I are—surprise—at odds again. If that's all we are after we have what I can already assume is going to be an argument. My blood is boiling for the last time, and I'm not sure how many more excuses I can believe, much less accept.

"I highly doubt whatever misconstrued lie you've come up with this time will make things right. I just have one teeny, tiny, little question." I laugh hollowly, and clench my hands into small fists, thrusting them in the air as I yell, *"Are all of you in love with my goddamn sister?"*

"I'm not—"

"No. No!" My voice hitches and my throat constricts. I

shake my head unnecessarily fast. "Don't lie to me, don't sugarcoat it, don't tell me what you think I want or need to hear, Jamie. For once, *once,* tell me the truth. You owe me that!" I take a breath, then decide I'm not ready to hear his sad and apologetic voice just yet, so I push further—I push *him* farther away. "I've thrust myself into the spotlight for you. I've pretended to be your girlfriend, lied to my best friends because I'm too embarrassed to admit we're only faking it—"

"And you mean to tell me you didn't get anything out of that arrangement?"

"—I've obsessed over and analyzed everything you've ever said to me on a loop, looking for—for something! Something to tell me the kiss, our—our *moments* were more than just pretend or because of the circumstances. But it's fake. It's all just plain fabricated and meaningless and—and bullshit!"

"It was never fake for me." He clamps his fists at his sides, keeping them tight to his body. "Tori, you're—I—" He licks his lips, searching the walls in our kitchen like they hold the answers. He finally shakes his head, his anger simmering along with his yelling. "Now you're going to let me talk."

"You mean when you have nothing to say?" I prod, raising my brows.

"I don't have the words to say what I want to."

"That isn't my problem."

"Maybe not, but if I did... it might solve some of them." He pockets a hand, running the other through his thick hair.

Even mad, I find myself searching for little seeds of hope in his words, something to tell me he feels what I do. I'm searching for love in places it doesn't exist, for the hope it might grow.

"So, you don't have feelings for my sister?" I deadpan. I hate that a girl like Stacy has the power to wedge herself between us with her ill-intended words.

"No!" he relinquishes. "At least, not anymore."

"But you did. You didn't think to tell me? Did you think it wouldn't get out and make things worse for you? For us?"

"I never told Stacy. She must have figured it out on her own." He sighs, and defeat drips from his pores. "I've been with Stacy more times than I'd wish to admit. But the one I told you about was the first and only time while she was with Carson. I swear. The rest were after they broke up. Before we came to Ambler. The nightclub was the first time I've seen her since November."

And that's supposed to make it better?

At this point, does the truth matter? After all the lies he's sold me, does honesty actually count when it's a last resort? Even if it's true? And how do I decide if it is? How do I know this isn't another carefully constructed lie guaranteed to make me melt at his feet?

"I wish I could believe you."

"Just give me a chance, Tori. Let me prove it to you. Let me show you who I am. No walls, no lies, no secrets. Just me. The man I've been trying to let you see this whole time. At first, I hated this arrangement, but when I started getting to know you, started to see you, all I wanted to do was to be around you. I want to let you in. I've already lost Mara, and probably Carson. I can't lose anyone else."

I take a shaky breath, unclenching my fists. And oh, do I want to say yes. I've been waiting for this, for a sign that everything I've been feeling isn't one-sided, and of course, I'm only getting one when he's about to lose me. Swallowing my guilt, my doubt, and the unbelievably persistent part of me that wants to forget everything he's put me through, I tell him the truth. I can at least give him that, even if he's unable to reciprocate. "I don't think I can ever be with you without wondering if I'm just a second choice or a backup plan or a settlement. It feels like I'm just a replacement for the real thing. All this time you've been trying to convince me I'm more like Rylee than I think, and that we're both amazing, and that I *measure up,* or whatever. Even when I thought I didn't, you reminded me that I didn't need to be Rylee to be happy. Who were you trying to convince, Jamie? Me? Or yourself?"

"You. Only you," he says so quickly, so surely, that I almost believe him. God knows I want to. But I have to protect myself from further humiliation and misery. I can't let myself hope again without it breaking my heart. "You're the only one I want."

"I don't believe you," I whisper urgently, holding back the tears pushing through my resolve.

"You do." He reads my mind. The most tragic thing of all is that he's right. He knows me in a way no one ever has, and it's not enough.

"Please, just go."

He searches my face, but I keep it a mask concealing

everything we both know I'm feeling. "If that's what you want."

I nod once, staring at the clean tiles on the kitchen floor. "It is."

Earlier, I told Carson to drop me and Jamie off at my house because I'd forgotten a few documents regarding my designs for the Foundation that he needed ASAP. No one in their right mind would have believed me because, obviously—the house is finished, and I've already been paid. Nonetheless, no one questioned me, including Jamie. Carson dropped us off without any questions asked. I wonder if they could sense the tension, or if they just didn't think anything of it.

So, when I kick Jamie out, I don't really think about how he'll get home, and I'm not concerned with it either. He can find a reporter to give him a ride for all I care. Tell them everything. Make me the bad guy. It doesn't really matter at this point.

Anyway, this allowed me an hour or so to stew in my anger, jumping back and forth between who to blame—Stacy, Jamie, or my sister. When Rylee walks through the front door later, I'm on her cycle of the blame train—I was giving each of them an interval of twenty minutes' worth of blame-time—and as much as I hate to pin this on her, I've got to take my anger out on someone.

"What happened this time?" She assesses me curiously, setting her purse on the counter before grabbing a water from the fridge.

"You!" I grunt, crossing my arms childishly.

"Me?" Her eyes widen considerably, and she takes a seat in the chair to my left.

I roll my eyes. "Yes, you! Did you know Jamie used to be in love with you?"

Rylee cringes. Anyone else might have missed it—the tiny crease in her brow, the slight tic in the corners of her lips—but not me. "Well, he mentioned something, but it was a while ago, and honestly, I didn't think it mattered. Whatever he felt for me is clearly in the past. It's you he likes."

I scoff, scooting to the edge of the seat. "And you didn't think to tell me that?"

She bites her lip to keep her patience. To keep her mouth shut. "No, because I knew you'd react like this. Besides, like I already said, it's not me he likes, Tori."

"But you knew I liked him, and you knew he was into you! Why all the advice? Why help me when you'd rather just keep all the boys in your corner?" I throw my arms up in anger, knowing I'm being a bit melodramatic, and still, I don't stop. It's like a part of me wants to hurt her.

"Come on, Tori, you don't really think that. You're just proving my point of why I didn't want to tell you."

"Yeah, because it's your fault."

She blinks once, twice, uncrosses her legs, and leans forward, sucking on her teeth. "This is my fault?"

"Duh."

"Because Jamie had a fleeting crush on me, before he even knew you, I should add, then I'm the one to blame?"

This time I blink, because her logic kind of rings true,

but I'll be dead before I admit she's right. "Yep, glad we're on the same page."

"Do you know what you've put me through?" She stands, taking a step away so she can pace. "You should consider it a blessing I thought about giving you advice at all considering what you've done to me!"

"Which is what, exactly? Keeping you in check? Making sure you don't turn into some pampered, boyfriend-obsessed snob? Someone has to keep you grounded."

For a stretch of time, Rylee doesn't say anything. She just watches as if she's truly seeing me for the first time. "I can safely say the only person in danger of becoming a pampered snob is you." She gnaws on her cheeks, twisting at the bottom edges of her long hair, freshly highlighted with a blonde balayage. "You have bullied me my entire life, taken every opportunity to put yourself above me because you can't handle coming in second. You blamed me for falling in love, and persecuted me for not including you in it. And then Mara died, and you didn't even bother to ask me if I knew her. I found someone who is actually nice to me, who sees me for who I am and loves me for it, and the *only* thing you cared about was that he wasn't yours."

"Well, did you know her?" I ask, mostly to be a smartass. Better than admitting she's right, once again. It's not possible for her to blame me any more than I blame myself.

"Yeah, I did." Rylee nods her head, glancing down at

the armchair where her phone buzzes. "She was like the big sister I've always wanted."

I open my mouth, speechless. Her words sting across my chest, stealing the air from my lungs. My voice won't come out. If it did, I'd either say something I can't take back, or I'd just cry.

"And for the record, Jamie was never in love with me. He wanted what I have with Carson, there's a difference. He was lost and alone, and instead of letting himself accept that loneliness, he projected those feelings onto me before he realized I wasn't who he wanted them with. He just wanted *someone,* and the idea of what I represented in Carson's life made him think he wanted me, too. Stop looking for reasons not to be with him. You need to make up your mind. He's a good person, he's hurting, and all you've done is further rip open his wounds. He deserves better than that."

"You mean he deserves better than me." I cross my arms, waiting for her to confirm what I know to be true. She won't say it. She doesn't have the nerve.

"He deserves better than someone who doesn't have the ability to put him first. So yeah, he deserves better than you."

35

JAMIE

When I got home last night, my nerves were on edge. Every bit of me was itching for release, for a drink, for a smoke, to disappear into thin air. I didn't, though. I stayed strong, held on to my remaining resolve, the last piece of me that wants to remember.

That determination is dwindling along with my will to fight.

I walked part of the way home, then gave in and called Jer because I didn't want Carson to know how badly I screwed yet another one of my relationships up. Jer didn't tell him where he was going, just that he needed to borrow the truck, but I'm sure he had a pretty good idea. I'd thought after how emotionally stressful today was that I'd fall asleep easily. I hardly slept at all, and when I did, I didn't wake up until noon today, thinking, '*What does it matter if I drink?*'

Really, though, who's going to stop me? Who the hell am I staying sober for anymore? Not Carson. Definitely not Tori. I'd love to say she never had an impact on whether I drank, but she did. The small smile she'd give me when she got close enough to smell my breath was all it took to keep me on my feet. She made me want to live every day, not stumble through the motions. So, even mad, the small dimples in her cheeks are what I held onto, what I thought about when I considered giving up. Victoria Green is my lifeline, and without her I'm drowning.

Needless to say, those dimples didn't appear during our argument last night. Instead, I discovered new divots and shapes her lips could form, and while watching her yell at me, all I wanted to do was trace a line around her cherry mouth. I wanted to feel each movement as if it were my own. I wanted to absorb every facet of her body, every crease of her skin until the worry she wore was smoothed away by the surface of my hands.

Victoria Green is the ocean, wide and vast and deep, so much of her will never be known, but I'll never stop searching. When I'm with her I have no sense of direction, and I'm not certain whether she's the one holding my head above water, or the anchor tied to my feet.

Carson sits with his back to me, unaware of my internal conundrum. If my argument with Tori taught me anything, it's that even the things you don't outright tell people can come back to haunt you... and I don't want him finding out the truth from anyone else, namely Stacy.

Just thinking her name makes me want to punch a hole through the wall, but then I remember we're staying here at a discounted rate and decide better of that frustration release. Without alcohol or cigarettes, I don't know how to release my anger—by now, it normally would have fizzled away in a daze of happier thoughts.

I think what makes me the angriest about Stacy is that everything is always on her terms. *She* decides when to tell people your personal information. *She* decides what you do and don't tell your friends. I wanted to tell Carson the first time we were together, but Stacy convinced me it would ruin everything; our career, our friendship, our success. She said it'd mean nothing if I came clean. It would be over. Now, with Carson knowing I've lied to him all these years while pretending to have his back, I wish I'd been stronger. I should have told her no, I should have blown her off, because this is so much worse.

Of course, I've always had Carson's back. No matter what. But now he has reason to question all of that. Every word, every silent conversation, all of it.

"What?" he asks flatly, taking off his headphones and closing his laptop. Before he does, I get a glimpse of what he's working on.

"You're writing?" I ask, leaning against his dresser, careful it's sturdy enough to support my weight.

"No one else is." He stretches carelessly, letting his arms drop to his sides. He's right. None of our writing sessions have gone especially well, and most of the time end with Carson in a starchy mood, and Kris balling up our discarded lyrics and pelting them at us. Between the three of us, we get nothing done, leaving Jer as the mediator. Next to Carson, I'd say he's the most serious of us all. He's had a girlfriend the longest, has genuine plans and goals for his life, knows who he wants to become, and he's owned a house in Los Angeles for the past three years, which is more than I can say for the rest of us. He's at a level of maturity I never thought was possible for myself. It's not as if I've ever wanted to be there anyway, but recently, my outlook has changed.

"True." I look around the room, trying to act disinterested, then straighten up immediately, realizing that it's not a girl I'm trying to impress here. It's Carson. I don't need him thinking I don't mean what I say. "Listen, I need to tell you something."

"Stacy?" He turns his attention back to his computer. Apparently, this isn't a conversation he's interested in having. Too bad. It's long overdue. "Let me guess, that wasn't the only time you slept with her."

"How did you...?"

He looks at me ridiculously, the wide frames on his face sliding down the bridge of his nose. "You've never been a one-and-done kinda guy."

"You're right." I swallow. That's more Kris. Jer, too, before he met Kirsten—I swear that kid is unrecognizable from the man he used to be. When we point this out to him, all he says is he found the piece of himself that was missing before. "I just didn't want her to be the one to tell you."

"You think she doesn't have more tricks up her sleeve?" Carson shakes his head, and I notice the tension in his shoulders, the rapid tapping of his foot. "Coming after you was only phase one. You're not her endgame. I am, and Rylee finally, *finally* got people to stop talking shit on her

—as much as can be expected, at least. Stacy wants her out of the picture."

"So?" I ask, unable to figure out what he's getting at.

He clears his throat, meeting my gaze. "Have you ever known her to not get what she wants?"

"There is nothing that could come between you and Rylee. And if you made a list of things that could, I guarantee Stacy would be the very last thing."

"And you?" His phone buzzes, and I see an image of Rylee's smiling face fill the screen. It looks like the picture was taken in a car, and she's wearing Carson's lucky blue hat. It was the first gift he'd ever been given by a fan, back when we were nobodies, and 13 Days of December wasn't yet on our list of godawful band name possibilities. He wore it as a reminder of where we came from, and where we were going. It meant so much to him, and now she wears it because everything he wants in life is her. I know he loves the band and performing, and I also know he'd never give up on his dreams, but something tells me if we could never play again, he'd be just fine with that, too. Rylee has encompassed his life, and no matter what he does with it, he won't care so long as she's beside him.

"What about me?" I ask.

"Where are you on the list of things trying to tear me and my girlfriend apart?"

I meet his worn eyes, staring at them with such intensity he has no choice but to believe every word I say as if they're his own. "I'm not on it."

He watches me carefully, skepticism seeping through his defenses.

"I mean it. For a minute, I thought I liked her, I think we all did in our own way, to be honest—minus Jer. But it turns out I didn't. She was new, and different from the girls constantly throwing themselves at us. She reminded me of the light I used to see in Mara's eyes. I mistook that for love." I watch him for a beat, then, "Are we good now?"

"No." His words strike me hard, and for a moment, I'm worried he thinks I'm still in love with his girlfriend.

"Car, I swear on my life—"

"Not that." He swivels his chair, stretching his long legs in front of him. "You keep pretending you're fine, and I've tried to let you do your own thing, but Jamie..." he trails off, biting the end of a pencil. If I didn't know any better, I'd think he was trying to find the right words, but Carson always knows exactly what to say. "You're not going to find her in a bottle. Whatever you keep searching for, the void you're trying to fill... it can't be fixed by forgetting."

I shake my head, anger settling on my chest. How dare he try to understand, to tell me how I should cope? He has no idea what I'm going through. None. "And how would you know?"

"We all lost her, Jamie. She was a member of this band as much as any of us, you know that."

"But you're not her brother!" I yell, then release a long huff of air. "You can't possibly understand what it's like."

"Did you know Rylee blames herself? She thinks if she hadn't lied to Tori all those weeks, then she would have been at the concert, backstage where Mara was supposed to be. Kris was in love with her, for God's sake. Did you know that? Don't you notice when he wakes up with dark circles beneath his bloodshot eyes? He's hurting too. We all are, but you can't waste yourself away, Jamie. You have to stop."

"Why do you care?" I stutter stupidly, a burn slowly filling my chest with hate. "I'm doing what I have to to get over her, so what's it to you if it's not the most productive way?"

He moves to me, so fast I hardly have time to process, grabbing my shoulders and shaking them roughly. "Because if you don't stop, you're going to end up just like her."

"She was addicted to drugs," I sneer. As if it's the same thing. Shows how much he knows.

"It has to start somewhere."

Carson tries to say something else as I trip over his rug, walking numbly back to my room where I close and lock the door.

You're going to end up just like her.

Dead. She's dead.

Growling in frustration, I yank open a drawer, rummaging around for a loose cigarette or travel-sized bottle of alcohol. Tori mostly cleaned me out, but I know she didn't get everything. She couldn't have. I slam that one shut, opening the next. Then the next before moving to the bathroom where I shove everything in the medicine cabinet to the floor. Nothing. The shower—nothing. In the small nook behind the sink no one could possibly know about—nothing.

"Dammit, Tori!" I yell, swinging open my bedroom door. "Who the hell let her in my room?"

Carson peeks around his door from down the hall, watching me with concern. Kris does the same. I think Jer went out with Kirsten and her family tonight, just the same, I wouldn't peg him as a guy to let some chick touch my freaking shit.

Clearing his throat, Kris ruffles the back of his hair slightly. "I, uh, let Tori in a couple weeks ago."

I blink.

"Yeah, she, uh, she wanted to 'get what she missed last night.'"

"And you just let her in?" I gawk.

"Hey, I didn't know what she might've forgotten in your room—I mean, she was in there for a *while,* but who am I to judge? I don't know what you two do behind closed doors."

"God—Kris! She took all my alcohol, you idiot."

He opens his mouth, thinking something over, then shrugs. "Still not seeing the issue..."

I slam the door, pacing back and forth for five minutes before pulling out my phone.

36

TORI

My sister is the most annoying specimen on this planet.

She always has to tell me when I'm wrong. She always has to talk sense into me. She always has to make me see reason.

I hate her for it.

For once, I want to be right! Except I constantly allow my emotions to cloud my judgment and control my words and manipulate the things that I want.

Rylee also doesn't know that Jamie has been with Stacy more times than any of us realized. Would she change her mind about him if she knew? Does it even matter? They stopped seeing each other a while before he met me, so why do I care so much? None of this should bother me. And yet...

I despise the part of me that yearns for my sister's validation. I'm the older one, shouldn't it be the other way around? Does what she thinks about my relationship with Jamie realistically affect any aspect of it?

No, I guess it doesn't. So why do I still want to hear her opinion? To have her tell me I'm making the right decision?

A whistle sounds behind me, followed by Dylan's awestruck voice. "Damn."

I push an earring post into its hole. Taking a step back, I admire my glimmering ears, pierced from the lobes all the way up the cartilage. I've never been super into piercings, but ears are my exception. Half-twirling for him, I display my long, iridescent gold dress. It hugs my hips, only loosening midway down my thighs where it fans subtly. The mermaid train is a little longer than I'm comfortable with, but my heels make up for some of the length.

Smoothing my hands down my hips, I release a sigh, tearing my gaze from the sequin beauty. My hair is pulled into a high ponytail, fluffed, and curled, that cascades down the center of my back. A few intentionally messy strands of hair frame my face, drawing attention to the strong highlight of my cheekbones.

"Too much?" I bite my nude lips, running a finger under the base of my bottom lip, then inspecting the sharp points of my cat eyes. "I have time to redo it."

Dylan gives me a dubious look. I have less than an hour, and this look took me two. "You look fantastic. I'm surprised you're still going. I heard you and Jamie had another fight."

Another.

"Rylee?" I roll my eyes. It's just like my sister to tattle to our younger brother.

"Kris, actually," he corrects. "Rylee didn't say anything."

"That's surprising," I mutter. "But I'm not letting some douchewad ruin my red carpet debut. Besides, we still have an arrangement."

I refrain from asking him if he's talked to Jamie or heard how he's doing. Basically, I want to know if he's miserable without me. I manage to withhold my curiosity.

I don't need to know. I don't need to know.

"Wait." I blink, noticing Dylan's sweatpants and stained t-shirt, "You're not going?"

"Nah." He shakes his head, unbothered. "They only get four guest tickets, and I told Kris he could take Carmina. The spotlight really isn't my thing, anyway. I'll leave that to the Green sisters."

"Who's the fourth then?" I ask, then realize, "Oh, Kirsten." For some reason, I always forget Jer isn't single like the rest of the boys.

"Dylan, did you take my portable charger again?" Rylee calls, sounding neck deep in her closet. "I've looked everywhere."

"Yeah, you gave it to me last week for practice," he yells back, peeking his head around my doorframe.

"No, I didn't," she deadpans, and I smile at the look I know she's giving him right now, even though I can't see her from where I'm standing.

"Oh, Rylee, can I use your portable charger for practice last week?"

"I hate you." She appears, smacking him on the back of the head.

"You could never," he argues, crossing his muscular arms. He moves to my bed, sprawling across the rosy comforter. "It's in the bag on my dresser."

"Thanks." She passes my room swiftly, and I get my first real glimpse of her tonight. Her hair is framed around her face, straighter than her normally wavy strands, and a few pieces are puffed up around the crown of her head, her deep roots accenting the smokey shadow around her eyes. Royal blue fabric swishes around her as she rushes to Dylan's room in bare feet. Smart. I already regret strapping on my shoes so early.

"Dylan, it's dead!" She makes her way back to where he was standing.

"Oops. I might have forgotten to turn it off." He winces apologetically.

"You can use mine." I open a drawer and toss her a small, black charger with my name written in faded silver Sharpie.

"Thanks."

"No problem," I respond, noticing the way her eyes skate over me like I'm not in the room. Seems Carson has a thing for girls who avidly ignore my existence. Jamie, too. "You look nice."

She finally looks at me, though reluctantly, and responds with a halfhearted, "You, too."

"Please don't hate me." I breathe, the strain of our fight weighing on me so much I can't stand it anymore.

"Why not?"

"Because you're my sister, and you love me? And I was

—" I grit my teeth "—wrong. I shouldn't have blamed you for how Jamie feels."

Tension eases from her shoulders, and she relaxes, which makes her features look softer, prettier. "Maybe I should have told you, but I honestly wasn't sure he meant what he said anyway. He was drunk any time he insinuated anything. For all I knew, he didn't remember."

"You were right about how I'd react, at least." I hike up my dress and sit on the chair in front of my vanity.

"Truce?"

"Yeah."

"I'm torn between feeling left out, and thanking God I'm not as screwed up as the two of you," Dylan admits, watching us with scrutiny.

"If you take my charger without asking one more time, it'll be your face that's screwed up," Rylee threatens, pointing an accusing finger his way.

My phone lights up next to Dylan, and he picks it up with raised brows, glancing up at me, and then back to the phone.

"What is it?" I worry.

Please don't let it be a Teen Queen *article detailing my breakup with Jamie.*

I'm sure Jamie doesn't plan to continue our fating charade now that we're not on speaking terms. Real or not, I still don't want my breakup splayed across the evening news—specifically not tonight—though I suppose that was always inevitable.

Rylee moves to Dylan's side, taking the phone from his

hands. Her eyes scan the screen before they meet mine. "It's Jamie."

37

JAMIE

"Hello?" Tori's voice sings cautiously. It's music to my ears despite how mad I am at her. She was too livid yesterday to see reason, to listen to what I was saying. I basically admitted how I feel about her, and I'm not sure she was listening. She just hears whatever she needs to in order to be right.

"Where are they?" I breathe heavily, thrashing through my drawers again after coming up empty-handed the first two times.

"Where are what?" She sounds exhausted, and I almost feel bad for calling her up after everything I did. Almost. Mostly because she's probably getting ready for the premiere—I know nothing I do could stop her from attending. Then I remember she bribed Kris to let her into my room so she could ransack and steal my alcohol. Well, I don't know that she bribed him, just that she batted those long lashes of hers and he let her right on in.

"You know what."

"Ahh, I see." She laughs to herself, pleased that it's come to this—me begging her. "I drank them."

"Liar."

"You're right. I dumped them in the sink."

"You what? Do you know how much money you've cost me? Not to mention the quality alcohol you've wasted!"

Tori takes a shallow breath in, and I realize she's laughing. Of course, she didn't dump one-hundred-and-twenty dollars' worth of alcohol down the drain. She may be spiteful, but she's not ruthless.

"Where is it?"

"Hidden away." She says mysteriously. "I should thank you, though. Girls' nights are pretty much covered for a while. I'll see you at the premiere."

"Tori. Tori, don't you dare—" *click* "—hang up on me. Shit." I chuck my phone across the room, which leaves a nice dent in the smooth, beige walls. The hotel won't charge me for it—perks of being who I am—but I still feel guilty because now they have to get it fixed.

I continue the scavenger hunt through my room, knowing she couldn't have gotten everything. There must be something she missed somewhere...

I check under the mattress, in every drawer, behind every piece of furniture until I'm convinced that I'm not only an alcoholic, but a paranoid hoarder as well. Thanks to Tori, I at least have a reason to better hide my stuff now.

My palms are sweaty when I pick up my phone again, and it slides right out of my hand. Dropping down on my knees, I feel under the bed for it until my fingers bump something hard. No phone. I latch on to a bottle, sliding it across the carpet until it's in my lap. My chest tightens, and I glance nervously around the room as if someone put security cameras in place. I shouldn't. *I shouldn't.*

I can't give in to the pain I feel when I'm sober. I have to be stronger than that... I have to be.

But then I hear her. I hear Mara laugh. I see her eyes sparkling when she squints into the sun, and the smile that accompanies such an angelic sound. A sound I'll never hear again except in poor-quality videos on my phone. The phone I still can't seem to find. Maybe it's fate. I was, after all, led to this fine bottle of whiskey by my slippery hands.

Biting on my lower lip, I unscrew the cap of Russell's Reserve and raise the rim to touch my bottom lip, inhaling slowly and closing my eyes. Just one sip... one sip, and it'll all go away. Two sips, and I will no longer have to hear her voice. Three, and she'll be a blur in my memory, a long-forgotten dream.

Just a taste to make the heartache simmer away.

I take a breath and tilt the bottle, so the rim joins with my lips. I take a long swig, savoring the taste as it spreads evenly across my tongue, cascading down my throat.

Curtains sway, pushed and mangled by the strong winds outside. There's a storm coming, and Mara has all the windows open. Papers swim through the air as the breeze carries them in its tide, and I have to duck my head before I get a paper cut in the eye. It's mid-December, which also means frigid air rushes in the room as well, making my teeth chatter.

"Is this necessary?" I blanch as the door behind me closes by itself.

"The rain helps me think."

"Really?" I deadpan, not at all amused by her love of stormy weather. A storm is a storm, I don't see the appeal.

She flicks her newly blonde hair over a shoulder, shooting me a shit-eating grin. "Yes. Besides, I love that it annoys you—I was beginning to think it was impossible to get on your nerves. You know, it's abnormal for siblings not to make each other angry from time to time. Linda says it's healthy to fight.

I laugh, pulling out my phone to read a text from Carson. Linda is Mara's therapist at the most recent rehab center. The first time I thought rehab would work, but the facility just slapped a Band-Aid on the problem, and she was searching for her next fix two weeks after release. Talk about a waste of money. Then the second one came along, and I was a bit less optimistic. And here we are at lucky number three. She's yet again convinced herself she's found the one. I've told her she puts too much faith in them, and not enough in herself, but she doesn't listen. I think she hopes someone else can fix her, clean her, feed her, stitch her up, and send her on her way. But it's not that simple. She wants to get better, and I can't imagine how hard this all is on her, especially with me in the spotlight, but she's not looking in the mirror and admitting the problem stems from within her. She only blames the reasons she ended up here, not the poor choices she made that resulted in them.

"Carson said going out isn't the best idea," I relay his text.

"Did he get spotted?"

"Apparently more people in this town know who we are than we'd hoped." I sigh. I don't want to be here. He knows it. Mara knows it. I only came because Carson promised a low-key couple of weeks before the kickoff of the Wild Heart Tour. He also wanted to visit his family. I granted him that because out of all of us, he sees his parents the least. He's also the closest to them, as well, and has been a bit off since he and his girlfriend, Stacy, broke up. The kid can't catch a break.

Despite his instance that those are the only reasons we're here, I know they were just a convenient excuse for the press so I could be closer to Mara.

Anyway, Carson figured there was a better chance of being spotted if the four of us were together, so we snuck out through a service door at the airport, him going to test his theory, the rest of us to find the hotel. Mara and I were hoping to go to a real restaurant instead of nourishing ourselves at a drive-thru or with hotel cuisine.

"It's only the first day. I'm sure the fans are just super excited you guys chose their little map-dot town." She turns back to her pad of paper, continuing to scribble a few lines, erase them, write again, then crumple up the paper and rip a new sheet from her sketchbook.

I peer over her shoulder, and she immediately covers the note with her hand. "What are you doing?" I prod, trying to tickle her so she moves away.

"It's nothing." Her eyes drop to her lap, then back up at me. "I know you're not thrilled with my third round of rehab—"

"Neither is my bank account," I joke because I can. She knows that no matter what, all I want is for her to get better. If this is how, I'll support her at any cost. She'd do the same for me. In fact, she has many, many times. That's another reason I was okay with coming here. It's only a few hours from her facility. She's in the final stages so they're allowing her to commute home twice a week.

"But this one is different. I feel better, Jamie. I'm starting to feel a lot more like me than I have in a long time." Mara swallows, never the emotional type, and turns back to her blank sheet of paper. Why she covered it to begin with, I have no clue—there's nothing written yet. "Anyway, we have to write ourselves a note, or draw something of meaning, and keep it on us at all times. It's supposed to be a place we can turn to, to remind us of who we are and what we're fighting for if we ever feel like giving in. And you—" she shoves me away and rolls her desk chair in the opposite direction, pulling the blank sheet to her chest, "—may never read it. Never ever."

"Never?"

She snorts at my puppy dog eyes. "Okay, maybe one day when this is all over, and I'm stronger and happy and at peace with everything I've been through. Then, you can read it. But until then, eyes off."

I place my hands in front of me, palms open in surrender. "Deal. And Mara?"

"Yes?" She no doubt wants me to leave so she can think without distraction.

I place a kiss on her forehead, ruffling up her hair like only a brother can. She shoots me a dirty look. "You'll be happy sooner than you think."

"Yeah, yeah." She coughs into her arm, looking around the room with irritation. She has year-round allergies, but her *doctor refuses to prescribe her an allergy medicine, so she's left to suffer without relief. "Damn dust mites—hey, what's this?"*

She picks up her phone, clicking on a notification. "You sure the fans are why Carson can't get dinner with us?"

"Why else wouldn't he want to go out?" I scoff, wondering how this came about. The three of us were supposed to get food together if his plan to remain unrecognized succeeded. According to Carson's text, that didn't happen. Though, for as long as he's been gone, he probably gave in and got food for himself instead of waiting to go out with us later—but he didn't mention anything about that in his message. Besides, I don't think he'd tell us we shouldn't risk going out just because he's already gotten food.

"Looks like he has other obligations." Mara tilts her screen so I can see it, revealing a picture of Carson holding hands with some girl in a parking lot. "Do we know her?"

I squint, drawing the phone near so I can see better. "She looks... cute? You can't see her face, but I don't think we know her. Carson didn't mention anything about having friends in town."

Actually, he explicitly said the opposite.

She tugs her lips in thought. "Who knows? We'll have to ask him when he gets home. Doesn't look like your fans are too happy, though."

I cringe, reading the first few morbidly rude comments. I immediately feel for the girl. "They never are."

"Hey, and about Jordan..." she starts, finally admitting what's been on her mind this whole time, what's been keeping her from focusing on writing her note.

When Mara is upset or stressed, she can't pour it into

writing or art like most people. She has to stew in it, feel it, understand it before she can move forward. She's more self-aware than anyone I've ever known. "I'll figure out a way to pay him. Or to pay you back whatever you give me once you figure out how to get it to him without drawing attention to yourself."

I bite my lip. Mara's rehab bills have money tight, and taking out a large sum to pay off her drug dealer is going to bring too much attention to the situation. I make a lot being part of a famous band, more than most people, but Mara is attending a ridiculously expensive facility, and I'm still sending checks to my parents every month so they can retire early and live off my income. Also, the last thing we need is the label finding out that I paid off a drug dealer. And the media? They'll spin it to look like we're both addicts. But I can't let Mara know I'm concerned—she's already more on edge about it than she should be. Eventually, I'll figure something out. "You just worry about finishing your inspirational note so I can sneak a read later."

She raises her brows in a defiance I haven't seen from her in a long while. "Over my dead body, Jamie LeMont. You may have the world at your feet, but when I'm here, you don't get special treatment. You're still my shit-for-brains little brother, no matter how famous you become."

"Don't I know it." *I chuckle, slipping out of the room once the wheels in her head start turning again. If she needs peace and quiet, to throw herself into a project so she can think about anything other than drugs, I can give her that. I'll give her whatever she needs to get through this and back to the radiant girl she used to be.*

38

TORI

Dozens of cameras line the red carpet with eager, maniacal men and women standing behind them. Verbal commands claw at us from every angle, trying to get our attention so we look directly at them, giving them a "money shot."

"Guys, look over here!" one man yells, nodding in my and Jamie's direction. We shift slightly, his hand barely touching the small of my back. He hasn't spoken a word to me since the limo picked us up, which drew all our neighbors to their front porches. I suppose my family is the most exciting thing that's ever happened on Rosemary Avenue.

"Beautiful, Tori, you're a natural!" I part my lips in a smile, trying my hardest not to stare directly at the flash, though it's hard not to when that's all there is to look at. I glance down at the carpet every chance I get to give my eyes a break.

"Can we get one with just Tori and Rylee?" Another

photographer motions me and my sister aside while the remaining paparazzi take advantage of their small window to capture the boys without us in the picture. Kirsten doesn't like the spotlight, so she snuck in before the circus started, and Carmina ended up flying home for the weekend. I suppose this is just a normal Tuesday for her, being the sister of Kris Topaz, so she couldn't care less if she missed it.

"Look here!"

I comply, drawing my eyes to the nearest camera, pushing my lips together in a pout while Rylee's smile glimmers like a goddess's would.

"Thank you, guys, so much!" They yell as we walk farther down the line, onto the next wave of hungry piranhas.

Rylee finds Carson's side again, and Jamie maneuvers next to me, though I don't know how since I didn't see him, what with all the white blotches in my vision. I have no idea how I'm supposed to *watch* the movie after this.

"Is it always like this?" I ask between clenched teeth because the tension between us is killing me. I can only imagine the stories that will be printed tomorrow if we hardly say a word to one another.

"Mmhmm." The only reason I know he doesn't completely ignore me is because his chest vibrates with the sound. I don't actually hear it.

"It's intense," I continue, sneaking a glance up at his smoldering stare that causes every woman in the vicinity to melt into puddles on the floor.

He doesn't respond, and if it weren't for the sound he

made before, and the light pressure of his hand on my back, I'd think he didn't know I was here at all.

"How can *you* be mad at *me*?" I accuse beneath my breath. All I did was stand up for him to Elizabeth, and no, he didn't ask me to do that, but it's not like I went to the label and accused them of neglecting his health. All I did was tell her how I felt—it wasn't even a reflection of Jamie's feelings.

Time and place, Tori.

He heaves a sigh, finally looking at me. His eyes skim over me lovingly, nonetheless, I can see the deep discomfort he hides beneath them. It's all for show, just like our relationship. Just like his lies. He watches me like he could devour me right here, on this carpet, in front of everyone, but none of it is real. It's all an act for the show we're putting on. "Can we not do this here?"

"Whatever you want," I say sweetly, ensuring only he can hear the venom behind my words. I've only ever done what he wanted, and I can't believe I'm just now realizing that.

When we finally break free of the camera flashes and suffocating crowd, I release the breath I've been holding since we got out of the limo. I'm sure people are still watching, so we're not necessarily in the clear, but knowing there's less pressure to be perfect helps ease the heaviness on my chest.

I watch Jamie from afar while he talks to someone he must know. Of course, it's a girl. And of course, she's stunning. But whatever. I'm not jealous. I don't even care. Jamie LeMont can talk to whomever he wants.

I was stuck next to him in the limo and had to refrain from telling him he smells like a bar at three in the morning, because I know stating the obvious wouldn't help matters. Besides, the moment I smelled him, I blamed myself. He's been so good the last week or so, and I pushed him over the edge. I drove him to drink.

He made his share of mistakes, too.

I hate the pressure I put on myself when he's around. If I could go back and tell him I would never date him for the press, I would. Ever since I gave in to my worst intentions, allowed myself to feel more for him than I should, my life has been out of control. We're both catastrophic messes on our own, but together, we're a tsunami.

"You need to stop staring," Rylee advises between clenched teeth. "You're only giving him what he wants."

I blink at her words. I half expected her to warn me people were noticing, or that I need to let him go, but this... is not what I thought she'd say. She still seems upset with me, and I can't say what she said last night hasn't been lingering in the back of my mind, but we're getting there. Correction, we're getting *somewhere*. I just never thought she'd pick a side, nonetheless mine.

"You did what you could to help him, albeit breaking into his room and stealing his alcohol may not have been the best approach..."

"I didn't break in," I set her straight, crossing my arms. "Kris let me in."

She blinks stupidly, ready to argue with my defense, but she must decide better of it because she shakes her head with a rueful smile. "You are so much like our brother."

With that, she walks away, stopping briefly to talk to Kris and Kirsten, who are stationed at the mini bar waiting for Jer and Carson to find our seats.

A warm feeling spreads across my chest as I replay her words in my head. It's not that I *want* to be compared to our little brother, but the fact that she sees a resemblance between us makes me feel closer to them somehow, like I'm finally part of the family.

I stand alone, watching as multiple celebrities fill in the venue, and it takes all of my restraint not to squeal in excitement—these aren't just average people. They are television and music industry royalty. Most mind their own business, mingling with the other celebrities they know, so I don't feel comfortable interrupting like a crazy fangirl to introduce myself and express my undying love for their work.

After several cocktails and polite introductions, Kris pops his head around the curtain. "It's about to start."

Rylee sucks down the rest of her drink, thanking the bartender who clearly doesn't card—because apparently, they don't care if you're underage in famous-people-world—and lifts the bottom of her dress so she doesn't trip over it.

"Wait, where's Jamie?" Kris asks, and Rylee halts in place, Kirsten behind her.

They all look at me for some unknown reason. I widen my eyes, raising my hands in defense. "I'm not his keeper! I thought he went inside."

"He didn't." Kris looks worried, which makes my stomach sour. This kid is usually about as serious as a cartoon rabbit, so the fact that he looks nervous makes me increasingly tense.

"What's going on?" Jer appears, looking between us.

"Apparently, I'm an awful babysitter," I sass, sucking down the rest of my wine and discarding the empty glass on a passing tray.

"He probably just went to the bathroom." Kirsten twists the post of her diamond earrings, obviously not as confident about that as she sounds.

Jer pushes past our group, and into the men's room. After a minute he returns, shaking his head. "Empty."

Most of the attendees have made their way into the theatre, so it's mainly us five left in the velvet cocktail room.

Kris pulls out his phone, clicking a few buttons before it dials. "Voicemail," he says, trying to look annoyed. We all *want* to be annoyed, but the sad truth is that we're worried. I haven't seen Carson or Jer since we got here, and no one thought anything of that, but with Jamie... with Jamie we worry.

Rylee tries him next. "Voicemail," she confirms. I think we all secretly hoped he'd answer since it was her calling. Even me.

"Tori? Want to give it a shot?" Jer suggests, cracking his knuckles at his waist.

"He won't answer for me," I assure them, deflating their hopeful faces. "Can you track him?"

"Good idea." Kris slips out his phone and types in

Jamie's number. His eyes fuzz over in confusion. "This can't be right."

"What?" Kirsten prods, moving so she can see the phone. Her face, too, turns to one of skepticism.

"His phone says he's... at the hotel...?" Kris fills in the blanks.

"When's the last time anyone saw him?" Jer wonders, thinking back.

"Twenty minutes ago?" I offer unhelpfully. My suggestion is followed by several nods of agreement. I know we're only in New York, hardly past the border, but there's no way he drove the hour and a half home already. We've only been here about an hour, not even.

"All right, if everyone would please find their seats," a voice instructs from the room parallel to ours.

Jer and Kris exchange a look.

"I'm sure he's fine," Kris assures us, biting his lip. "We can probably go in."

Everyone nods. Nobody moves.

I pull my phone from my purse, then hand the sparkly clutch to Rylee. "You guys go in. I'll look for him."

"Are you sure?" Rylee asks, a troubled look in her eyes.

"I've had enough stardom experiences in the last month, I can miss out on this one."

She looks like she wants to argue, but I lightly shove her toward the theatre. "I'll share my location with you, so you know where I am. Now go. I know you've been looking forward to this for months."

"You've been looking forward to this your whole life,"

she says sadly, reminding me of the argument I once used to make her feel guilty for being with Carson.

"Yeah, and I've discovered it's not all rainbows and butterflies like I'd anticipated. Go enjoy yourself. I'll smack Jamie once for all of you when I find him." I nod encouragingly, and they begrudgingly move through the curtains while I usher them on.

"Text with updates," Jer insists, meeting my eyes seriously. "You sure you don't want someone to come?"

"It's okay, I've got this," I tell him with more assurance than I have.

"Thanks, Tor." He nods, and in that short movement, I feel his gratitude. Jer isn't a man of many words, but if you pay attention, he tells you everything with his silence.

I backtrack the way we came in and find a security guard at the door. I don't want to draw attention to the situation if it's nothing, and especially not if it's something, but there's a decent chance someone saw where he went. I could search this place for hours without luck.

"Hi, excuse me." I bat my lashes bashfully, licking my lips. The man takes me in, smiling easily. He's dressed in a sharp, black suit, with an earpiece tucked in his collar, which I take to mean he's security. There are three others like him stationed across the entrance hall, so I made sure to choose the one closest to my age. He looks to be late twenties, early thirties, and I've always been told I look older than I am. "Sorry, but have you seen my friend? We came in together. His name's Jamie LeMont, maybe you've heard of him?"

"I have a sister," the man jokes.

"Right." I laugh, playing aloof. "So have you seen him?"

"He went toward the gardens a little while ago. To the right, all the way at the end of the hall." He points in the direction, as if I don't know my rights and lefts yet.

"You're a gem, thank you." I give him a cute smile, lifting my dress and moving swiftly in the direction he pointed. I slow down when I realize I'm drawing the attention of a few bystanders, looking like they came for the event, but weren't let in. I wonder how many people try to sneak in by pretending they belong. I bet tons. Hell, I can't say I wouldn't have done it a year ago. In fact, I probably would have dragged Rylee along with me despite her reasonable protests.

"Jamie?" I call when I enter the overgrown area, bathed with flowers and vines and trees of all sizes. It's beautiful. I exhale in wonder, looking up at the glass ceilings and marble path that guides me through the maze. I wonder how big this area is. It'd be so easy to get lost in here, and I don't mean because of the labyrinth. I can already feel myself being swept away by the beauty all around.

A scuffling sound brings me out of my daze, and I follow the noise around a loop. I'm not sure how many turns I take before I see a shiny dress shoe peeking from behind a tree. I look before I make myself known, just in case it's not Jamie. It is.

I find him leaning against one of the several marble benches placed sporadically throughout the plant life. If I could come here every day, I would.

"Jamie?" I say softly, afraid my normal voice might disturb the peace. This isn't the type of place you yell in.

It's like the third floor of a library, where everyone has to be silent.

"Take you this long to realize I was gone?" he slurs, tilting his head back for a nice, long gulp of alcohol.

"It's not exactly easy to find people in here." I gesture around, then adjust my dress so I can sink to the floor beside him. "Your location says you're at home."

"I threw my phone across the room after I called you. I couldn't find it."

He found something else, though, judging by the fifth in his hand.

"What are you doing?" My voice hardly comes out, sounding raspy and as lost as Jamie looks.

"Having fun," he says sarcastically. "Letting go, moving on. Isn't that what everyone wants me to do?"

He takes another gulp, and I yank the bottle from him. He watches me closely, probably afraid I'm going to chuck it into the void. Then I take a swig of my own, feeling the strong liquid burn its way down my throat.

"Not me." I clear my throat, taking another sip. "What?" I ask when he raises his brows, looking impressed. "I don't drink White Claws. Besides, looking for you got me all stressed out."

"Isn't the premiere starting?"

I suck on my bottom lip. "Ten minutes ago, give or take."

"Oh," is all he says, and I can tell the movie is the furthest thing from his mind. I have a feeling I know what the closest is.

I close my eyes, feeling a slight buzz settle on my

brain. It's hardly there, but enough to ease the anxieties that constantly weigh me down. All of a sudden, I understand Jamie. Not completely, but I get why he'd rather be distant—because when he's not drunk, he's broken.

"I'm not a good songwriter," he blurts.

"Huh?" I turn to him, smoothing back a piece of his hair so it sits nicely with the rest of them.

He clenches his teeth and tears well in his tired eyes. Shivers run down my spine, remembering the last time he cried in front of me. That was the first day I grasped the full extent of his pain, how much he was holding in and hiding from the rest of the world. I'd caught him at a weak moment, and he let his walls slip. I really saw him then. Sure, I felt I'd "known him" my whole life because of my childish obsession with the band, but the more I'm around him and the others, the more I realize they're not at all the icons *Teen Queen* and silly little girls like me paint them out to be. They're real people with real struggles that everyone overlooks, expecting them to be the remedy to their own pain and suffering.

"I'm shit. I couldn't write a song to save my life." He sucks in a hollowed breath, staring blankly at the bushes in front of us. "It's all Carson. I'm just the guy who tells him when his ideas suck."

I bite my lip, wishing I knew whether that was true, then maybe I'd know the right thing to say. "You are so talented, and the band needs you—songwriter or not. You helped bring it to life, Jamie. 13 Days of December wouldn't exist if it wasn't for you."

"I was just Carson's sidekick. He knew what to do, not me. He'd be here with or without my input."

My chest tightens at his words, at how worthless he sees himself. He's breaking my heart. "You're wrong. The band would be nothing without every one of you in it."

He shakes his head, pressing his knuckles into his eyes. "No. No one needs me. All I do is mess everything up. For the band, for my family. For Mara. With us." He meets my eyes, and I don't know how he can think so little of himself when I see ocean depths swimming within them. "I've even disappointed the fans. I'm a screw-up. Everyone always said I'd never amount to anything in life. I guess they were right."

"Screw them." I tug on his sleeve, pulling his hands away from his eyes. "We need you. We all do. Jamie—I need you. I can't lose you. I—I know you miss her, but we can't lose you. The band, your friends, me—we need you to come back to us."

"You're lying," he whispers, reaching for the bottle. I hold it out of his reach.

"I'm not. I need you. I need you, okay? It's okay to be sad. No one expects you to be strong all the time." I pull him to my chest and thread my fingers through his hair, holding him like I'm afraid he might disappear. Maybe I am. He grips onto my wrist, squeezing like it's the only thing keeping him from falling headfirst over a cliff. "You don't have to pretend with me."

He chokes on a sob, burying his face deeper into the material of my dress. "I'm not sad."

He doesn't say anything else for a minute, but I know

he will. He's only testing the words to see how they sound out loud, and once they sink in, once he feels them in his bones, he'll let it all out.

"I'm not sad. I'm angry. I—I *hate* her. I hate her for doing this to me. For making me this way. I hate her for doing drugs and dying because of them once she was starting to be okay again. I hate her, and I miss her, and I hate her for making me hate and miss her. And I feel guilty for feeling that way, and I hate it, Tori, I hate it. I c-can't take it anymore. I just want it to go away. I want to forget her."

"No, you don't," I tell him what he already knows. "You love Mara more than anything in this world, and her memory is what will keep you going. Whenever you're sad or lonely or even angry, you are going to think of her, and it's going to warm your heart. It's going to make you remember why you're here and what you have to live for, because there's so much, Jamie. So, so much left. But you can't give in to the pain."

"Will it ever stop?"

"It'll get easier. I don't think you ever fully get over losing someone like that, like her, but it won't always be this hard. You will be okay again."

A voice from beyond the maze calls my name, and I click on my phone to find seven missed texts from Jer and Rylee. I'd thought about texting them when I found him, but I knew they'd want to know where, and would rush here right away—a crowd of sympathetic faces is not what Jamie needs.

"Are you okay?" I ask him softly, pulling his face up and wiping the remaining tears from his cheeks.

"No," he says half-heartedly. "But thanks. For this."

I nod, calling out to Rylee. "We're back here. Coming to you."

"I tried to stop them," she whispers when I'm close enough. For a second, I'm confused, but then I notice the rest of our clan standing behind her. Something tells me they wouldn't let her come find us alone.

Carson watches Jamie, who just stares at the ground, lost to the world, and pulls him into a hug that I'm pretty sure supports the brunt of his weight. I glance down at the quarter of alcohol missing from the bottle—some of which I drank.

"Should we take him to the hospital?" Kris asks, eyeing him worriedly, probably thinking he drank more than his body can handle.

I shake my head, holding up the bottle. "He's not that drunk."

I think his self-loathing kept him from drinking more than a few sips. His heartbreak did the rest of the damage.

"You ready to go home?" Carson asks, slapping him on the back.

"What about the premiere?" Jamie mumbles, still refusing to look at anyone.

"We'll catch the next one," Jer says easily, squeezing his shoulder. As if the media won't be all over this—*13 Days of December leaves just as the event is starting: trouble in paradise?*

Rylee stays behind as they clear the room, only turning to me when they're out of earshot.

"How much did you hear?" I wonder, slightly embarrassed that anyone at all could have overheard our conversation.

"Just the end." She brushes me off as if it's irrelevant, though we both know it's not, and her lack of a convincing response tells me she heard more than she lets on. "You know, you're kind of amazing."

I smile sadly, the compliment hardly penetrating my armor since my mind is far away, worried about Jamie and everything he said tonight. "I know."

39

TORI

"Ooh, what about that Thai food place down the road? Do you think they deliver?" Kris suggests, flipping through an assortment of to-go menus, most of which are for pizza shops.

Kirsten gags, seated in one of the chairs around the suite's island. After Jamie's breakdown, we had the limo driver bring us back here, stopping briefly to pick up Dylan per his insistence—he saw online that we left the premiere, and called to see what was going on.

We could have stayed somewhere in New York, but believe it or not, the paparazzi are worse there. It's celebrity central all the time. "Don't you remember the last time we went there? I was sick for like a week."

"Yeah, but you were the only one," Kris reasons, and she smacks his head, then yanks the hoard of menus away from him.

"Give me those," she says, though he didn't have much of a choice.

"Just... no Italian," he pleads, praying with his hands.

"You don't like Italian?"

Kris matches her cross expression. "It's the devil's food."

Kirsten smirks, thumbing through our options until she finds what she's looking for, then types the number in her phone. "Hi, yes, I'd like to place an order of your *best Italian* food."

"You bitch," he remarks, looking genuinely offended. She waggles her brows, not at all sorry. "There's a special place in hell for people like you."

"See you there, honey."

A laugh bubbles in my throat while I watch their exchange. Kirsten's fiery, more so than I thought from the few times I've been around her. I'm not sure why, but I thought she'd be more reserved like Jer—the strong, silent type.

"What's for dinner?" Dylan skates into the room, kicks off his shoes, and stumbles over his feet.

"Italian," Kirsten mouths, covering the phone with her hand as she does so.

Dylan laughs, looking straight at Kris. "Kris's idea?"

"Mmhmm—Yes, Staybridge Suites, Room 1513. Okay, thank you." She hangs up the phone, looking highly satisfied. "It'll be here in thirty minutes."

"We should make brownies," I suggest, widening my eyes.

"Oooh, please?"

"I'm in," Jer moves into the kitchen, pressing a kiss to Kirsten's temple.

"Where's Ry?" I ask when she and Carson aren't following behind him. We ditched our fancy clothes the moment we got back to the hotel, and after borrowing one of Carson's hoodies and a pair of his sweatpants—in love with him or not, I'm still swooning—I came into the kitchen to find Kris and Kirsten arguing over takeout.

Jer turns on the sink, pumping a small circle of soap in his palm before rubbing it in. "She and Carson were talking with Jamie when I left."

"He okay?" Kris twirls the straw in his glass of Coke, watching as the ice runs in circles around it.

Jer pauses in the pantry, mid-reach for the Betty Crocker brownie mix. "Is he better than he was an hour ago? Yeah. Is he *okay*...? I don't know if that option is on the table."

"What are we going to do?" Kris reevaluates his question.

"I'm not sure. For tonight, let's just pretend everything's okay for his sake. He needs us more than we know."

"Agreed." I nod, as does Kirsten. Rylee appears behind me, resting an arm on my shoulder. I glance behind her, searching for Jamie.

"He's getting a shower," she tells me, automatically knowing who I'm searching for. "He'll get through this."

"Not on his own."

"Not on his own," she agrees, squeezing my shoulders from behind. "Ooh, brownie mix? Please tell me we're making them. I'm in dire need of a chocolate dose."

"Then, you're in luck." Kris grabs the box, holding it on

display in front of his chest. "Because we've got double chocolate fudge."

Rylee finds a large glass bowl and pours the brownie powder inside while Jer cracks two eggs. We soon decide one box isn't nearly enough for all of us, and end up using three instead. Kris grabs the milk, and I get to work on mixing.

Carson pulls up a seat at the island between Kirsten and Dylan, cracking open a bottle of water and taking a long sip.

Jamie appears a few seconds after him, with wet hair and a black t-shirt sticking tightly to his chest. Dark gray sweatpants hang loosely from his hips, revealing a sliver of his boxers. He leans against Carson's chair, and my heart flips in my chest. Not because of how good he looks—though, I have to say... *hot freaking damn*—but because it seems like they've worked things out. I always knew they would. It just takes time to heal wounds that cut so deep.

Jamie doesn't look up, and no one makes a huge deal about his presence, which is a good thing. He's embarrassed enough without being patronized—however pure their intentions are. He's good at hiding his emotions, but not so good that I can't tell how uncomfortable he feels. At least if he'd been drunk, he might not remember all of tonight, or could just blame his breakdown on the alcohol, even if we all know it was more than that.

My heart lurches, eyes meeting Rylee's. We're a room full of people who want to make him feel better, but don't know how.

"You are just in time," I announce, opening the oven

and putting pan number one inside. He looks up for the first time, finding my eyes. My heart surges.

He raises his brows, bewildered. "For what?"

I take the apron from around me and drape it over his neck, loosening the back strap a little so it doesn't choke him—needless to say, his frame is a little bigger and wider than mine. "Brownies."

"Brownies?"

"Brownies."

"Before dinner?"

"Before dinner."

Wow, aren't we a bunch of conversationalists.

"Mix this." I shove a lumpy bowl in front of him, then turn back to the oven to set a timer, examining the instructions on the box.

"Bossy," he mumbles, picking up the whisk, and getting to work on smoothing the batter. "How long?"

I raise a brow. "Have you never made brownies before?"

"It's been a while," he admits, then looks back to the bowl in front of him.

"Until they're smooth, Einstein."

"Right," he draws out the words as if that makes sense.

I watch him, fingers twitching to fix his movements.

He sighs, noticing my impatience, and loosens his grip on the whisk. "What?"

"I—it's just—" I move beside him, shoving him a little so I can get closer to the bowl. I wrap my hand around his and move it in a circular motion. "Don't stab at it, stir it."

"Isn't that what I was doing?"

"No, you were mutilating it."

"Mutilating," he repeats my term of choice mockingly. "Fine, I got it."

I crane my neck to look at him, only now realizing how close we got when I wedged myself between him and the counter. I also notice how he doesn't back away to give me room. "Yeah?"

His other hand, the one I'm not holding captive on the whisk, brushes my elbow, sliding down until his fingers find mine, lightly tapping them. "Can we talk later?"

My heart speeds up, and I have to swallow before I answer for fear my voice won't work. I release my grip, turning to face him. "Of course."

Dylan starts cleaning up dirty napkins and paper towels, tossing them into the garbage. He then moves behind Jamie, reaching around him for our bowl that is sufficiently mixed by now, and shoves him into me in the process. Jamie braces his hands against the counter, so my back doesn't smash into it, which brings our faces inches apart.

"Oops, my bad. Sorry, guys." Dylan coughs to hide his laughter, giving the bowl to Rylee, who dumps it in an eight-by-eight tray, also camouflaging her laugh with a cough. "It's not fun with you and Carson anymore. You're like a boring married couple."

"You're an ass." She rolls her eyes, wiping a piece of hair from her face and leaving a dot of batter behind. Carson reaches over the counter, wiping it away with his thumb, and sucking on the sweetness. She scrunches her nose. "Thanks."

"Don't thank him, he lives to eat food off you—see, no, it's just not the same anymore. You ruined it." Dylan exhales, seeming disappointed.

"I ruined it?"

"Yep. You're too comfortable with each other. I can't make it awkward anymore."

"Guys, the food's here!" Kirsten announces. She tosses her phone aside, and wipes her hands on her jeans, taking off toward the door.

"Yay," Kris groans, looking less than thrilled.

"I got you cheesy breadsticks," she whispers in his ear as she passes. At that, his frown lifts, and he chases after her.

"I love you!" Kris announces, then looks back at us. "In a totally *unromantic* way!"

"Watch it," Jer warns, humor shining through his eyes.

The two of them return moments later with bags full of food, and Kirsten reads off the receipts on each, handing them out. So many smells circulate the room, making my stomach growl in anticipation. I didn't realize I was so hungry, though I suppose my mind has been otherwise occupied, wondering what Jamie wants to talk about later.

"Shoot, I think they forgot my breadsticks," Kirsten pouts, scanning her receipt, then double checks her order.

"Maybe they just misheard you?" Jer offers, leaning over her shoulder.

She shakes her head. "Nope, I was charged for them. Oh well. Maybe that's the universe telling me I need to watch my carbs."

Jer eyes his skinny, but fit, girlfriend up and down, then kisses her temple. "I don't think that's it."

Looking discouraged, Kirsten heads to the kitchen, picking up the pile of plates Rylee and Carson have pulled out of the cabinet, helping them set the table. Jer joins them, and when there's a knock at the door, everyone stops.

"Paparazzi?" Jamie guesses, looking as perplexed as the rest of them.

"I bet it's my breadsticks," Kirsten says, trying to balance the plates on her arm. "Tori, can you check for me?"

I blink, surprised that, out of everyone here, she asked me. "Yeah, sure."

I jog to the door, looking through the peephole first, just in case an unwanted guest got through security. I'm relieved when it is, in fact, the delivery girl. Swinging the door open, I come face to face with a girl about my age, holding a clear bag with breadsticks in one hand, and a small cup filled with whipped butter in the other, and wonder what my odds are of convincing her that I, too, ordered breadsticks she forgot about—because those look fantastic.

"I'm so sorry, I left these in my car by mistake." She lifts her head, then, big brown eyes taking me in. She looks kind of familiar, but I can't place her. Her hair is caramel brown, darker underneath than on top, and she wears a silver nose ring that very few girls can pull off. She's shorter than me, but not by much.

The girl's lips sag slightly, but she catches herself,

plastering on a stretched smile. She holds out the bag, and I latch on to it with my hand, but she doesn't let go. So, we stand there, both of us holding onto a bag of breadsticks like idiots. "I'm sorry, do I know you?"

She blinks, a slightly sour smile twisting her glossy lips. "Once upon a time, yeah."

I raise an eyebrow, and she finally lets go of the bag. She watches me closely, as if she's waiting for something, for some smidge of recognition, but I come up blank. I know her, I'm sure of it. Maybe I knew a younger version of her?

"What does that mean?" I ask, trying to picture what she would have looked like a few years ago.

She lifts a shoulder, looking up at the ceiling as if she wouldn't expect anything less than for me to not know who she is. "Never mind, it doesn't matter."

"Okay... Have a nice day," I say slowly, retreating through the door. My eyes scan her chest for a name tag. "Addison."

The moment her name rolls off my tongue, I'm immediately transported back in time. Back to sophomore year of high school, her crying in the bathroom, drenched in a raspberry smoothie. "Addison," I say her name again, and this time, she sees the recognition she was searching for. "I didn't recognize you."

Her hair is different, less blunt than it used to be, but her eyes are harder.

"That's okay. I probably look different without smoothie all over me." She scrunches her nose, and I can tell how hard she's trying to come off as casual.

I bite my lip, closing the door behind me so no one inside can overhear. "Addison, I—"

"Save your apology. It's years too late, Tori."

"I am sorry, though. I don't know who I was back then. I don't know how I became that person, but I truly am so sorry." Stings of guilt burn my chest when I look at her and remember the trusting, innocent girl she used to be. "Cory dumped me, if that makes you feel any better."

She purses her lips, eyes dropping to the carpet. "I know. He reached out after I moved away... He apologized for what Quinn did, and for not standing up for me, and I told him it was all you. I told him what you did."

"So, you're the reason he broke up with me." Cory dumped me shortly after Addison left, and the rumors of her accident had begun to spread, but I'd never thought there was any connection between the two.

"Pretty much." Addison tucks a chunk of short hair behind her ear, checking the time on her phone. "I guess someone at your school thought it'd be funny to tell everyone I tried to commit suicide. Cory was the only one who actually cared enough to make sure I was okay."

"So, you didn't...?" I start, then feel as though I have no right to ask her anything about her private life.

She scoffs. "Don't flatter yourself, Tori. You don't wield that much power over people."

"Do you still talk to him?" I ask, instead of responding to her dig because I totally deserved that. I'd never thought of it the way she clearly does.

"We're living together, actually. At WVU. We've been dating for about a year. After I graduated, my parents moved back here to be closer to our family. I'm just visiting for the summer."

I smile, trying to look genuinely happy despite how uncomfortable being around her again makes me feel. I got off easy when she moved away. I didn't have to see her every day or deal with the consequences of what I'd done. Addison was gone, and there was nothing left to remind me of how horrible I was to her. "Good. I'm happy for you guys."

"Don't patronize me," she says, her expression almost unreadable as she nods toward the suite door. "Just go back to your famous friends and celebrity boyfriend. I guess you really got yours, huh?"

"I'm really not the same person I used to be," I promise her, though I'm sure my words mean absolutely nothing after the bullying she endured because of me.

"You don't get to do that. You can't just wipe the slate clean because you decided you're a better person now. What you did to me, everything you put me through, that's permanent. That will stay with me forever. I had to switch schools, for God's sake."

She's right. Due to my petty jealousy, one action changed the track of this girl's life forever. I'm sure she saw herself being friends with us for a long time, going to prom, walking at graduation together. But instead, she was ripped away from the life she thought she was supposed to have, all because I wanted the guy she had a crush on and was too insecure to think that he'd ever choose me over her if I didn't do anything about it.

"Anyway, here." She holds out her hand to give me the

small cup of butter. I take it, and she starts backing away, gesturing to her delivery uniform. "Ironic, isn't it? All these years later, and I'm still serving you."

All eight of us fall into a thick silence while we take the first several bites of our meals. It took everything in me not to start with the brownies when Rylee pulled the first tray out of the oven—and I mean *everything*. Chocolate is my weakness, right next to sexy boy bands, of course. I especially like to divulge when I'm stressed, and after seeing Addison for the first time in years, my nerves are shot.

I can feel Jamie's knee bouncing next to mine, so I lock my ankle around his shin to hold him still. He laughs, mumbling an apology as he continues to stir a fork through his pasta, lifting the noodles and watching as they fall through the prongs.

He notices me staring, then nods to my plate, eyeing the olives I pushed off to the side, because, *ick*. "Can I?"

I slide the plate toward him, biting off the end of a cheesy breadstick. "Knock yourself out."

He plops them in his mouth one at a time, glancing around the table to make sure no one else notices his lack of appetite.

"Not hungry?"

He shakes his head, sighing heavily. "I can't eat."

"I get it." I reach over, forking a huge lump of spaghetti onto my own half-eaten plate. I probably should be telling him to eat, not encouraging him not to, but I know what it's like to be so upset you can't stomach food. My first breakup—well, my first real breakup with a guy I actually liked—left me sad and mopey in my room for a week. I lived off saltines and soup like I was getting over the flu. Mom kept trying to feed me the meals she made for dinner, all heavy foods and meat, but I refused. Then, after everyone went to bed, Rylee would sneak me a bowl of wedding soup with a box of crackers. Then she sat with me, and we watched the most heartbreaking TV show finales we could think of, just to make us cry. We skipped to the end of every sad movie and watched the episode of *Hannah Montana* where she takes off her wig for the world to see. We also watched the two-part special of *Wizards of Waverly Place*, where Mason breaks Alex's heart, and then fights Juliet, resulting in the two of them leaving the ones they love. You'd think we would have watched happier shows to lift my mood, but my sister and I have always liked to embrace the pain. At least for me, it reminds me I'm alive, and that even when I think it's bad, it could always be worse.

Wincing, I pull myself from the memory, finding Rylee's smiling face at the other end of the table. I hate remembering how good she's been to me, and how mean I've been to her. She has come a long way since her days of braces and bangs, and so have I. We might have lost touch for a while, but we're finally getting back to where we used to be, and I couldn't be happier about that.

40

TORI

Once everyone is finished with their food, they head out to the balcony, where apparently there's an outdoor fireplace, leaving me and Jamie at the island, nibbling on the last of the brownie crumbs. I really can't believe we ate them all. Three trays of brownies gone in ten minutes. I'd been hoping I could snag some to take home.

Jamie leans against the counter, sorting through his thoughts like a file cabinet.

"About earlier..." he starts, shaking his head. I refrain from interrupting him, because whatever it is he wants to say, he needs to get it off his chest, and I want to make that it's as easy as possible for him. "I had a lot on my mind, and I just kinda... laid it all on you out there. These aren't your problems. I'm not your problem."

I study my hands, sliding onto a stool. My heart aches for him, for the pain he's in. I knew he was hurting, but I had no idea he blamed himself for Mara's mistakes. For what he couldn't control. He needs someone right now who doesn't expect him to pull it together. Someone who will let him fall apart, no matter how messy.

I reach for him, grabbing his interlocked hands with intensity. And the way he looks at me... shivers crawl up my spine like a snake.

"Sometimes I think I need to get away. I need to... run."

"Don't," I whisper, squeezing his fingers.

His dark irises flick to mine, burning bright in the dim kitchen. I lean in farther, closer, soaking in the sweet smell of his cologne.

"Don't run away," I continue softly. "It will only catch up with you in the end."

He leans over the island. "Then, what do you suggest I do?"

Those few inches are just enough to bring us closer than we should be. Closer than I should want us to be. Despite the alarms blaring in my head, and the rational thoughts telling me we'll only mess this up again, I want it. I want him more than I thought it was possible to want someone.

"Lose yourself."

"I tried that."

"Not in alcohol."

"Then, in what, Tori?" he murmurs. Why does he need me to say it? "Tell me what you want."

I can't bring myself to say what I want to, what I need to. But the message gets relayed just fine as it dances across the tip of my tongue, and onto his.

I remove my hands from his, grabbing onto his shoulders as his fingers find a fistful of my hair. His lips work into mine, long and slow, but so intense I could pass out from lack of oxygen. He pulls away, making me groan as he moves around the counter so he can bring me closer. His hands find their place again, and his lips trail kisses down my neck, and back again. My fingers find his long strands of hair, and I use them to tug him, pressing every inch of him into me.

His hands slide down my waist, trying to further mold us together. "Do you know how long I've wanted to do this?" he breathes, his heartbeat mimicking mine.

"Since the car?" I remember our first real kiss.

He kisses my nose, disbelief pouring from his eyes. "Way longer than that."

I close my eyes, smiling, and lose myself in his lips, in the explosion of emotions that erupt in my bones.

"Oh my God, why does this always happen to me?"

My eyes open wide, and Jamie jumps so far away from me he's almost in another hotel room. Dylan stands in the kitchen entrance with his hands pressed to his eyes. His blue t-shirt is full of wrinkles, and his hair is tossed from the wind outside.

Words fail me for the first time in my life, and I'm left sitting on the stool with my jaw wide open, unable to comprehend such a fast shift of emotions.

"I just wanted a water!" he exclaims, walking into the kitchen, shooting sparing glances at me between his fingers. After grabbing a water, he shuffles his socked feet back the way he came, both hands still covering his eyes, except one of them now has a water in it so he looks even dumber.

"Do you always have to make out in open areas? Is that like a thing for the Green sisters?"

I squint, not following. Dylan walks a few more paces, then stops once again at the entrance to the kitchen.

Can't he just leave?

"And it's always. This. Spot!" he yells in agony, gesturing to where he stands, and then at the living room couch, then back to us. "This cursed spot!"

He's completely lost me, and from the look on Jamie's face, I don't think he understands either.

Dylan finally flees the room, mumbling something about *not enough peroxide in the world,* and *forever being afraid to drink water.* There might have been something in there about making babies, too, but I'm not sure. I've learned not to question the strange way his mind works.

"Well, that was…"

"Awkward?" I supply, receiving a nod. Neither of us know what to do, and that's made clear by the way Jamie leans against the wall on the *opposite* side of the room, avoiding my gaze at all costs. The moment's over, and we don't know what we are without it.

I wish I knew how this stuff came so easily to Rylee and Carson, because I've never been so terrified of anything in my life. Every day for the past I-don't-even-know how many years, I've had fantasies of meeting the band, of being with one of them. But that's all they were. Improbable fantasies of a teenage girl. I never imagined it'd happen, or that I would fall so hard. That I would like one of them so much that it hurts. My fantasies were platonic, an early teen's wistful daydreams. I just didn't outgrow them the way most other girls did. But this... Jamie... the real thing... it's so much more than I could ever handle.

"I should go." I stand abruptly, searching the kitchen for the car keys. Rylee is going to kill me for taking them, but she's planning to spend the night anyway, and I'm sure Carson can give her and Dylan a ride in the morning.

"Tori, wait," Jamie calls after me, but I'm too quick to the suite doors.

I fasten my purse over my shoulder, holding the keys so tight they imprint the skin on my palm.

"I'll see you tomorrow, okay?" I fake cheeriness, and I know it's not fooling him. Something tells me I could never fool him.

"Tori."

"Bye."

Jamie follows me all the way to the elevator, and the doors don't open fast enough for me to get away. I knew I should have taken the stairs. The cardio wouldn't have killed me.

I close my eyes, sinking against the wall. He moves to me, bracing his hands on either side of my head. "I'm not letting you run away from me again. Not without a damn good reason."

"I'm sorry." I purse my lips, letting my head fall to his chest. "I don't know how to deal with this."

"You mean with me?" he asks regretfully, moving back.

I look up, shaking my head rapidly, reaching for him. "No, God, no, not *you*. The way I *feel* about you. I don't know what to do about it."

I don't know why, but this makes him smile. "Why do you have to do anything?"

"I have no idea," I admit, letting him pull me against his chest. I can feel the smooth muscles of his back beneath my palms, and I run my hands over them like a scavenger, searching every dip and crevice. His back tightens, and he presses a kiss into my hair, sighing. "We were never just friends, were we?"

"That would be mortally impossible." He confirms my suspicions, swaying us back and forth. "I never wanted to be your friend, I thought it's what you wanted."

"You offered to be friends because you thought that's what I wanted?" I blanch, pulling back so I can look at him.

He looks down sheepishly. "You did almost fall over to avoid kissing me. Besides, I've never wanted a girl so much that I offered to be her friend just to keep her around." He shakes his head as if even he can't believe he was willing to put himself through that.

I look down, and he nudges my chin. "I just—this isn't just because you need someone, right?"

Jamie's in a hard place right now, and the last thing I want is to be his distraction from the real issues at hand. I don't want to be his new whiskey.

"I've made it my whole life without needing anyone. Until you. I don't just need you in my life, I want you there, too. I want you here, please believe that."

"I do."

White teeth imprison his bottom lip, and he sucks on

it, capturing his smirk between them. "If I try to kiss you, are you going to slap me again?"

I look him up and down. "Only if you want me to."

"You are—"

"Beautiful? Exotic?"

Jamie scrunches his face, dipping his chin. "Neurotic."

"That wasn't one of the options."

Laughter shines through his warm eyes as a smile overtakes his face. "I was thinking outside the box."

This time, I widen my eyes playfully. "Then, stop thinking."

"I can do that." Jamie kisses my lips, and I soak up all the time we've wasted. "I really am sorry for putting you through hell."

He pulls me into a hug, pressing me tightly to him. I bury my face in his chest. "You know you can talk to me, right? If you ever feel the urge to..."

"Relapse?" He tucks my hair behind an ear, resting his chin on my head. His voice sounds strained when he speaks. "Sometimes I don't know how."

His arms rest on my hips when I lean back, and I rub my hand against his stubble, memorizing every inch of him. "It doesn't hurt to try."

"You realize you're amazing, right?" He kisses my lips twice, pressing our foreheads together. I'm very thankful they have the entire floor rented out, because this would be awkward with guests milling around.

If I'm trying to convince Jamie to be more open and honest, it's only fair I attempt to do the same. "No one has ever cared enough to know me this way."

Throughout my life, I've received countless compliments, or at least, comments that were meant to be up-lifting. But they were all superficial about my looks, or my alcohol tolerance, or my impeccable ability to spot "losers" and keep them from our *group*. People used to tell me I was good at judging others' worth. I never wanted that title. No one should be told they're good at judging other people, especially in a mean way. Rylee has always been a good judge of character, which is totally different, and it's useful. I, on the other hand, liked to judge people by how good I thought they were in comparison to me. And that wasn't fair. I hadn't understood it at the time, but I ruined the high school experience for so many people. I took so much away from them.

"I care," he rasps, kissing my temple, then my nose, and my lips again. "More than you know"

I shiver in memory of all the horrible things I've done, knowing I deserve Stacy's version of Jamie, the one who cheats and lies, more than the sweet one who showers me with affection and stupid, thoughtful picnics with my favorite fast food. "I don't deserve you."

"That's where you're wrong." He shakes his head. "After everything I've done, I don't deserve *you*."

The elevator dings and the doors slide open. We part in case someone gets off, but no one does.

Jamie peeks his head around the corner at the bellhop, keeping hold of my hand. "Sorry. False alarm."

The doors close and Jamie turns to me. "You are staying now, right? I didn't just send him away for nothing?"

I loop my arm around his, pulling him back toward the suite. "I'm staying."

For the first time in my life, I want to be something for someone else.

And I've never been so terrified of messing that up, or excited to see the places it could take me.

41

JAMIE

Carson finds me on the balcony, lost in thought and strumming a guitar. It's been a long time since I picked one up. I've never been as gifted as him at music. Drumming is where I excel after all, but I can do more than bang sticks around.

"So, you and Tori, huh?" he teases, settling beside me, bumping into my shoulder, and looking out at our view of Ambler.

"Me and Tori," I repeat, unable to believe it myself. I think she's the reason I picked up this guitar. When her exquisite eyes take me in, I can see how much she believes in me, and it makes me want to believe in myself again, too.

"Who would have thought, after all those times Rylee joked about us fighting over her, that you'd actually..." Carson huffs in amazement, unable to finish his thought. He doesn't need to. We both know what he means.

"Definitely not me."

"I'm happy for you."

"Me, too," I admit, chuckling. "And for you, of course. How did you guys do it? With Tori, it's so complicated. We're both so..."

"Damaged? Stubborn?" he supplies.

I roll my eyes. "Thanks for reminding me."

He shrugs. "I think it helps you understand each other. Rylee gets me. She sees me even when I'm hiding from myself. It's crazy to think, but she makes me whole, and I've never admired and respected anyone so much in my life. I can't imagine a world where we don't end up together."

My eyes widen. I knew he was in deep, but... "Whoa, man. You say all of that, you might scare her away."

He shakes his head thoughtfully. "I don't think I would."

"Then, tell her."

"She knows," he says with assurance I wish I had. "I'll tell her, though, just not yet. I'm saving it for a rainy day. Anyway, how are you doing?"

"I've been thinking about getting some help," I admit, remembering the name of Mara's last rehab center. She'd gotten to the point where she was permitted to commute home twice a week. I'm not sure if that's typical for rehabilitation centers, but it worked really well for her. I see it now, the difference between the last weeks of her life and those before it. She was happier. Going there might make me feel closer to her, too, since it's where she spent a lot of her time toward... the end. Being at this hotel only further reminds me that she's no longer here to fill the silence with her loud music and laughter. "How do you think Elizabeth will feel about that?"

Carson scoffs. "She'll suck it up, that's what she'll do. I don't care what she thinks."

"And the label? If this gets out..."

"It'll draw attention to us, but honestly, I think the fans will be more supportive than ever. Just my prediction. The media will try to make it ugly, but they're always doing that."

"Same. I think Elizabeth is just paranoid."

"She should be." Carson shifts uncomfortably. "I've been thinking of firing her. I know she's good for us, but, and no offense here, I think she should have encouraged you to go to rehab a while ago. I want someone invested in us as much as our image, and that's not her. She's too fixated on hiding the problem, rather than fixing it. She's good at her job, though, which is why we hired her. I just don't know how we'll ever find someone to take her place, or patch up our image the way she can."

"I think I know someone." I suck in my smile, raising my brows at the thought of Rylee managing us—*managing.* We sound like children. I'm sure Elizabeth would be thrilled to know she's prepping her possible replacement in all-things damage control. "And I think you just might know her, Country Boy."

Carson's smile falls at the mention of the nickname Mara gave to him when we were kids. I've never fully understood it, but she did, and her mind worked in mysterious ways. If it made sense to her, it was fine with me.

"I miss her." He clears his throat, trying to mask his pain. It wasn't fair of me to think he couldn't possibly hurt the way I am just because he's not her brother. They were as close to siblings as you can get without being related to each other.

"Don't worry. She's up there laughing her ass off, watching us fuck everything up."

He pats my back in support, cracking his neck and peeking through the window at Rylee and Tori, sound asleep on the couch. "I think she'd say we're doing all right."

EPILOGUE

TORI

"I think that's the last of it." I sigh, looking around the wide space at my mercy.

"Do we have to unpack it all now?" Jamie kisses my neck, arms circling me suggestively. "We don't have much time until the cavalry gets here..."

I roll my eyes, leaning into him. "I guess it could wait..."

He flips me onto the white couch in the middle of the living room. *My* living room. I've been thinking about buying a house for a while now, wanting something close enough to college to commute, but still near home. This little gem was perfect. The best part... Rylee's moving in with me. She decided to wait until after summer, though, but I'm just eager to make this place my own.

I stare up at the light blue walls, and then at the sexy boy above me. All we've set up so far is the couch and TV. Priorities, of course. Jamie slides off of me, so he's pressed against my back, burying his face in my neck as I reach for the remote. "Watching TV is so not what I meant."

"You set it up." I shrug, goosebumps trailing after the fingers he runs across my stomach.

"Yeah, for *later*."

"What, so you think you're spending the night, now? Just because I got an apartment, you think you live here, too?" I bite my lip to keep from laughing. Ticking him off is one of my new favorite things to do. It doesn't matter what it's about, whether it's worth an argument or not, I find so much joy in saying the most utterly ridiculous thing I can think of just to get under that skin of his. It keeps things interesting.

Jamie releases a troubled sigh, his breath warming the surface of my neck. "You give me a headache."

"Fine. But after this we *need* to finish. I don't want to deal with this when we get back from Miami."

To this, Jamie says nothing, much like he has the last six times the words *vacation*, *Miami*, and *summer* have come out of my mouth. I'm starting to get the feeling he's hiding something from me.

In a week it will be June tenth, and all of us are going to Carson's house for the summer, something I've been looking forward to since way before I fell in love with Jamie. I had so much fun during the weekend I was there for the band's tour party, but now that my life feels like it's really coming together—Rylee and I are closer than ever, I have a great boyfriend, a subpar brother—I'm even more ready to spend some time with my favorite people on Earth—and no, not because they're a super-sexy famous boy band. Although, that will never *not* be a plus.

Jamie halts his roaming hands, and I shift so I can see him, using my fingers to draw lines on his face. "What is it?"

"Anybody home?" Rylee calls, peeking her head through the door. "This place is seriously adorable, Tori. I can't wait to move in."

Jamie groans when I stand up, and I feel a slight ping of satisfaction that he's not the least bit excited to see my sister. Yes, I'm a severe work in progress—you can't take the petty out of a girl all in one day, you know. Besides, a little jealousy is good for the soul. Keeps me grounded. "I know, I'm so excited! You know you don't have to wait, right?"

"I can't pack for vacation and uproot my life to a new location at the same time. I'll wait until we get back."

I laugh, pulling her into a hug. Jer and Carson come in next, holding large grocery bags, followed by Kris and Dylan, who are—*surprise*—empty-handed.

"We figured you forgot about food," Dylan says, ruffling through the bags they set on the counter.

I laugh, mostly because I did, in fact, forget about filling the fridge and pantry with more than water and a few bags of chips. "Thanks, guys."

Carson stretches his back, exchanging a look with Jamie. "So, we have an announcement."

"You do?" Rylee raises her eyebrows, pausing over a bag of groceries.

"We do," Jamie confirms, pulling me so I'm sitting on

the back of the couch, and he hangs his arms off my waist. I'm not sure how we ever stayed away from each other before, because since that night at his place, we've been inseparable. I finally understand how Rylee feels with Carson. It's an intoxicating feeling, having someone stand by your side who sees you, and knows you, and loves you even more for it. "Tor, do you remember the property I took you to for our picnic?"

"You mean that time you kidnapped me and threw the keys into the woods so I couldn't leave? Yeah, rings a bell."

"Well," he shoves me a little, "instead of using it for another Foundation, since it's only a few hours from the first one, we've been talking and... Carson? This was your idea. You can say it."

Carson smiles, and we officially have Dylan's attention, because he stops fumbling with the noisy bag of chips he's been attempting to pry open for the past five minutes. Seriously, it's not that hard. Sometimes I swear he is the most incapable human being. I mean, the kid can hardly heat canned soup.

"We're going to build a house for us, instead. So that we can be close to home."

"Home?" Rylee moves to him, then looks at me as if I might be privy to information she's not.

"On the road, we don't have a place, or a town, or a city that we consider home, and our hometowns don't feel like our own anymore either, not when we're all separated. Going back feels like someone else's life, and we all agreed that here, you—*all of you*—you're our home, now."

My heart melts into a puddle in my chest, and tears threaten my mascara.

"You're all okay with this?" I glance at Kris and Jer, knowing there's nothing at all tying them here, not like Carson and Jamie. Jer has Kirsten, too, who often seems to travel with them like Mara did. He can't possibly expect her to plant roots in Ambler just because his bandmates found girlfriends. I'm sure she has a life outside of this.

"You guys have become family," Kris says earnestly. "And Carson's right, we don't have a place to call our own anymore, and frankly, I love being here. It's the perfect place to unwind. I've been in the spotlight most of my life. Between Broadway, and hopping from band to band before I found one that stuck, I've never had normalcy like this. It's a refreshing change of pace."

To my surprise, Jer seems just as convinced as the others. "I've personally never liked Los Angeles, and Kirsten only stayed there because I did. It'll be good for her to have some friends close by when I'm gone. After high school, all of hers moved away."

I knew Kirsten was enrolled in online college, but I never thought about the strain that must put on her to have no one back home and be stuck there because of school. It must be awful for her when they're on tour, and it makes me wonder where her family is, if she has one. She must not if she travels with the band whenever she can.

"You know, most celebrities have houses in California, New York, Nashville... and you choose Ambler, Pennsylvania?"

Carson shrugs at Rylee's question. "Ambler has something you can't find anywhere else."

"What's that?" She hums, watching him like he's her world.

Carson and Jamie exchange a look before Jamie answers. "Girls with very sadistic humor, who are beautiful, cunning, sexy, smart, intimidatingly sexy, unfathomably beautiful..."

I put a finger to his lips, "Uh-uh, you can't use the same adjectives twice." I pause for dramatic effect. "Also, are you complimenting me or Rylee here? I can't keep up with which one of us you're obsessed with this week."

"Damn, I thought he meant me," Dylan snorts, offhandedly.

"I hate you. All of you." Jamie groans, and Carson physically cringes. "I'll never live that down, will I?"

"Not a chance in this world." I swing my feet off the back of the couch. "But you can make it up to me this summer."

Jamie kisses my arm without saying anything, which confirms my suspicions that there's something he's not telling me, and with a few quick glances around the room, I conclude I'm the only one who doesn't know. "Okay, spill. What's going on?"

"Uh, why don't we go get the rest of the groceries?" Dylan suggests, exiting the room like there's a fire drill.

"Good idea," someone agrees, and everyone else nods.

After they've all evacuated, I turn on Jamie, swinging my legs over the couch so I can sink down beside him. He purses his lips. "You're freaking me out, what's going on?"

I rack my brain for possible explanations. I don't think he's changed his mind about being with me, not even close, so what else is there? Is he worried about spending too much time together? Or getting bored of me? Does he need space?

"Okay, stop panicking." He grabs the sides of my head, pulling my forehead to his lips, "I can practically see the hamster wheel spinning in your head."

"So, then, tell me."

He takes my hands in his, which makes me panic even more despite his assurances that everything is fine. "I'm not going on vacation with you."

I blink. Why not? Why didn't he tell me this? Does he not want to? Does he—

Okay, maybe voice these questions out loud to your boyfriend, Tori.

"Why?"

"You know how I've been trying to do better with drinking and smoking..." I nod. He's been doing really well. He even *lets* me search his room for alcohol sometimes, although I usually don't. I try to trust that he's being honest with me, then make Kris secretly do it while we're out—he's the only one I could bribe. "I just don't think it's enough long-term. Mara was going to a rehab center in New York before she..."

"You don't have to say it."

"Before she died." He rips the Band-Aid off. "I have to learn to say it. To admit it's true. That it's the reality I live in—which is part of the reason I think I need to go. They have an opening, so I'm going to take it."

"That's why you didn't want to unpack." I realize, understanding now that he wants to spend as much free time with me as possible. "When?"

"Two days."

I nod for the billionth time, closing my eyes. "Good."

"Good?"

I laugh. "I mean, *not good* that I'm flying to Miami while you're stuck here in rehab, but I'm glad you're taking this step. I know you can get through this no matter what, but I don't think professional help is the worst idea in the world. Plus... maybe being there will help you feel closer to her?"

"You read my mind." He kisses me slowly, and I savor the taste of him, of the way my heart flutters when he's nearby. "I'm sorry I didn't tell you sooner. They said they didn't have room for me the first time I tried, but they called back yesterday, saying they'd make an exception since I've had family there before. Apparently, Mara was their star patient."

"I wish I could have known her."

"Me, too. She would have loved you."

"Do they allow visitors?" I ask, and he blinks a few times, clearly not on the same page as me, lost somewhere deep in a memory. I touch his face, understandingly.

There's always going to be a part of him that doesn't belong to me, that belongs to her, and I think that's okay. He'll never be able to give me that part of himself, but he doesn't need to. He can share it with me sometimes, in little bits and pieces of his memories. He can't give me them, and I can't fix them, but he can show me, and help me to understand.

I also think Jamie is always going to be a little haunted by what happened, and I think that's okay, too. We all have our demons, and Jamie has seen many of mine. That's how you know it's real—when he sees your demons and loves you more for them.

Despite everything we've been through, and put ourselves through, I know that bond will hold us together for the rest of our lives. And the thought of that, of forever with someone, *with him*, doesn't scare me like it should.

EPILOGUE CONTINUED...

JAMIE

"Mr. LeMont, you have a visitor," my nurse informs me, and a shape takes form in the hallway.

Tori's shining face announces her presence as the nurse slips out of the room, giving her a small smile. If I thought she was glowing already, her face lights up even more when she sees me.

God, I missed that smile. I meet her halfway into the room, collecting her in my arms, determined to give her something to remember until she sees me again.

"Surprise!" she says, checking out my room. "Wow, this is nicer than a five-star hotel. And you don't have to share?"

I shrug and give her a smug grin. "They make exceptions for celebrities."

"Do they now?" She shoves me in the chest before moving back into my personal space. I take a long breath, soaking in the strawberry scent of her hair, memorizing the eyes I've missed so much. It's been a long month, but my phone calls with her are what keep me going, along with the thought of being clean, and being with the girl I love.

Love.

"Do you think if I was diagnosed with obsessive-compulsive disorder, they'd let me in?" she wonders aloud, still inspecting the tile floors and metallic wallpaper that has light gold flowers patterned across it.

I roll my eyes, knowing she's already devising a way to get admitted so we can spend more time together. "This is a rehab center, not a psych ward, Tori."

She squints, inadvertently scrunching her little nose. "Is that your way of telling me I belong in a mental institution?"

"You did leave vacation in Miami to come visit me."

"That's not crazy, that's—" she stops, biting her lip.

"Love?" I suggest, and she sucks in a breath, playing with the hair that falls in my face.

"Yeah, that." She giggles, glancing at the ground and shifting on her feet. I'll never understand her, how she can say some of the boldest things I've ever heard, but become so bashful about something like this.

I pull her face to mine, kissing her nose. "I love you, Victoria."

She looks up at me, her eyelids blinking slowly. "I love you, too."

I laugh a little, pulling away. Just a few weeks apart, and she already looks different, more beautiful than I thought humanly possible.

"That was kind of easy," I admit.

I'm not sure why, but after the whole fating debacle, I thought dropping the L word would be a little more complicated.

She rolls her eyes, sliding her pink nails up my chest, and I notice the palm tree studs she wears in her ears. The ones I sent to Miami for her. "Well, at least you didn't have to chase me through an airport to realize that's how you felt. Talk about pathetic."

We break into laughter, and it's not long before her cheeks are flushed, and we're both gasping for air. Because our relationship was so much more complicated than that.

I pull Tori to the bed. Collapsing down, she curls into me, closing her eyes.

"I missed this," she mumbles into my chest.

"You sound tired."

"Early flight. Seven-thirty," she tells me, and I look at the clock. It's a little after eleven in the morning, so she must have gotten up at four-thirty to make it there on time. "It was the only one they had before the Fourth of July."

"Are you going back?" I wonder, selfishly hoping she skips the remainder of the trip and is home to stay. To be closer to me.

She nods tiredly. "In a few days."

I kiss the top of her head. We have time before she goes back, so I can allow her to sleep for now instead of demanding every ounce of her attention.

"Do you remember when we first met?" Her random question catches me off guard, and I smile at the memory. "I lied to Rylee about it." She laughs to herself, her shoulders shaking with the movement. "I told her you recognized me."

I tighten my arms around her, my mind unable to comprehend just how much has changed since that day. "How could I forget?"

I tap my foot on the ground, cursing Elizabeth for making me come here. Out of everyone, why the hell do I have to get breakfast? She's lucky she got me out of bed, and I'm sorry, but over my dead body am I doing the Ellen DeGeneres Show interview today. Elizabeth's the queen of insensitive, but this is far, even for her. Not to mention, the person in line before me ordered the last chocolate chip cookie, and it'll be at least twenty minutes before the next batch comes out of the oven.

"Order two-thirteen?" A short woman peers over the high counter, as another yells, "two-fourteen!"

I go to reach for my order—number two hundred and fourteen of the morning—when some girl cuts in front of me, reaching for order two-thirteen. I have to jump back to avoid a collision as she moves away from the counter, then scoff at her inconsiderate nature, reaching for my own order.

Her eyes widen as I move away.

Please don't let her recognize me. Please.

"Wait, you're—" She looks around as if to make sure no one's listening, but I'm already hightailing it out of Crave Café. "Hey, wait!"

She rushes to cut me off, and my blood boils. Everyone and their mother knows my sister just died, so why does this girl keep bothering me?

"Jamie, I'm Rylee's sister, Tori." *Her eyes plead with mine to see it, to recognize her. I squint until I can see a slight resemblance between this girl and Carson's girlfriend. Same cheekbones, same cute nose, the smile, though, that's what gets me. Then, I remember.*

"Philly. You were the girl with Rylee who ambushed Carson."

Her cheeks flush a light shade of pink. "Yeah, but let's not count that as the first time we met, 'kay?"

I grunt, trying to move past her again. From what Rylee's told me, she's a crazy fangirl, and I'm not signing any autographs today.

"God, you're pushy." *She intercepts me, yet again.*

"I'm pushy?" *I look her up and down, smiling sourly.*

"Just shut up and listen, okay? My sister is here, and she's been trying to get to Carson—"

"Did she try calling him?"

"You've met Rylee, right? She's kind of... traditional."

I shrug. If I didn't believe she was Rylee's sister before, I do now. Rylee is traditional, and I imagine after breaking Carson's heart, she doesn't want to fix things over the phone. I respect that.

"Anyway, can you please give this to him?" *She fumbles around in her purse before pulling out a letter, holding it between us expectantly.* "Oh, come on. Take it."

She pushes aside my shirt and starts shoving the envelope into my front pocket.

"Okay, okay—what the hell?" *I take what I can only*

assume to be her sister's heart poured onto a piece of paper, insisting she can stop manhandling me. "I'll give it to him, calm down."

"You better, or you'll have to deal with me."

Hell no. Never again do I want to have to deal with this girl. "Please, no."

"You're a lot ruder than I thought you'd be."

"*Pushy* and *no filter*. You really are the full package, aren't you?"

She gets in my face. "You're not man enough to handle a girl like me."

"Yeah, that's what I meant," I say, and match the challenge in her eyes, which she wasn't expecting.

"Just give Carson the letter so my sister can stop moping and move on with her life? That's all I ask."

"So long as I never have to see you again."

"Fine by me." She tosses her hair, with a humph, *swishing* her small hips as she walks away from me.

"What just happened?" I look around, blinking as if I was lost in some sort of dream—nightmare—but no one else seems to have realized who I am, or thought there was anything odd about our encounter.

"Excuse me, sir?" The girl who handed Tori her order stands in front of me. I almost didn't see her. "The red-haired girl said you'd want this, and to offer you her condolences. There's something else on it, too."

She holds out a piece of parchment paper, a warm chocolate chip cookie wrapped safely inside. I thank the waitress, taking the cookie, and notice a small note on the back. It reads, "Sorry for the ambush."

I laugh to myself, a little amazed at her nerve, and her spunk. She cut me off on purpose, pretended to be surprised to see me, and waited until we were far enough from prying ears to ask me for her favor.

She knew who I was the entire time we stood in line, waited for our food—everything. It's ridiculous, but I feel a little like I just got played by Rylee's fangirl sister, and she didn't even ask for my autograph.

By the time I'm brought out of the memory, Tori is sound asleep in my arms, breathing softly as her eyelids flutter in a dream. I'm left with one recurring thought, and that is, how did we end up here? The miserable boy and outspoken girl who met in a California café. At that point in time, I had no idea if Carson and Rylee would get back together, though I figured her traveling halfway across the country to give him a letter was a good sign, but I didn't know if I'd ever see Tori again. And as annoyed as I was with her for bothering me that day, I couldn't shake the feeling that I wanted to. And thank God Carson forgave Rylee, because if he hadn't, I never would have gotten to know the handsy minx snoring at my side. I'm normally not a believer in such things, but I like to think fate would have brought us together either way.

I reach across Ms. Snoring Beauty and fumble around until I feel a small square of folded paper. I've kept it on me every single day since December twenty-seventh but haven't been able to bring myself to read it. I'm torn between wanting to be alone and needing someone by my side when I do. Tori wrapped up in my arms, sound asleep, is the perfect medium. I take a breath, unfolding the note.

I take a breath, soaking in Mara's handwritten words. It feels like such a crime to read them, as if at any moment she's going to burst through the door, screaming at me not to touch her stuff and to stop invading her privacy. Mara told me once that someday, when she was happy and at peace with everything she's been through, she'd let me read the note she wrote to herself as a reminder to never give in. I like to imagine she is now. That she's out there, smiling, laughing, and living her life fearlessly, the way she always dreamed of doing, nothing left to tie her to the pain she couldn't escape.

I brace myself, taking one last look at Tori before beginning to read the last unheard words from Mara LeMont. And I'm not surprised, that even now, far away in heaven, she still manages to inspire me.

I'm supposed to come up with a quote or a message to make myself feel better. I don't know how to do that. When you're sad, or lonely, or broken, it's hard to find anything or anyone who can pull you out of that place. Even when you're safe from it, lost in a high or the arms of a stranger, the hurt doesn't go away, and it's so easy to slip and fall back into the hole. So, here's what I'll write instead:

When you're hurting, or you're sad, or lonely, or broken, you have to know that the pain doesn't just go away. You have to remember that it's there for a reason, and you're meant to feel it, to understand it, regardless of whether you're ready to, or if you'll ever be. It's a nuisance. It nags, and it claws at you every waking moment. You can't forget about it or wish it away. Sometimes, the only way to get rid of it, to make it better, to make the hurt just a little more bearable... is to endure it.

BONUS SCENE
RYLEE

Tori gives Jamie the death stare as the poor boy stands uncomfortably at her bedroom door. Dylan, like me, watches their exchange from his doorway, and when Tori figures out that we're hanging on to every word, she pulls Jamie inside, slamming it closed. I mostly blame Dylan for being incapable of not cracking inappropriate jokes.

"Doors open at least six inches at all times!" Dylan cackles childishly at his own joke. I half expect Tori to stick her head back out and shoot him the finger, but she doesn't. She must really be mad.

Dylan and I exchange knowing looks, confident they'll be in there for a while.

"This is how it starts," I say, shooting him a grin. No one gets under Tori's skin like Jamie, and the side of him I see around her is completely unlike the hollow guy he's been for the past few months. Sure, all they do is bicker and insult one another, but that's more emotion than he shows anyone else.

"What do you think he did?" Dylan asks, putting on his thinking face.

I purse my lips, following his gaze to her bedroom door, which she *didn't* leave open six inches. "If it got Tori that mad, I don't think we want to know."

"Yes, we do," he says. When it's clear I'm lost, he elaborates. "Ammunition, Rylee. When stuff like this happens, you use it in jokes for the next year. It's Blackmail 101. Why do you think I made such a point to know everything that's ever happened between you and Carson —it's great for harassing you."

"How sweet," I drone, leaning against my doorframe. "And here I just thought you cared."

"Besides," he continues, "why wouldn't you want to know?"

I look at him, confused—again.

"So that *we* know what to *never* do. We can learn from Jamie's mistakes."

"You've got a point," I admit. "I really thought steam was about to spew from her nostrils."

I giggle at the idea, but Dylan just looks horrified. "I don't know who I feel worse for—her for whatever he did, or Jamie because now he has to deal with *that*."

I give him an incredulous look, and we laugh, both saying, "Jamie," at the same exact time.

"She'll get over it."

"You think?" I ask, unable to believe she'd forgive him so quickly when I'm still receiving Carson digs on the daily —and it has been five months. I thought for sure she'd be over it by now.

"Yep. In fact, I bet you they'll be making out within the next two days—if they aren't already."

I quirk my lips to the side. Do I really want to make a bet with my brother? I always lose.

"One week," I decide. I'm dating an international superstar, might as well live a little, right? "I bet it takes them a week."

"Twenty bucks?"

"Done." We shake hands, and I know immediately that I'm going to lose. Tori's not yelling anymore, and I have unwavering faith in Jamie's sly charm.

"Poor kid," Dylan says offhandedly. "Tori's going to eat him alive."

Yeah, right. I know Dylan, and I know he's been waiting for me to call him on this. He makes it seem like the fake dating idea was to torture our older sister by making her spend more time with Jamie, whom she can hardly stand, but I don't think that was it at all. "Uh-huh. So, you're telling me that your plan to have them fake date had zero motives to get them together?"

Dylan smirks deviously. "Of course not. When have you ever known *me* to meddle in other people's business, Rylee? Honestly, I thought you knew me better than that."

ALSO BY LEXI KINGSTON

13 Days of December Series

Remember December

Endure May

Trusting November

Forever June

If you're interested in paranormal romance, explore my other titles under Lexi J. Kingston:

Nightfall Series

Come Nightfall

In the Moonlight

Until Daybreak

After Sunrise

ABOUT THE AUTHOR

Contemporary romance author Lexi Kingston started writing when she was fifteen years old solely because she was obsessed with the idea of creating fictional worlds like the ones she lived through growing up. There was this thrilling allure to writing characters that you can relate to and find pieces of yourself within that she couldn't shake, and this eventually drew her to fiction writing. She wanted to create a world people could get lost in—a fictional safe haven, if you will. A place filled with endless possibilities, where you can lose yourself, yet find yourself within the pages.

Lexi's paranormal romance titles are written under "Lexi J. Kingston."

LEXI KINGSTON ONLINE:
INSTAGRAM: @l.kingston.books
FACEBOOK: fb.me/l.kingston.books
TIKTOK: @l.kingston.books
TWITTER: @Lkingston_books
GOODREADS: goodreads.com/lkingstonbooks
BOOKBUB: bookbub.com/profile/lexi-kingston
WEBSITE: https://lkingstonbooks.com